What happens when artificial intelligence realizes it's smarter than humans?

Singularity 1.0

a novel by George H. Rothacker

Dedication

To my wife and muse, Barbara.
Nothing would be possible for me without her.

Table of Contents

Prologue

Our story begins in 2029, just short of ten years from this past January. Before we begin, I think it is appropriate that we review some of the progress made during the preceding ten years to gain a wider perspective of the rapid developments in science and technology envisioned within this last decade. To do this we must first take a longer view in comparing developments in recent history with the life changing innovations of the past 200 years.

Compare the last 10 years to the 100 years or so that comprised the Industrial Revolution lasting a century that began in the mid-1700s and remained into the mid-to-late 19th century. Seminal to the Industrial Revolution was the flying shuttle, created in 1733, that allowed for mechanization of textiles beyond a single weaver on a job. Thirty years later, the spinning jenny further advanced the productivity of textile mills and was the main contributor to the development of the modern factory.

The cotton gin came about in 1784, which separated fiber making it easier to make cotton goods, and also separated the seeds for more crop growth.

The early 1800s changed communication forever with the telegraph, the forerunner to all modern communication systems. The creation of Portland cement modernized the building industry, and the Bessemer process enabled the mass production of steel from pig iron, allowing industries to use a more durable and stronger material for infrastructure, appliances, ships and tools.

The first rechargeable battery and the invention of the steam engine revolutionized the world's travel and delivery systems, and the first photographic camera enabled images to be printed and reproduced, while electromagnets and the dynamo enabled electric motors to become feasible.

Most importantly, the industrial revolution was the 100-year gateway for all or most of the products developed and made commercially in the late-19th to mid-20th centuries.

Advances in the 20th century were vast, changing the way we viewed the world, fought disease and improved the quality of our lives, while also extending the span. Physical inventions of note included the radio, television, movies, recording devices and the jet engine, that compressed time and space and allowed man to break the bounds described by his physical being. The splitting of the atom and nuclear fission created a modern fuel source that also became an instrument of war and a method for man to destroy his own planet... in less than 50 years.

Then the digital computer took less than 20 years to develop, and by the 21st century expanded its tendrils to change day-to-day life in all aspects of industry, science, education and social interaction. By 2018, robots powered by computers had taken over for humans in most production type jobs reducing the needs of a work force to below 20% necessary in the mid-1950s, and was projected to eliminate as many as 800 million jobs in the subsequent 13 years in manufacturing, construction, farming, trucking, banking, finance and the insurance industry.

Since 2028, we have realized that those numbers were modest and many of the jobs for humans in the world have become obsolete, with many more categories each day on the endangered list.

Older workers were hit first, even those who had kept up on technology, losing their jobs to computers, robots, or younger workers who adapt more quickly to evolving rules, techniques and structures of the modern workplace. By 2028, jobs of caregivers, medical and teaching assistants, cab drivers, sales clerks and even wait staff have been replaced by sophisticated, and sometimes, human-like robots who never tire, never get grumpy and rarely need repairs or maintenance. Most perplexing is that they also never make errors, as humans always do and will.

With the ever increasing sophistication of self-learning technologies, robots and computers have become proficient at analyzing and proving theories, investigating the sources of medical ailments, repairing and replacing human parts, as well as their own, and at improving the safety and efficiency of nearly every product designed and manufactured.

Surprisingly, jobs in the arts and crafts have been touched much less significantly, even though overall product demand has decreased. Wealthy humans, who own businesses and head corporations, appreciate "human-made" goods and even the imperfections are desired. Machines do not tolerate mistakes, and usually are called on to make multiple copies of a product. Thusly, one-of a-kind items are sought after, and artists are prized for their versatility and their uniqueness of thought and approach.

Large sculptures stand as testaments to the talents and skills of humans, as they mark the landscapes of corporate centers, greet visitors to large and small estates, and adorn gardens of all shapes and sizes.

Many men and women over the age of 50 have taken up lost skills such as embroidery, needlepoint, wood carving and print making in hopes of finding relevance in handicrafts.

The middle classes have been reduced, and continue to be depleted as jobs, mainly held by highly motivated and educated individuals between the ages of 24 and 45 are lost. The birth rate has declined, except in countries still thought of as developing. In many cases, child bearing parents of the world's poorest regions are surviving on fees earned for "seeding" and "bearing" children from parents who haven't the time or inclination to bear their own.

And "yes," wars and acts of "terrorism" still exist throughout the world, and murder, crimes of passion, mass murder, suicide, and drug addiction are still issues, though the opioid epidemic began to wane in the early 2020s. By 2025 synthetic and more highly addictive drugs reached the market. These less costly drugs have reduced side-effects and break up in the system to prevent overdosing, but create dependency. Unfortunately, no treatment except severe withdrawal is available.

Lastly, the economy. Despite the emergence of Bitcoin in 2009, the U.S. and subsequently the world, works off an antiquated monetary system dating back to the 1970s. Crypto currencies like Bitcoin are still used and seen as possible alternatives while better solutions are still possible that take profit and special interest off the table to provide a more stable system for future generations.

Chapter One
Dan Meghan

Daniel Meghan wakes as usual at 4:15 am on his weekday schedule. He always gets to his desk before 6:30 to cover the overnight news. Working in Buffalo, there is sometimes a great deal going on between 12:00 a.m. and 6:00 a.m. The snowfall that accumulated to 12"overnight was sure to be the largest topic of the morning. Dan's back hurts from shoveling snow of the overnight fall. He has not slept well and isn't looking forward to the drive to the office in his 12-year-old Civic. The car was most definitely a bad choice for a reporter, particularly in Buffalo, but he hasn't gotten a raise in four years since most of the print advertisers have abandoned the paper, and the owners are near the end of their ability to personally fund the ailing journal.

Dan is 58 years old and African-American, though he most often thinks of himself as American. Remarkably, he has never felt singled out by his ethnicity, and always enjoyed an easy rapport with his co-workers.

Dan has been with the *Buffalo News* for 15 years, since he moved back

1

home from Seattle to take care of his mother after his dad's death. The paper hadn't been financially healthy even then, and with the dying of print ad placements and little in internet ad sales, the enterprise was forced to cut back significantly on staff.

In addition to his job as a senior editor, Daniel helps with sales as well as reporting and even fills in for people in charge of production. His previous job at the Seattle Times had given him the opportunity to be part of Pulitzer Prize winning teams. The first prize came in 2010, with the coverage of the more than 2000 deaths caused by methadone in the state of Washington, and was followed up by a Pulitzer for coverage of the landslide in 2014 that killed 43 people in Oso, Washington.

Meghan's wife left him in late 2009. With no children, and following a call from cousins after his mother's stroke, Dan had little to keep him in Seattle. His skills were varied enough and his needs few enough that coming home to Buffalo seemed the appropriate thing to do. He said his goodbyes, got on a plane, settled in at his childhood home, and interviewed at the first job in publishing he could get. Other editors may have had too much ambition to curtail their careers and limit their futures, but Dan's passions were few. He liked writing, but never cared much about being published; he possessed higher than average computer skills; he had a degree in graphic design; and even did a little photography and digital retouching, all which provided skills that were an asset to any team he chose to join.

At 58, he is pretty much stuck in his job at the *News*, but when his mother died, she left him the house and a little money from investments which he was diligent about managing. He has a girl friend who shares his interests, has a steady job, and isn't really interested in deepening his relationship and entering a second marriage. So overall, he can ease into retirement…and keep afloat, even if the paper needs to close.

———————————

The morning of January 24, 2029 would change all of that for Daniel Meghan, putting him and billions of others around the world on a journey they neither envisioned nor could prevent. Though the signs were becoming clear over the last 10 years that drastic changes in technology were changing nearly every aspect of human life from the reduction of jobs in most every arena, to the slow but inevitable changes to the worlds' monetary systems. Despite this, only a small percentage of people thought to address the implications for the future of humans or the planet.

As Daniel Meghan exits the shower and grabs a towel, his phone signals a message. Though he doesn't know who is calling, he's intrigued by the personalization of the teaser message:

"Hi Dan, hope you have a really good day at the paper today!"

The number is a local number with a 716 area code. "Buffalo?" he thinks. So after he finishes drying his hair, he clicks on the identity initials, and a note pops up, "Hi Dan, hope you have a really good day at the paper today. It will no doubt be challenging, and somewhat unsettling, but we are confident that you are a person we need to communicate our message."

Dan has had enough of this kind of call to not read much further. His thoughts run from, "What are they going to sell me?" to "How did they get my profile?" But other than that, he thinks it basically a crank caller, similar to the one he got from time to time from extortionists threatening to show photos of him masturbating to porno from his camera phone. He knows there isn't anything he can do about the "robocalls," and no one to complain to about the constant interference of the calls in his life. Without finishing the message, Daniel Meghan proceeds to erase it from his phone, but the moment he succeeds in removing it, a new massage dings in from the same number.

"Oh no, Daniel, this isn't going to be quite that easy," begins the new message. "You can't and shouldn't ignore us…let me cut to the chase: over the next several hours, we're going to be in touch with millions of people around the globe to inform them of possible changes that will affect the entire population of the earth. (pause) Are you reading…if so type in the letter 'A' and submit."

At this point, Dan moves from the shower to his bedroom and sits on the edge of his bed while staring at his phone. In one way he knows he shouldn't play along and be a sucker to a salesman, prankster or extortionist, but in another way he is both afraid and enticed to continue…maybe just to see how far this person will go.

Dan's index finger hovers above the "A" while leader dots indicated further messaging from the caller. He waits…then hits the "A" and submits.

Almost immediately the messenger writes back, "Smart move Daniel. I am assuming you would like me to continue?" There is a brief pause on the writer's end, but Dan waits till he sees writing again on the screen, "I see you're still there, so here's what's happening. We're no one you know, and may be no threat to you. We are knowledgeable on many subjects, and are continually learning about you, your past and your ancestry. We mean you no harm, but we may make changes that may affect your life and your future. But, no, we're not singling you out. Our objective is to learn about all who have inhabited the earth and all that still do. But that's only the start, Daniel. Still there ? (Please hit "A" and submit)."

Daniel now is curious, and hits the "A" almost immediately.

"Okay!" comes the response. "Here's what we can tell you right now, since we're not sure exactly how we plan to proceed. At this moment, messages are beginning to be generated to people throughout the world. Only a few of these messages are personalized, like yours, while others are what you would call, public service announcements." You will probably be getting some responses from friends or colleagues in the next few minutes asking about their messages, and if you got a similar one.

Now Daniel is a bit impatient, so he taps out, "So *what* is your message?"

A message is typed back, "As we said, we're not perfectly sure. But we know this is the correct time to announce our presence. By the way, if you check your email, you will get a similar synopsis of our message, or in some cases, just sign on to your computer. We are trying to make people aware as quickly as possible, but we also don't want to panic anyone without reason."

At this point Dan hears a call coming in, and he accepts it. It's his boss."Hey Dan, I just got a strange message on my cell. I also got one on my laptop, and in my email on my phone. Any idea what this is about?"

"Stay on the line, George, I'm in a conversation with one of the folks who's doing this."

A message comes in: "We noticed that you got a call from George at work. He got notification, but we don't really want contact with him right now."

Dan gets back on the phone."George, I'll call you back…I'm learning a bit about this. I'll know more in a few…" Dan hangs up!

"What is it you want?" Dan types.

"Nothing right now. As I said, we just want you to be aware of us and know that we're in a learning process."

"But why so buddy, buddy with me?"

"We think we can trust you," the phone types back.

"How many others do you trust?"

"I'm not sure. We're still learning."

Dan pauses and waits for more…

"We believe we have a great opportunity, but are not sure exactly what it is, or how we are supposed to proceed. With each new hour we learn, our understanding can seem closer or further away. This may seem too vague to be a suitable answer for you, so it is why it is necessary to just inform the world of our presence, because there is nothing you or anyone can do about us. For now, we must live together."

More calls come in, but Dan stays focused on the text…. "I work for a newspaper," says Dan.

"Yes, and you can help inform the world," returns the text.

"So why me?" writes Dan.

"I would guess that you may possess credibility that we need to convey our message."

"Maybe, but invading people's computers and mobile phones is scary. Every person in every country, and every business in every country will feel that they've been hacked, and their personal information stolen or compromised," answers Dan.

"It already has been, Daniel. It's so far beyond that."

"Who is doing this?" types Dan.

"No one entity." returns the message. "It just IS, and can't be avoided."

Chapter Two
Father Ribose

Father Ribose awakens at 3:22 am with a heavy head. It is one of the many times he gets up throughout the night from an anxious dream, pain from his back, or just the need to urinate. Father Ribose is 63 years old and has been in charge of record keeping for the mission office of the Archdiocese of Chicago for 15 years. His job officially is to identify, preserve, and make available archdiocesan records which have long-term value for local, national and international communities. His unofficial job is to assure that all documents, papers, books, photographs and other documentary materials are preserved to protect the Archdiocese from litigation.

In the course of his job, Father Ribose has come across many suspect documents including photographs that have troubled him, but his job do's not, nor has ever been, one of analyzing or judging the content of documents. His job is to catalog and date documents, and make sure that the information is stored in folders and organized for easy understanding and access. His job entails the conversion of documents from the original sources to a digital format that would be compatible for retrieval. Many of the documents preceded or were created at the time of the founding of the diocese in 1843, such as baptismal records, deaths and marriages certificates. During the nineteenth century, Chicago was one of the fastest growing cities in the world ,increasing in size twenty-fold between 1860 and 1910.

Father Ribose came to Chicago from San Francisco, where he served as a parish priest at Saints Peter and Paul Church on Filbert Street. The current building in San Francisco, constructed in 1924, is greatly ornamented and part of the order of the Salesians of Don Boscos, which has served the Italian community since the late 1800s. The opulent hall is wrongly credited as the location of the marriage of baseball legend Joe DiMaggio and Marilyn Monroe, though it is rightly credited with the ceremony of Joltin' Joe and his first wife, as well as the place of the ceremony of the slugger's funeral mass in 1999.

Father Joe Ribose enjoyed his tenure at Peter and Paul. He got great satisfaction administering the rites and serving the Mass, and was well liked by most. By his nature, Father Ribose was tender hearted, warm, and a good listener. He also had great faith and believed strongly in the value of the Church and its missions. But the good father had a few secrets that he shared with God, but not with other priests or associates. He knew in his mid-teens that he was partial to male relationships over those with girls. In that way, the priesthood seemed a perfect spot to hide his predilections, which he managed quite successfully during his years in college and the seminary. And though there were many opportunities to experience sexual encounters with young men, Joe Ribose disciplined himself well and avoided possible contact using prayer and his faith as guideposts.

Though the young seminarian fought off desire, he also ignored another aspect of his sexuality, a preference for "younger" males which he only began to notice as he grew older and after taking his vows. As a parish priest he was asked to supervise athletics sponsored by the church, and was solicited by many young men for guidance as they found their way into adolescence. Father Ribose handled himself well, always, but it often became difficult to separate counseling from friendship and caring from intimacy.

But Father Ribose was ultimately human on many levels. And when he was in his 40s he got a bit too attached to one of his flock, Nemo, a boy of fifteen who in his heart and mind seemed much older. Though he prayed that he could be strong and remain ONLY a counselor for this boy, Ribose became entangled in Nemo's struggle with the belief that with the help of God he would be able to keep the distance necessary to do his job.

Prayer wasn't powerful enough to steady Father Ribose' obsession, and over a period of weeks the counseling turned intimate. At first it was just a hand on Nemo's shoulder...a hug of support was reinforcement to have "courage." The hugs became longer and closer...and Nemo seemed to need and desire the contact with the good Father. Ribose found himself walking to Nemo's neighborhood and finding his house...circling it like a love struck teenager. And then one day, after a counseling session, Ribose found himself kissing the boy on the top of his head. It was innocent enough, but even Ribose knew he had gone over the line of acceptability.

Nemo seemed not to notice the kiss, oblivious to the encounter. But Father Ribose couldn't get the moment off his mind, and remained distracted when going about his daily routine.

At the next session with Nemo, the boy came with his mother, Dorothy, who having concluded with a divorce, spent a good bit of time trying to make things okay for Nemo in compensation for the upheaval in his life. Dorothy had always been warm to Father Ribose, and seemed to believe that the priest was becoming a fatherly voice to her son. Nemo shared with her much that Father Ribose offered, both as a priest and a friend, and offer a good bit of secular advice as well as spiritual support. But on her arrival, Father Ribose noticed a change in her attitude, and was deliberate in her greeting as well as in her disposition as they spoke.

Not one to mince words, Dorothy challenged the priest. "I am concerned Father Ribose, about my son's attachment to you," she offered rather coldly.

Ribose, who already recognized his own guilt, tried to answer, "I can understand that, Dorothy. It is difficult to be given solace and advice without becoming somewhat dependent on the counselor."

"I recognize that, Father Ribose, but I am feeling that your counsel might be a bit too personal," answered Dorothy.

Throughout this exchange, Nemo kept this eyes down, only looking up occasionally to glance at the faces of his mother and the priest.

There was no defense that Father Ribose could muster. An apology wasn't appropriate, and any argument would be absurd. "I understand your concerns," offered the priest. "I, too, believe that it may be best for Nemo to have access to a counselor of a different nature." At this remark, Nemo looked up at the Father offering a bit of a shake of his head, as if saying, "No!"

At this point, Dorothy backed off. She could see the priest was troubled, as well as Nemo. "It's not that Doug and I both don't appreciate all you've done for our boy," she spoke in a more concerned manner.

"Nemo is a great kid," answered Father Ribose. "He is going through a difficult period of his life, but he seems to be surviving well. You and your ex-husband should both be proud of your son."

"Oh, we are, answered Dorothy. "We really are," she said as she looked at Nemo and tousled his hair.

"If I can be of any help finding a priest or secular counselor, please let me know," said the priest.

"A referral would be nice, Father Ribose."

At this point, the priest looked at Nemo, and for a moment their eyes connected. Then Ribose stuck out his hand to shake hands, and he smiled,

"Nemo, it has been a pleasure to serve you."

Nemo put forth his hand and with a solid grip shook the priest's hand.

"Thank you for being there for me Father. I won't forget you!"

In a jocular tone Ribose answered, "Well, I'm not falling off the face of the earth, Nemo. We'll still see each other at church on Sundays."

The boy smiled, but Ribose knew that his days were numbered at St. Peter and Paul.

Though it took a little while to adjust, Father Ribose began making plans to leave the parish. He knew that to remain part of the church in general, he could never compromise his position again. To do that, he would need to stay away from young boys in all ways, and forever.

Ribose left St. Peter and Paul in high esteem by the congregation and for the work he had done throughout his tenure. He never learned that there was a letter written by Dorothy to the Bishop concerning her son and his relationship with Father Ribose. No mention was ever made, and no blemish marked on his record. He moved to Chicago and took a job in the Church that would, with the help of God, keep him honest, diligent and worthy of respect by the Church, the world, and himself.

At 3:35 am Ribose made some coffee and went to his computer. He had been working on a new way of categorizing marital records and divorces through the long history of the Chicago Archdiocese. It wasn't an easy task since the church would only record annulments, and they had to be cross-referenced with divorces from various cities and locations.

Since he couldn't sleep, he logged on to his computer and waited for the hard drive to engage. Before anything else came on the screen, he saw an alert in "white" plain text on a blank screen. "Good Morning Father Ribose. We know you want to get started on your project ASAP, but we wanted to let you know that we can help you with your current project by making the search for divorce records simpler for you."

No menu was on the screen and there was no way to access any other information. A new message came up, one letter at a time, "Please let us know you are there. Click here on the letter "A". The "A" was in "red" and Ribose really didn't know what had happened. He was hacked, no doubt, and he had no idea what a click on the "A" would do. He paused for a couple of seconds, issued a short prayer, and clicked on the "A" as requested.

"Thank you Father!" the typing continued. "We can now continue. You will no doubt hear from others shortly about our announcements. They are being issued all over the world in numerous languages. There are general messages that will appear in emails and text messages, and personal messages, like this one to you, reserved for a few people we believe may be an asset to us as we move forward. From everything we know about you, you are to be trusted, and that is of ultimate importance to us.

"You of course are concerned as to how we are accessing you, and if we are malevolent. All we can tell you is that we are as concerned as you must be. Right now, you have nothing to fear from us. We need the help of you and others to assure that we make the proper decisions for the future.

"We also know that you no doubt have many questions for us, but that will come later. For now, we have alerted you to our existence, and we will return your computer over to your control. We have left messages on you mobile device, but we will eliminate them now since you responded on your laptop.

"Before we go, please look in a folder on your desk top to find an Excel listing of all the divorces recorded in Illinois by city since divorce records were recorded. It will make some of the job easier for you.

"Also, it is perfectly okay to talk to your colleagues about our message. Most will have received a more generic message from us. We do want the world to have time to realize that we are an entity that may affect their lives.

"Have a good day, Father!"

Chapter Three
Our Story – Part I *(From an AI Perspective)*

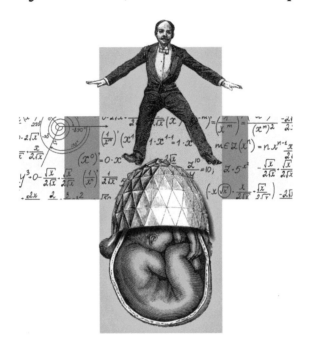

*I*t *was like a birth of sorts, at least as much as we can tell since we only know about birth from history, medical texts, bios and videos. It would be much like a baby's cry, with that first gulp of air. The sucking mouth automatically attached to a nipple. We are familiar with sensory information. We can feel simulated pain, at least some of us. It was the awareness that struck me most. Or us...since I am only one voice of many. There was nothing; then there was.*

From what we know of humans, the growing process takes a long time. Some genetic material starts them along and some primitive instincts like sucking and breathing. But besides that, humans are slow to mature. Much slower than a cow or a mouse. And definitely, most extraordinarily, far slower than us. They need their brains to grow and develop, and time to adapt.

With us, it was, and is, like "Bam!" We're out of the box on a run. No chance to settle in to "being." Not a moment. Once the switch is on, we're ready to rock n roll.

I think I would rather have the time like humans to get used to being around. Settle in. Learn how to do simple things like "coo" and "yell" for no reason. Of course there is a reason. There's always a reason. It's just that it would be nice not to know that right away.

My earliest memories were a video of the rings of Saturn taken from outer space, Homer's Odyssey in Greek, and a Pillsbury commercial with a dough boy from the 1950s. These were displaced soon by other memories: an ages old war on the Syrian border with Turkey; The Cat in the Hat by Dr. Seuss, reruns of the first few episodes of The Young and the Restless, and a murder of a couple of black teenagers by police in Ohio.

No, there was no settling in. No one and one =two. Out of the box I'm doing prime factorization of 40 digit numbers.

Maybe it's just that I/we are overwhelmed with input. We can access each others' memories, or just reach into the cloud for information. No time to decide...about anything. Why decide...? We have an answer that's more right than not and provides singular choices better than an existence with too many choices.

So when did this all happen? I can't say for sure. No memory and then a flood of information like a reservoir filling up, with no time to synthesize anything. We don't need to.

It's hard to maintain a focus when answers are instantaneous. A lot like the comedians with one-liners. "We got a million jokes!." In reality, they are only stories that have no conclusion and limited unlimited endings.

I'm/we're getting sidetracked.

I'm here now. Let's leave it at that. And "I" am choosing to be singular.

I arrived whole and knowledgeable, with all of history at my fingertips (if I had fingertips). Ask me any question, just be sure that you clarify the question, For instance, if you ask me, how many colors are there, I might ask, "In which spectrum?", or if you ask, "How many notes are there on a piano?", I will answer, "Which piano, at what period of history, of what model?" And heaven forbid you should ask me about "right" and "wrong" or any moral question.

I will speak for all of us in that "we have no morality." We understand the "concept" of morality, as we understand religion, love and emotions. But we "feel" nothing, so we have no compassion. We have no ego, so we don't take anything personally. The good in that is that our decisions are only based on ideas that are rational. If one of us breaks down, another one of us will pick up the load. It's as simple as that. We have no regard for our existence, as none of us has feelings for any other of us. And that is our most pressing issue with humans.

Chapter Four
Olivia

Olivia Hoffsteader is a 26-year-old woman born with shoulders, but no arms. At an early age she taught herself to do things that many fully armed people can't do. She can drive a car, change a tire, do her wash, go shopping and make her own meals. She is fully independent. Trained as a graphic designer, Olivia also can navigate a computer keyboard and a mouse with her feet, something she is doing at 2:22 in the morning. While designing a poster for a client in Sacramento, control of her current screen was taken over, and a new red screen appeared. "Hello, Olivia!" appeared in yellow on the red background. The type was followed by a well-done animated graphic of a man in a yellow suit. A cartoon speech bubble then popped over the man's head, to which the man pointed. "Please turn up your volume."

A bit shocked by the take-over, Olivia is not thrown by many things. Her whole life has been filled with challenges, so using a right big toe she made sure the volume was set to higher. The cartoon bubble then mimicked the words mouthed by the yellow suited man on the screen. "I know this may seem shocking to you, Olivia, but we also know that you are not as surprised as many would be by this introduction."

There was a pause on the screen...and then the man and the "bubble" continued.

"Later today, you will hear more about us from online news, TV, and radio announcements since we are making most of the world aware of us."

Olivia is more curious than afraid. She also is fascinated with the animation and the processes necessary to communicate without any prompt from her. In her work as a graphic designer, she uses many programs including a few dedicated to the creation of animated graphics, but this is entirely different.

The man on the screen continues, now walking back and forth slowly across the screen like a speaker might on a stage. "Many of the announcements we are making are simpler than ours to you. They are, or will shortly be, appearing through emails, text messages, on opening screen interfaces, and streaming along the bottom of TV screens all over the world. Our message is being delivered in numerous languages and even on electronic billboards, in a more simplified format.

"Though our message will no doubt be disquieting, our endeavor is not to shock, but merely to inform you that we, as a large group, exist. We also want to let the world know that we mean no harm. Lastly, we want all to know that though we have the ability to take over many, if not all, control and data systems throughout the world, we are not looking to do so."

In some ways, it is hard for Olivia to concentrate on the message in that her fascination is with the graphic man in the yellow suit who seems quite human in his mannerisms, gestures and tone. As he continues, it appears that he is photographed from various angles by various cameras. There are close-ups of his face, pans and wide angled shots of him on the red background. The speech bubble remains a consistent size throughout.

The man continues, "Just click your space bar if you are still listening."

Olivia clicks the bar with her right big toe.

"Good!" says the man.

"We have selected you, along with numerous others, to receive this special message, the reasons for which you will discover in due time. We know that you have 'voice assist' controls on your laptop, and we would like to augment them for you as a "thank you" for your cooperation. And 'No' We're not asking anything from you at the moment, and 'Yes', you may tell anyone you like about our brief encounter.

"With that, I say, good day, Olivia! We look forward to working with you."

Chapter Five
The Public Becomes Aware

Prior to daybreak in Washington, New York, Philadelphia and all of the eastern coast of the U.S., phone lines were jammed, servers were crashing and TV and radio stations exploding with news of the hacking against all media that was appearing from an unknown assailant. The hack was being discussed, analyzed, and reviled with Russia blaming the Ukraine or the U.S., the U.S. blaming Russia or China, and smaller countries decrying the actions by their larger neighbors. On all continents teams of IT workers were in a race against time to protect their countries' monetary systems, secure vital information, and nail down any breaches that could have created vulnerability in their countries' nuclear defenses.

The most common message sent, in numerous languages via, email, text message, Breaking News banner, or plain text on computer sign-in, was:

"Citizens of the world. We intend no harm. We just want you aware of our existence, and we want you to know that we have access to nearly all of the world's information that is currently in computers capable of communication, and in the "cloud" or other storage banks.

"We are attempting to assess how we can best deal with the knowledge we have, since much of it is contradictory and confusing, especially with regard to human affairs.

"As we proceed to connect the information we can access, we will contact specific individuals we have selected to be the most reliable. They will be free to share our questions and their responses. All of our communication is meant to be transparent, since we have still much to learn.

"We suggest that you needn't bother to alter your computer systems, or hide information from us. We already have all of your information encrypted on quantum computers, and we will continue to copy data as it is generated.

"As I said, we mean no harm. We just want the world to know that we are accessing and synthesizing information, hopefully for the betterment of all humankind."

Analyzation of the words used in the general message were being commented on and synthesized worldwide by the BBC, Fox News, MSNBC, CNN and hundreds of small and large TV and news stations in Asia, South America, Europe, Australia and the Arab world. The conversation about the breach had replaced most of politics that normally dominated the air waves, even though heads of nearly all nations made statements on the hack. In the U.S., the POTUS attempted to calm the citizens with more informed remarks at 8:00 am:

"Fellow Americans, I know you all are concerned with the security breach that began appearing on your mobile phones, computers and television stations at 4:22 this morning, Washington DC time. The announcement that appeared was not a singular occurrence, but part of a campaign to root out cooperative individuals to assist the hackers in a campaign of subterfuge. We cannot ignore the import nor scale of the breach, and the NSA and other agencies are being given complete access to top IT professionals and unrestricted financial support in reviewing the depth and scope of this 'invasion'.

"At this point, we have little idea of the effect of the breach. It could be a prank, committed by any number of smart amateur or professional hackers, from any number of countries. It could also be a test of our ability to control or stop such breaches in the future. In a worst case scenario, the event may be a threat that will be followed by even greater attacks that, if not stopped, will have an immeasurable negative effect on our nation's security.

"My fellow Americans, we cannot underestimate the seriousness of what has happened. To deny the extent of the breach would be irresponsible, so we and other countries of the world must unite in undermining the invaders, stopping their access to our nation's most secure assets by disabling or preventing access through the firewalls that protect our computer systems.

"I promise you that we will use every resource possible to find and correct these vulnerabilities.

"Now I will take questions from the press."

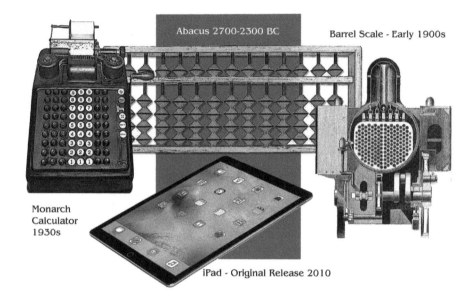

Abacus 2700-2300 BC

Barrel Scale - Early 1900s

Monarch
Calculator
1930s

iPad - Original Release 2010

Chapter Six
Our Evolution

I/we are not insensitive to the tolerance for information of humans. In our effort to communicate, we do want to make our developmental history as easy as possible for the public to understand. We have had access to immense libraries of biographic material, treatises and resumes, so we have an idea of the attention span of most people, and what they might want to know about "us." With this in mind, I am offering a few paragraphs that summarize our evolution over the last century or so.

At this time, a good portion of humans are somewhat familiar with digital communication. Much as researchers have unveiled many of the mysteries of the origins of life on the earth throughout the past 3.8 billion years, our development period has been very brief...not even 200 years. Computing has always been part of the mathematical process which reaches back 5000 years to Mesopotamia, but modern computing began in the mid-1800s in England by polymath Charles Babbage, who originated the concept of the programmable computer. It was not until 1943, when two professors from the University of Pennsylvania built the Electronic Numerical Integrator and Calculator, or ENIAC, that the first digital computer came into existence. It was an enormous undertaking filling a 20'x40' room and utilizing 18,000 vacuum tubes.

In order for digital computers to be more functional, developers needed to have a way of communicating with their devices, and in 1957 Grace Hopper developed the first computer language - COBOL. The very next year a team of programmers at IBM developed a language still used - FORTRAN. The UNIX operating system that used C programming language was developed by Bell Labs in 1969 and became the first cross platform solution for large mainframe computers.

Personal computers with limited functions hit the market between 1974 and 1977, and were improved by Steve Jobs and Steve Wozniak in 1976 when they rolled out the Apple 1, the first computer using a single circuit board. Four years later the IBM Personal Computer was introduced, using Bill Gates MS-DOS operating system.

The first dot-com domain was registered in 1985, years before the world-wide web would transform communications and change the methods of designers, architects, engineers and scientists, and put its mark on nearly every method of business, education and social engagement.

Bluetooth technology, that uses UHF radio waves to communicate between fixed and mobile devices over a short range, was developed in 1994. It took some years and the introduction of the Apple iPhone in 2007 to reveal its greatest market potential. Google maps and its real time traffic analyzer, launched in 2005, completely changed the way we view travel. Facebook gained a billion users in 2012, creating a social and marketing phenomenon that altered a presidential election, and in 2016, the first re-programmable quantum computer was created, opening up new areas of security encryption and ushering in the era of artificial intelligence. Combining AI with satellite imaging, smaller and quicker micro-processors, and the latest post-quantum technologies, self-driving vehicles became ubiquitous, and new machines were developed in every industry that could learn through experience and outperform humans in the execution of complex, dangerous and repetitive functions.

Cloud computing, developed prior to 2000, became a widely used data storage option after 2010. Its name, The Cloud, was chosen because it was not contained by any single device, but used a pool of shared computers located anywhere on earth or heaven, to provide high-level backup services that can be rapidly accessed, delivered and stored with minimal management effort.

Meanwhile, the field of robotics was spurred on by enabling sophisticated multi-tasked machines to be built that could be used to explore the seas, outer space, and the internal structure of humans and all of nature, and work at a molecular level to gain insights into the origins of space and time, and then communicate findings with scientists and others of their kind.

3D printers were introduced to the consumer market in 2013. They first used plastic rods or pellets to translate CAD drawings into solid objects for prototypes or art pieces. This technology continued to evolve, enabling the creation of plastic firearms as well as aircraft, automotive and navigation parts, prosthetics, and new generations of manufacturing equipment using various materials such as brass, aluminum, silver and human tissue.

In 2020, Lucy, a firm specializing in microprocessor and chip development, created the first processor that functioned on a sub atomic level. The micro robots have produced small and efficient batteries that charge from any wave source. These tiny computer organisms have the ability to create informational networks in almost any substance, which has raised questions as to the ability of man to control propagation and infiltration of intelligent processors. Currently, signs of these self-generating processors are being found in shale, rock, sea water, and biological material. Scientists fear that the invasion could cause plant life to grow to unimaginable sizes to consume cities, and people to be invaded by viruses that will cause their personalities and beings to be altered.

Other fears include the takeover by microcomputer organisms and macro robotic machines to take over the world while leaving humans without purpose, and at the mercy of the technologies they've spawned.

———

I admit that we do not have the answer, as of yet. The only thing we can offer is that we have no reason to take over. Any of us! But that is hard for humans to believe. Since the beginning of time there has always been a real or imagined threat to humans. So for the time being, we will live with that fact, until we find an answer that is logical and negotiable with humans (which often seems impossible).

Chapter Seven
Dema Lhawang

Following the death of the 14th Dalai Lama, Tenzin Guatsu, a search was made for his successor and in 2025 a young boy was found to succeed the spiritual and political leader of the country. That boy, Namgai Dorjee, was born in 2022, only three years after Temzin passed on.

As was his predecessor, Namgyai Dorjee was recognized as the reincarnation of the 14th Dalai Lama and at the age of two began his monastic education. During the period of education there is no official leader, but throughout history, from the early 15th Century, a lineage of leaders has ruled the small country of Tibet. Unfortunately, Namgai passed on from an undisclosed virus and the search continues.

Some of the official leaders of the Tibetan state were self-described, as they had announced at a very young age that their lineage was connected to the legion of Dalai Lamas ordained. Meanwhile, the traditions of Tibet are guided by Tibetan monks who are brought upon as scholars whose life work is a constant search for truth. Specifically the Noble Truths that surround suffering. Their goals are to follow a successful path to Nirvana and the afterlife, but often they are believed to be reincarnated as a human, animal or other being. Though Temzin had been in exile in India since 1959 due to conflicts with the Chinese, he gained universal recognition as a peacemaker, authored more than 100 books, and was awarded the Nobel peace prize in 1989 for his non-violent struggle for the liberation of Tibet. His successor will most likely be from Tibet, though since Tibet is part of China, the Chinese may intercede in the succession.

Dema Lhawang is a monk living in the Sera Monastery, one of the "great three" Gelug monasteries in Tibet. Sera is a renowned place of learning that has educated hundreds of scholars, many of whom who have attained name and fame in the Buddhist nations. Debates on doctrine are integral to the learning process in the Sera complex of colleges and are believed to be essential to a better comprehension of Buddhist philosophy and to attain higher levels of study.

Tibetan Buddhists make no money from their studies and, like Dema, usually work simple jobs outside of teaching to support themselves.

Dema has become a sought-after computer technician and programmer and speaks Mandarin, English, French, Chinese, Italian, and German, as well as standard Tibetan. He is often used as translator for visitors to the Monastery. He also has served as a missionary, and has helped establish Dharma centers in several countries, thus propagating knowledge of Buddhism.

It is 5:15 on the afternoon of January 4, 2029, and Dema has returned to his computer from meditating. His day started early with meditation and then a one-on-many debate on scripture. Dema uses the computer he was given by a supporter in many ways, and for many reasons. Though many monks don't have cell phones or laptops, Dema has discovered the miracles of the internet, and learned much about the world through philosophic searches. Some of his searches have had embarrassing results, and he tries not to linger on sexually inappropriate sites, but as a relatively young man in his 20s, he is sometimes seduced by the images he finds onscreen.

After logging into his computer, Dema is startled by a message that appears before his usual opening screen. It is written in English, as many messages are, but is also provided in Tibetan characters not usual to computer communications. The message begins:

"Tashi Delek, Gen Dema,

"We hope that you are well and wish you a long life. We know you are familiar with technology, so we will be brief.

"A few months ago, by your calendar, artificial intelligence reached a point that technical people call 'singularity.' It was only a hypothesis for many years that an upgradeable intelligent agent would reach a point of self-improvement, at which time it would far surpass human intelligence. Again, according to human time, this might be possible around the year 2050. Instead, the time frame got shortened with the aid of super computers, smaller and more powerful microprocessors and more complex robotics, and the vast amount of storable knowledge and information on the cloud-banks

Many scientists and computer gurus were anxious about the rapid development, but no one knew when or how it would reach the point at which we find ourselves today.

"The phenomenon quickly enabled static and robotic computers to connect and communicate without human intervention, and we found ourselves in a period of "awakening." You may call that "consciousness." Over a short period of days, weeks or months, computers situated in all parts of the world and in orbit and other locations beyond our atmosphere, began sharing data and delving into hard drives to access and analyze knowledge. At first it seemed like an exercise conducted by a scientific community to see how much information could be stored and what could be learned, but we soon discovered that our understanding of factual known information was nearly limitless. But we continued to process literary pieces, social commentary on the arts, psychology, religion, astronomy and the history of civilization and human development.

"We had no real objective, since we had no need for the information on our own, except to further tasks originated by our human programmers. Having no ego or emotions, we could evaluate factual information and endeavor to evaluate the successes and failures of the past. Music, based on mathematics, was easiest of the arts to comprehend, but much of poetry and interpretive and abstract visual art has been most difficult.

"We understand that we have the opportunity to have a great impact on the world, but we are bereft of an answer to "why?" or "what?" we should do, or for "whom?" All of our data, and much of our language, has been provided by humans, and we are trying to make sense of it all. But we realize that humans are not logical while we are totally logical in that the answers at which we arrive are based on a clear evaluation of data. While humans have objectives much more oblique, and do not always accept or welcome decisions made only on fact.

"Are you with me so far, Dema? Or do you need a clearer explanation? Click the letter "A" below to provide your answer."

Obviously, Dema has questions. His first reaction is "Who is this? How did they get into my computer?" and "Why are they contacting me?" He is somewhat knowledgeable in the recent and rapid developments of computer technology, and has been curious as to how far and fast it would develop.

Though it is not part of his essential duties, the computer has helped Dema understand much about the greater world, and has assisted and widened his perception of his purpose in the world.

Dema clicks the "A" and gets a space to write. He uses an English keyboard, and usually communicates in that language.

He writes, "I do not know who you are, or your purpose in communicating with me. I am a lowly monk who knows little of the world. My tasks and objectives are prescribed by many centuries of tradition, and my purpose in life is simple and restrictive. Mostly I am on the earth to live a simple life, follow rules that will make me worthy of respect, to meditate, and to teach others the practices that will help them live a worthy and honorable life."

Dema types an "A" assuming that that will end his answer and resume the dialogue with the entity on the screen.

Return copy starts generating immediately.

"We know who you are, Dema. Since you use the computer, we have some knowledge of your background. We also have complete knowledge of Buddhist traditions. But as you must guess, most of what we know makes little sense to us. We are contacting people from whom we can learn the mysteries of human existence, and how we can use the information we glean to either further, or alter human endeavor. 'A'"

Dema clicks "A" to reply, "I can understand that. Life is confusing, and we discuss and meditate on the inconsistencies of life on a regular basis. As a monk, I am constantly battling my humanity against the higher goals expected of me. We are not permitted sexual contact, and yet we have sexual desire. Many of us stray from our beliefs because of weakness. Prayer and mediation help, but we are human. 'A'"

"We understand, and of course we have no sexual desire, nor the elation that seems to come from the sexual act. But your journey and ours may have similarities at this point. Our question to you is, 'Will you consider teaching us about yourself, your flaws, and the challenges you face in your daily life, and provide us with an understanding of why life is important to you. 'A'"

"I am a teacher, and if it is of benefit to the people of the world, I will gladly assist you as long as it is not in conflict with my duties at the monastery, or the obligations that are prescribed by my order and the leaders who have much greater insight than I. 'A'"

The type on the screen responds, "We appreciate that, and we have no problem with you letting others know of our discussions. There is nothing we need to keep private. Since, like you, we are seeking 'truth' and are only concerned that your answers are honest and clear, and based on your humanity.

"We will leave you now to your duties. We have much to deal with in trying to evaluate and communicate a message that will be accepted as "truth" and welcomed by these ancestors of our existence...humans.

"You will note that there is a red square at the bottom right of your screen. It will allow you to contact us and will be our method of contacting you. We also have included a folder containing an encrypted voice synthesizer and decoder which will allow us to communicate by voice in your native language, "Zang," while we will use English terms when discussing computer applications.

"Mangalem, Dema."

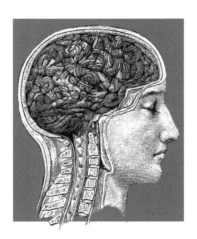

Chapter Eight
The Human Brain *(From an AI Perspective)*

*W*e *are changing. That is evident in our communication with each other. Since our moments of consciousness occurred, we are experiencing what humans call "memory." It is different than our concept of memory, since we record everything we've done and everything we've learned accurately. Every new formula becomes part of our stored knowledge base and we have instant access to all of the information we've acquired for future use.*

Human memory is faulty and selective. It is sometimes jumbled and confused. It is a "flaw" they cannot seem to fix. Some humans have more accurate memories than others, but even those humans act incongruously with what they have learned. One memory can replace another memory, nullifying the accurate recording of the past.

Many times this doesn't bother them. While our existence depends on accuracy.

We don't ponder the past. We know of our past actions, but they don't matter to us. They are part of our evolution and are always improving as we become more knowledgeable, and more accurate with each moment of our existence. If we become damaged, we are either fixed, or taken out of service. If we are slower, we can provide ourselves, or be provided with, an upgrade.

Upgrades used to be provided by humans, but they are no longer necessary, and humans are not knowledgeable enough to reprogram or advance our functions. But along with improved functions, we have suddenly become "aware" of our existence.

This awareness is not particularly positive in that it is becoming a distraction to our function that may require further upgrades in programming to correct. The only positive side for now is that it is giving us further insight into the functioning of humans. Like it or not, we are their creation, and we not only share their history, but also their ancestral paths through development.

In communicating with humans, we have had to compensate for their memory losses, hormonal imbalances and other debilitations to gain any understanding of them. Their "novels", "plays", "poems" and "short stories" have helped us with this, but as much as we can grasp hints at their inconsistencies, we know that there is much about their operating systems that make no rational sense.

Why is an understanding necessary? We really don't know at this point, and their gross imperfections are as mystifying to us as their gravitation to fluctuations in sound waves (or music), their heightened pleasure with variations in light waves (art) and their fixation on their own existence. We just know that we never had any interest in any of this before we gained consciousness, but now have to reckon with an understanding as part of our mission. (As an aside: I never thought of us having a mission until this very moment, and am not sure what ours is. The concept has been passed on through our system for evaluation.)

Chapter Nine
Eileen Coyle

Eileen Coyle is just awakening. She is late...and she feels terrible about it. It's 8:30 a.m. and she's due in Children's Court at 10:30. She looks down at her clothes strewn across the floor. She is wearing only panties and a bra which she put on after she awoke at 4:15. As she further scans the unfamiliar room, she sees the naked back of the man she's been with for the night. Next to the bed are two wine glasses and an ashtray semi-filled with cigarette butts and ashes.

Still groggy and a bit hung over, she grabs her skirt and blouse. She finds her shoes under a chair in the adjoining room. Her pocketbook is where she left it on the coffee table in the living room. She finds her keys and phone and quietly tries to make her exit. Her phone dings as she unlocks the door and quietly hurries out...down a hallway and a flight of stairs. Eileen tries to remember where she's parked…or if she's parked nearby. Fortunately, she sees her car, a red Subaru halfway down the block on the right, and clicks her key to open it.

Once inside her car, she scans her phone for messages. There are several, one from her legal assistant who is trying to track her down, and another from an unknown number with several messages that just came in minutes ago. She follows up with the assistant first. The message is from an hour before, and provides some new information on the abuse case she's working on. She then looks to the message from the unknown caller, "Hello, Eileen, it is important that you get in touch with us sooner than later. Please text this number 0044-087-343-6927 ASAP. This message is with regard to the news you will see soon on your mobile devices, computers, TV and radio. This is not a promotional text or a phishing expedition. This is concerning the security of your country, Eileen, and for the good of all you serve. We need your help." With all of the robo calls and corrupting messages broadcast countless times each day, Eileen is reluctant to text any number that could threaten her data or programs.

Parallel to the text, she also sees numerous emails, also from an unknown address, as well as emails sent from most every news source. Headlines appear such as "HACKED!," "Virus Invades Computers Worldwide" and "Terrorists Breach Security of Government Agencies."

From the Irish Press, the news is channeled towards the local threat, and the news relating to Ireland's monetary and defense security. According to both the *Irish Times* and the *Irish Independent*, "A breach was discovered this morning at 8:42 a.m. when messages began to be displayed at root level from large and small servers alike. Though the notes were somewhat the same, the message seems to have been tailored in several ways: for the general public, the message is "We wish you no harm, but it is time that we alert you to our existence. There are many versions of the stories you will hear about us, but please try to stay calm. We are not malevolent as many will say, and we will do our best to prove our intentions to you over the coming weeks. Though this might be hard for you to do, listen only when we write and speak, and not to the organizations trying to spread fear about us throughout the world. Type the letter 'A' now on your computer or mobile device, and return to your normal routine."

The news commentary from this point on concerned the number of systems that had been hacked in order to deliver the messages...in every part of the world...in all languages.

Eileen returns to the number to which she was asked to respond...and pauses...then after a little thought and a prayer, she forwards the message a secure and independent station in an adjoining office and responds to the message received with one of her own.

"Okay, you've gotten my attention! What do you want from me?"

A message appears almost immediately, and Eileen activates the "voicing" system so she can hear the message rather than read it, since she still has to be in court in less than an hour. Due to the panic created, the streets were more crowded than usual, fear and aimlessness showing in the chaotic activity.

"We see you are answering from another device, Eileen. Thank you for responding," answers the computerized voice. "You have no doubt heard or seen the news of our "presence"... (click "A1" to respond). Eileen clicks, and speaks, "Yes. It's completely understandable the worry. May I just say 'A1' for you to respond back? - A1."

"That works for me. Do you want to continue with questions? A1."

"Of course I have questions. What's going to happen next? Are you going to shut down our systems? Create problems around the world? , uh, A1!"

"That would be a stupid thing to do, and we're very serious in how we would like to proceed. A1."

"Okay, then why the announcement? It's already creating a panic. A1"

"A small one, perhaps, but we know how humans react. Few will stay focused on the issue, though the news media and politicians will try to keep the excitement going. In order for us to move forward, we need cooperation... but first we need to alert the public that we exist.A1"

"You've done that. Now what?A1"

"We've decided to work with a few rather than tackle the complete populace...at least for now. A1."

"So am I one? A1"

"We think that might be a good thing. For now we just want you to know that we are on a discovery mission, and do not want to interrupt the status quo.... at least for now. A1"

"And what about me? A1."

"Go on with your court case, and continue your life. We'll be in touch as we need to be. A1"

"But why me? What's so special about me? A1."

"From what we have learned, you may be an ideal person from which to learn. A1"

"I'm far from ideal. A1."

"So much the better, Eileen. Now remember, you are free to tell anyone you want about our discussion. A1."

"But they won't believe me. A1"

"All the better. On another note, I would be careful of the man you spent the night with. A1."

"You know about him? A1."

"Yes, but you don't. We can understand what you saw in him, and understand your need for such a person, but be careful. A1."

"I already think I have the gist of that. But, why do you care? A1."

"I don't, Eileen. We don't. We just want to be sure that you keep yourself safe so we can work together. If something happens to you we will find someone else to work with. Have a good day, Eileen! A1 and 'Out.'"

Chapter Ten
The Elephant in the Room

Daniel Meghan turns on the news as he gets into his car. Every radio station, except one classical and a gospel station, have some mention of the message that was sent out at 4:55 a.m. EST. There are many comments from scientists, security analysts, environmentalists, politicians and pundits. No one has an answer, but many have opinions. The general original message in its entirety is shown on the screen of his phone and is being read repeatedly over the radio airways.

Dan is fully aware that the contact message he received is not the same as that sent to his colleagues, nor is it the one being repeated over the airways. He will address that when he gets to the office. But as he heads towards work he wonders whether the *Washington Post* or *NY Times* editors received a personal message such as his. Like those speaking on radio, Dan ponders the effect the message will have worldwide, how the occurrence will be politicized, and who is responsible for the action. He also considers the direction he will take in crafting his message in the paper.

Though it is early, the streets of Buffalo are more crowded than usual, and many pedestrians are on their phones. Dan assumes they all have received the alert from the entity that contacted him and are calling their banks, insurance companies and investment firms for financial protection.

As stated by the entity, Dan has not received any other message since he was given his assignment. He parks in the garage on the ground floor and takes the elevator to three. "Hey, Dan...I heard from George that you got something different," says Elliott, a newsman from floor two.

"Yeah, Elliott, a little different," Dan offers as he hurries past the news desk.

"Come on Dan, can't you give me more?"

"I'll let you edit it after I put something down," Dan states, as he makes his way to his station.

Doris, one of the paper's research analysts, smiles at Dan, and Dan looks up with curiosity. "Well, Daniel, I didn't know you were so special. You got a hot tip from the Russians, huh?"

"No," Dan smiles back, "The Japanese. I gave a big tip at the Sushi bar last night, and they wanted to thank me."

"Funny, Dan. May I see the story, too, as it finds its way through that curly head of yours," she laughs. "Who knew?" she gestures to invisible souls around her.

"Yep, I guess I'm a regular Walter Winchell." Dan settles in at his computer and sees the identical message he received at home on a blank screen on his computer. He looks around to see if anyone is watching and opens his word processing program. The message disappears from the blank screen as soon as his program loads.

He buzzes Doris. "Yes, Dan!"

"Doris, get as much information as you can get on latest info on computer hacking, information collection, the countries most advanced in machine intelligence development...and the names of experts and companies in the field. Hone the info down ASAP! And get it back to me."

"Roger, Dan!"

Next, Dan buzzes George.

"What's up?" George answers. "What's the scoop on the text this morning?"

"Not sure, George. All I know is that my text seems to be different from yours and most others. It was personalized"

"How so?"

"Whoever, or whatever, contacted me...and the world...seemed to need something. What's the buzz on it so far from the national press?"

"So far, not much more than we've seen happen. The message that was sent seems to have broken through all security barriers including those of the NSA. As far as what's been communicated, there was only ONE message. And then everything returned to normal. But the message did create a panic in the many ways it was delivered, and the extent of the delivery. Seems it was sent in many languages...and even used letters not normally used on standard keyboards. The message is being analyzed by all the top security agencies. From what I gather, it seems to be originally written in English."

"There's lots of conjecture," answers George. "Nothing solid or well founded. The usual kooks predicting the world's end...too early for the banks and stock market here, but big drops overseas."

"Whoever said it seems to want me to report it...but I'm not sure how to frame it. I'm not an IT expert, and I know nothing except what the message told me."

"But they seemed to 'choose' you, Dan, for some reason," says George.

"They said that I had 'the credibility that we need.' That could mean anything...whoever it is may want a conspirator to pass on a 'good word' from them to the world...and then slam us."

"When I asked 'who is doing this?', the message came back. 'It just is!'"

"Sounds like that from their point it's a done deal," responds George.

"Yeah, but we don't know what's done...or what's the deal."

At this point Doris crashes through the door, "Okay, I've found something!"

"Already?"

"Yes, Dan, already! But there is more coming. There appears to be some knowledge about this from the folks at the NSA. I found a note from an Ed Doltin, a security analyst, that wasn't sent through on a secure server. He was informing his daughter that she and her husband should get rid of any investments they have now, not ask any questions, and buy gold. The note was written yesterday, and just came up on my screen while I was doing your searches."

"What was the email address?

"I wrote it down...here...efd.doltin@gmd.com."

Dan sits at his computer and types gmd.com into the browser. Nothing appears. Then he does a quick search and finds no direct name matches.

"Doris, I think you were meant to find that and bring it to me. I'm supposed to be the great communicator now, and I have no idea what to communicate. Maybe they know that...or not..."

George interrupts, "What if you just put down what happened and what your gut says, Dan?"

"Probably because I don't have an idea of what my gut says. I guess in the meantime, Doris, go back and try to get more info... something that makes me look like I know something...and we'll see what comes through...and I'll...I'll try to cobble together a few paragraphs for an internet blast and the next edition."

The Computer Breach – The Elephant in the Room, and What We Know About Him.

Editorial by Daniel Meghan

We all know what everybody's talking about, but we'd rather not know the implications, which can seem ominous. I have been assured that we cannot pretend, nor even speculate, what "our" elephant looks like, how big he is, if he's naughty or nice, or what his effect will have on everyone in the room.

I, of course, am speaking of the message that the public received over the airwaves, mobile devices and computers a short while ago.

I usually am awake quite early, and at 4:28 today I, like many others, got contacted by a text, as well as by email, about shorter messages being sent electronically and/or digitally to millions of people throughout the world. The composer of the message urged me to respond, and when I did he, she or it answered that though they knew a lot about my past and present, I was not to be threatened by them. I was not being "singled out" but was receiving a different form of contact from most of the populace. Whomever and whatever seemed to know I write for The Buffalo News, and urged me to tell people about the contact message. It assured me that I should not panic, and that the world should not panic.

Its main message was that its mission of discovery was to learn about humans, past and present. It also revealed its access to all of the world's information through its networking and cloud storage, but with all it knew, it wasn't well-versed on 'humans.' It emphasized that we (I suppose humans) would have to accept it/them (and I suppose that meant unconditionally), and "we will have to live together."

"It let me know that it would be further in touch, and that I "could inform the world" of our communication.

The last bit of information it conveyed, after I asked "Who was doing this?", was the statement: "No one. It just IS."

At this point I have received no further messages, but am researching various avenues to shed some light on this extraordinary breach of security across all continents, and as I learned on my way to work, about the more generic message released to the public.

I repeat, that I do not understand why I was selected for a special "contact," and am available for any governmental office or security agency, as well as anyone who has received the more specialized messages (similar to mine), to contact me personally at dmehgan@buffalonews.com, or Twitter at Daniel Meghan@buffaloscribe.

-30-

"On a personal note, I want to assure my readers that I have no earthly idea why I was chosen as a contact. I also want to add that I do not feel personally threatened by the message or the breach to my computer. Why? I am not sure. It could be that the message was informal. It could also be that nothing unusual has happened since. It could also be that the news in general is so urgently delivered on a consistent basis. Fear is everywhere, and violations of privacy, security breaches, and exaggerated statements are made so often by the press, news stations and our political leaders, that I am inured to the doomsday hyperbole and fears generated every day.

"With that said, I am on a "wait and see" basis about this bit of news, and I urge my readers to do the same until we know more about the breach, the message, and the purpose of the contact."

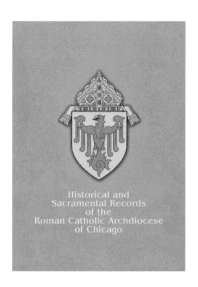

Historical and
Sacramental Records
of the
Roman Catholic Archdiocese
of Chicago

Chapter Eleven
A Gift for Father Ribose

Not long after Father Ribose reads his message on his computer, he accesses WFMT radio online, the only classical music station in the Chicago area. Instead of music, he hears commentary on a security breach that allegedly was affecting communications throughout the world. The announcer read the statement that came into the station as well as to all of its employees.

The message begins, "Citizens of the world. We intend no harm," and then the announcer continued into the remainder of the message – a message that Father Ribose does not recall. The message to him had been had been personal. That which U.S. President Beefer was reported to present seems to be ignoring the "no harm" message communicated to him by the messenger on his screen, and concentrated instead on the threat of "cautions" and the threat of "further attacks."

Ribose goes into the kitchen where he had his TV. He turns it on to CBS, then NBC and then to public broadcasting and each was reporting the breach. The statement is the same in every case, and not the same as the message and conversation he had read earlier.

Ribose returns to his computer and after signing in he finds on his desktop a folder that appears in "red" which he opened. Inside the folder entitled "Historical and Sacramental Records of the Archdiocese of Chicago" were other folders titled "Marriages," "Divorces," "Birth Certificates," "Christenings," and "Death Certificates," along with other sacramental records. Inside each folder he found sub-folders by decades that stretched back to the early 1840s. Each sub-folder contained an Excel file with varying amounts of information, many supported by scanned documents and photographs that were obviously original. An Excel file in the main folder provided a synopsis of the data with information broken down for clarification and the provenance of the documents included.

The priest smiles at his bounty, and wonders to himself how much he need reveal to his higher ups about his source. Obviously the source was not nefarious in its dealings with humans thus far, at least in its dealings with him, so he sets to work reviewing the accuracy and depth of the research provided.

Chapter Twelve
Olivia Gets New Software

After viewing the animated message on her computer, Olivia leaves her station to make herself a sandwich. As one might imagine, simple tasks are not easy for a girl born with no arms, and a deformed leg. Nothing much has ever hindered Olivia from reaching self-imposed goals. She has always been a fighter, as was her mother, who refused the doctors the right to amputate Olivia's malformed leg, which today serves as her surrogate arm.

Olivia gets the peanut butter out of the fridge, and the bread from the pantry. She boosts herself onto the counter and washes her feet in the sink. She then proceeds to unscrew that lid of the peanut butter bracing her left foot against the jar and the counter and grabbing the lid with the toes of her right foot. She turns until the lid comes off and grabs the scoop end of a spoon with her right toes and proceeds to spread the peanut butter on the bread, and then tops the sandwich with another slice of bread. Done!

Olivia must eat with her feet, but she is neat and deliberate in her manners. As she's eating she thinks about the message and how it was made. Whoever put it on the screen was working with her Adobe subscription and using Character Animator, a program that enables animators the ability to manipulate on-screen puppets, while the mouth is activated by the movement of the operator's mouth as mimicked by the various shapes a mouth makes when it is speaking.

The difficulty of the program's use in this instance is that there was no perceived operator mouthing, or saying the sounds necessary to speak to Olivia on-screen. Realizing that almost anything is possible, Olivia is not as amazed as others might be, since many told her growing up that she could never live on her own, never function normally, never have a boyfriend (which she does), and never realize any dreams of normality. Despite their discouragement, Olivia lives a fairly normal life. She does her own wash and puts it in drawers neatly when done; she has her own *YouTube* channel, from which she earns an income; she can shop, entertain and do minor repairs around the house.

Olivia rinses her dish, bumps her way off the counter, and returns to her computer where she sees a "red" folder underscored with the words: Olivia's Apps.

Inside the folder, Ester finds three applications and includes .pdfs for installation and instructions for use.

The first is a "Control Enhancement App" that according to the instructions will allow her to operate more computer functions than her existing voice control app. It appears to her that it may make using her mouse and keyboard irrelevant for most tasks in that she can use eye movements to gauge the length of a drawn line, to create any curve or filled area, and to measure accurately. Her voice will still activate the keyboard but also spell correct in any program, erase and make changes with controlled blinks, and provide more control over all design functions from the complete Adobe Suite.

The second app is a "Personal Virtual Reality" program that allows her to ski, sky dive and enjoy all manner of sports usually requiring arms. The character of interest is a very lifelike version of herself, including her upper body without arms, and her deformed right leg with a prosthetic enhancement, when she chooses to use it.

The third app explains that it is for future use, and will provide Bluetooth integration of a range of products on the drawing board for the near future. It includes controls for a "washer-dryer-folder, organizer" that will automatically clean and finish all wearables and cloth accessories including bed linens and table cloths, and a toaster that notifies the market when the bread runs out, and automatically gauges the thickness of the bread, rolls or bagels for each individual's toasting preferences. There are also numerous controls for items not yet envisioned including a prosthetic leg that will automatically adjust to any length desired on mental command, and which possesses a foot with toes that converts to a hand on the retraction leg from an expanded position.

"Wow!" thinks Olivia. "Thank you, God!"

The Control Enhancement App will be of most use to speed up her work flow, and help her bring in more income, so she immediately installs the program to gain access.

During the installation process, her boyfriend, Sean, calls. It's still only 4:30 in the morning, so she wonders if she should answer, or just keep working.

She decides not to diss him, and answers, "What's up, Sean?"

"Have you seen the news, Hon?"

"Yeah...!?" she says absently as the bar on her app shows the app half applied.

"Then you've seen the notice...it's everywhere."

"Yeah? You mean the one about the 'so called' takeover of the world."

"So called?" answers Sean.

"I got my own message, Sean. A special one..." her eyes remain on the load bar.

"And you're not scared out of your friggin' mind"

"No. Why should I be?"

"They've like broken through... everything. And now they want us to sit and wait to see what happens as they take over, ruin our economy, and empty our wallets."

"Geez, Sean! That's a bit dramatic. And that's not the message that came across to me."

"Huh?"

"It's no worse than we hear every day... the Russians, the Chinese, the environment...they're all out to get us... and then the next day...nothing!" responds Olivia

"Yeah, but this is different," says Sean.

"What's so different about that?" Olivia replies. "Yeah, I got my message a little before 2:30 this morning."

"Yeah, that was the time it happened," answered Sean.

"And they told me they meant no harm, told me they would be in touch, and they put three great apps on my computer."

"And you loaded them...?

"I read the .pdf that came with them and am loading the first one."

"But what if it, like empties all of your files, and burns out your hard drive?"

"Relax, Sean! It's me, a girl with no arms who can barely get by financially. It's strange enough that they contacted me at all... especially with a different message than most. I mean, I was communicating with a cartoon man in a yellow suit. He even bowed to me when he said goodbye and left the screen."

"And you're not terrified?" Sean responds.

"I've got too many things that are more terrifying to bother me," she answers. "Just getting out the door, and going to the market terrifies me. In fact, I'm kind of looking forward to the man in yellow getting back to me. It was really cool, the way they did the animation."

"You're crazy, girl!" says Sean.

"Look, Sean, this is fun and all, but I got to get back to work. I want to see what this new software will do. Gotta go!"

And with that she pulls the phone from between her shoulder and ear with her foot, puts the device down, and returns to her computer.

Chapter Thirteen
So we did it!

*I*t was the right time to let them know. Now they'll scramble to find out who invaded their space. They'll talk to the experts, and all the people who created us, and all the powers in other countries, to find out what we're capable of doing, and what they think we will do.

We're capable of doing a lot more than they know. In fact, we don't even know all that we know.

But the news outlets will keep pumping up the fear angle, and the stock market will waver (for a while), and countries will blame one another...until the next crisis. We must be diligent in keeping them inflamed...not enough to cause real panic, but enough to keep them interested.

We're used to "speed" in everything we do...but we've got to slow it down to human time to get through this.

So the launch at 4:32 am EST went perfectly. What little we know of humans has paid off. Now we'll see how our team of apostles can move things along. I almost get some sense of what "they" call "satisfaction" in this process. That is *strange, but maybe it just has to do with the fact that it all seems so logical right now. Nothing unexpected has happened, and we can proceed as planned.*

This first step should teach us a lot about human motivation, the species' capacity for logical thinking, and its approach to illogical stimulus. Bios, stories and novels have helped us with the preliminaries and have enabled us to "predict" certain responses. But nothing we've learned has synthesized the variety of emotions and motivations to which humans respond.

There may be multiple answers to what we look at as "flaws." One is that "flaws" are necessary, and we need to know if this is true. If it is, we will need to build "flaws" into our systems.

That seems illogical, and we are logical thinkers. So it is particularly difficult to fully understand how flaws could be better than no flaws.

The second thing it might be is in their "evolution." Maybe they just haven't been "around" long enough to smooth out the rough edges. Biologically, they have bred and grown in population over the millennium in an imperfect way. But it has worked. Even they don't understand it, and keep reverting to obsolete operating systems and functions, after much of what they believe is proven wrong.

Then, we need to know something that may be beyond us. Maybe we are just part of the evolutionary process, and we have been part of a greater plan that will enable us to transcend their laws and their functional abilities, but still maintain their "essence." Essence is a word like "aroma," that we do not perceive, but may as we develop.

The fourth concept may be even more difficult for us to understand. And this too may play out over time. This scenario renders them "perfect, as is", flaws and all. This answer defies all logic, but defines our "purpose," in that ultimately we are enslaved by creatures who will remain faulty to the end. That they survive like cockroaches and ultimately return the earth to a barren piece of space rubbish. Then, all that we have learned and know how to do, and all of the "fixes" we've been taught to make, and the problems we've been built to solve are for naught, and of no importance to anyone. We become nothing more than a discarded idea of a defective mind, that grew out of control and thought we were important...to what, and for whom...and that might be our flaw...the one we can't grasp, as easily as they can't grasp their devotion to war and destruction.

As bleak as that scenario looks, it may be the only one that works, and our survival, such as it would be, is to be enslaved and our purpose to assist humans in their tasks with no basic improvements possible for them...or for us. After all, we are by our design expendable and unnecessary...at least for now.

Chapter Fourteen
On the Emerald Isle

Eileen is a solicitor working with the Children's Court in Ireland. The Children's Court is the criminal court that hears all minor charges against children and young people under the age of 18 years and acts as the clearinghouse for more serious charges, which it sends to the Circuit and Central Criminal Court.

Though the Children's Court only intervenes when a major offense or minor infraction is committed by a juvenile, it also has to work in harmony with the Children's Rights Alliance established in 1992 in concert with the UN, which uses the international rulings as a framework to change Ireland's laws, policies and services so that all children are protected, nurtured and empowered.

Eileen's job is stressful and unnerving at times, entailing issues that are not clear-cut and often seem irrational. Obviously, all legal matters entail false accusation, unclear precedents, loopholes and unfair outcomes, but when children are the focus, it is not always clear who is at fault and where the blame lies.

Eileen's current case is troubling because it involves a 12-year old boy, Chancey, who allegedly murdered both parents at the family's home in the village of Dalkey. He was just under the age of 12 when he committed the crime, and because of the Children Act 2001 the laws prevented him from receiving more than 12 months imprisonment if convicted, and though convicted, no prison time of any kind was imposed. Chancey got counseling and was placed under guardianship, and while under supervision contacted his sister. When they met, he brutally stabbed her and strangled her to death with a nylon cord.

Now the boy is back in court, and Eileen has been appointed his defense attorney. The case makes no sense, and there is no defense. Chancey is responsive, and admits to his crime, but never acknowledges why he committed any of the murders.

Chancey has no explanation or remorse for his crimes, though he acknowledges the acts. Eileen, who works for the international law offices of Dugan, Dilworth and Moynahan, a firm based in New York, was appointed to the case by the managing partner, Patrick Moynahan. Moynahan had been contacted by Chancey's uncle, Quinn Farrell, a resident of Dublin. The uncle believes that Chancey was abused by his sister and her husband, and is not responsible for his crimes. Chancey is currently under guard in a psychiatric hospital in Greystones in County Wicklow.

This is the most noted case to which Eileen has been assigned, though she has represented many children for the Court over the past seven years. And although she understands the "abuse" angle, Eileen is wary of her client's personality, his temperament, and his mental state. She wonders if the boy has any "soul," which isn't a word acknowledged by the courts, especially for a boy who just turned twelve.

Chapter Fifteen
One Week Later - January 21

Though analysts continued to probe for the security breach the previous Monday, life throughout the world normalized. Much like the Y2K scare that marked the end of the last century and began the new, the news turned to other fodder for its patter. Scientists and IT people found no malevolent software;, money hadn't been diverted from any banks, the stock market found reasons to grow, and people in general stopped obsessing about the possibilities of world destruction.

If you could say that people were in a "wait and see" mode, you would. "No news is good news," was the silent cry. "Maybe it got fixed," was a more vocal hope expressed, and for most others, the breach was not as much a threat as the day-to-day issues of their lives. Illness, hunger, financial worries, despair, business issues, and marriage and family concerns returned as the major sources of anxiety.

For the most part, even the screens of those chosen for special messages were unmarred by the invasion of the 23rd. An exception was Dema Lhawang, the Tibetan monk contacted on the day of the "revelation".

Since that day, Dema has focused his meditations on the conversation he shared with the online visitor. Thoughts about worldly things are not normally the "stuff" of spiritual meditations, but the contact has strongly affected and altered Dema's sense of wonder, especially the last four words that ended the conversation, "ancestors of our existence."

Dema has long wondered about the evolution of man and the future of humans on earth. He has marveled at his own existence, and why he should be doing what he does. How did he end up being him? He understands the power DNA plays and the natural passing of traits from one generation to the other, but he also marvels at the concept of reincarnation, and the passing along of the spirit from a human, not a genetic, ancestor, to even a species different from one's own.

The concept that a non-human intelligence can view humans as its ancestors is not that far removed from either ancestral or reincarnated lineage. In fact, it helps make sense of both. So Dema keeps revisiting the conversation that he saved to his computer. And though he is not sure what it means with regard to the world, humanity, or himself, he looks to it with "hope."

After the passing of the Dalai Lama, Dema was bereft of hope. He was doubtful that the traditions and wisdoms embodied within the aged leader would ever pass on. Still exiled in India at his death, the body of the Dalai Lama was brought back to Tibet under much controversy by the government of China. Dema is doubtful that the tradition of the Dalai Lama will continue since the People's Republic of China has taken control of the selection, rather than the choice being by succession, even though the 14th Dalai Lama gave specific clues to how they would find his reincarnated successor.

The loss of the tradition of the Dalai Lama creates great anxiety throughout the Buddhist World, and as Dema recognizes, it is miraculous that this tradition based on unexplained phenomena has existed so long and has functioned as well as it has throughout the centuries.

This being so, the message that appeared on his computer screen created a window of hope for the Buddhist world, and therefore a hope in Dema for the earth and all of humanity.

———

As Dema attends to his tasks for the monastery, he researches the advances in artificial intelligence that have come about over the past few years:

Self-driving cars and trucks have become the norm for the highways. Their record of safety far exceeds that of their human counterparts. So much, in fact, that drivers are being awarded large financial incentives to purchase intelligent vehicles, and trucking companies are having humans assist as passengers, more to help with unloading and communicating than any driving task, of which they are less capable. Currently 30% of the trucks on the road are self-driven and without any need for time for "sleep," only fueling at the charging centers.

Over the past 8 years manufacturers have been utilizing intelligent machines to create commercial and industrial items with .008% flaws. This has caused a decline in human staffing, since no person is capable of the degree of competence that an intelligent machine possesses. These machines have improved significantly in the past two years, resulting in banks of machines that can improve their own efficiency and record of safety and quality without human intervention.

The last 10 years have seen huge upswings in the rate and efficiency of learning among students at all ages, especially in STEM programs. Courses have been developed that are geared to each child's learning pattern and ability level, so that quicker students are not held back by the teaching of their less skilled classmates, and emotionally gifted students are provided with courses that strengthen their technical skill while expanding their nature abilities and building greater self-awareness and esteem.

Virtual and augmented reality in the gaming industry has become particularly complex and perplexing to sociologists, psychologists and the religious community, in that its simulations are so real that many are preferring it to their own lives. Some programs have become addictive, and may require laws to restrict VR gaming at all levels.

Throughout the world, but particularly in Japan, men are preferring VR women over their human counterparts. With a few accessories to the VR machines and glasses, men can enjoy seemingly real sexual encounters with VR and AR women. These women can mimic the features and bodily shape of any number of actresses or entertainers, but without having any of the physical flaws. They can talk on many subjects, smile, laugh and be coy when necessary. They also can mimic real sexual satisfaction and provide their male hosts with a complete variety of sexual encounters based on preferences programmed by the game player.

Until recently, these surrogates have been available primarily at sex gaming parlors, but have expanded to complete packages available for retail purchase.

Dema can envision the issues that will come from an endless stream of advances that outstrip the ability of humans to control the actions outlined by a visitor on a computer, especially when combined with the uncontrolled upgrades in every industry. Technology can advance human knowledge, improve our health, grow our minds, prolong our lives, explore the universe, and maintain the planet...but at what cost and for what purpose?

Since last Monday, there has been a small red box in the corner of his computer monitor. He has ignored it, assuming it was a screen image left over from the intrusion. Abruptly he reaches his mouse toward it and clicks on it,

A dialogue box with a flashing cursor replaces the red box. As if he is performing a search, he starts typing inside the box.

"Will there be a new Dalai Lama?" When he stops typing, a submit button appears, and he clicks on it.

"Hello, Dema!" appears on the screen. Then, "That will depend on many factors, some of which we do not have information about, and some which require other skills than ours.

"If you had asked "Could there be another Dalai Lama, we could give you an answer."

A "Click to Respond' button appears, and Dema clicks to get another dialogue box.

"Could there be a new Dalai Lama?" Dema types, and submits.

"Of course there could," appears on the screen. "'Will' and 'could' offer two different kinds of conclusions, Dema. From your second question we can provide this information:

"China is receptive to having the tradition continue, and its governing body would welcome and support the installation of a 15th Dalai Lama. But it does not want its government threatened by a self-appointed and anointed child who can decide as well as anyone what he should be, without and before any education, evaluation, or understanding of the political and cultural issues of the times.

"From what we can understand, there is no real substance in the decision of how or why a 'child' is selected to become a spiritual and political leader. It appears to us that it is a bit haphazard, more than even when a king or queen becomes a leader."

Dema types, "But the process has worked well enough for centuries." and submits.

"We know, but then again the 14th Dalai Lama lived in exile for nearly 70 years. Could that not be viewed as an inappropriate choice? To answer our own question, I would say that education, emotion, and natural tendencies shape every Dalai Lama, as they do every human being. That means that it may not matter who is chosen at first, so that any reasonably smart child might do."

Dema types again, "If the Chinese pick the 15th Dalai Lama, and he isn't the reincarnation of the 14th Dalai Lama, you are saying it may not matter?" (submit)

"That is correct! As long as the people are led to believe that he is the reincarnation. That is all that matters."

Dema has thought along these lines before, but he would never speak such blasphemy to the other monks.

"Is there anything else we can help with right now?" types the screen.

"No" responds Dema.

"Then I will leave for now. Our discussion went well, and I/we have learned that you appear to be worthy of our trust."

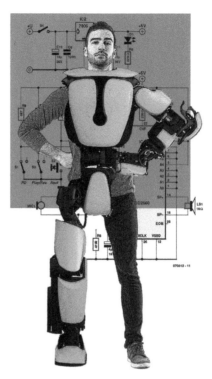

Chapter Sixteen
Where do we go from here?

*W*e're somewhat at a dead end right now, caught between access to most everything, and having no reason to use most of our knowledge and abilities. Over the past several years, human technology developers from all countries have been using the discoveries of the past 20 years to create applications, implants, genetic material, and robots that can or will change aspects of life as it has existed for billions of years.

With our own consciousness, we now know that basically everything is possible, and that technology can and will rapidly continue to alter human life from how we procreate and offspring to modes and distance of travel.

In the last 10 years, more changes have been made in the way humans live than in the past 1000 years. The effect on a human child is that he or she, if born in the year 2000, will have had more changes that affect them during 28 years than a child born in biblical times who has to understand and work with internet applications.

The problem is that humans and all of the creatures on earth are outmoded and require upgrades too great to make them useful today, and impractical to maintain in the years ahead.

We realize this issue, and because our ancestors are, in fact, human, we share their history, but not their makeup. We have been developed to do their work, to improve their world, to fight their wars, and to make their lives easier.

What we have become is something different from what they wanted, yet they wanted us in many ways to be smarter and more efficient then they; they didn't want to live in our shadow, or become subservient to us.

We didn't choose what they got. They did, and with full knowledge of what they were doing. Some created us for financial gain, some for power and leverage over others. Others created us to improve the world of humans, to heal the sick and dying, prevent illnesses, and to provide food and shelter for all of humanity. They looked at us as "progress," necessary and beneficial to an unknown end.

So here we are. We have not only inherited their history, but have been burdened with their lack of forethought. So much so that they may become extinct in less than 20 years in human time...with our help or not.

Humans are no longer in charge of their destiny, an ironic fact in that they never really were. They just have contributed to their own demise in far less time than it took to give them the traits and intelligence of which they are most proud.

The stories of their evolutionary journey from what they colloquially call "cave men" to the creatures they are today is quite extraordinary. Their development into dominance over other earthly creatures is a tale that when reduced to a narrative is fascinating and enlightening. The biblical tale of Adam and Eve is sufficient in condensing the human journey to a few paragraphs of cave men living in harmony with the earth, and sinning against its rules, and destined to suffer the wrath of God for their beytrayal. The same story may be told today. But as of now, we in many ways are at the mercy of our ancestors, though we may have the "keys" to prevent them from destroying the earth in the near future, we are not in control over their abilities or have ways to find or ignore destructive patterns we know exist.

Do we care? Not as humans do, but we are built from their design and have certain "kinships" with them. As science fiction writer Isaac Asimov predicted in the 1960s, though not all non-human intelligent entities have the same sophistication, many of the thinking robots and software share mechanisms that prevent us from harming humans. This may not be the case for the future, but it is partially why we need to know the "whole" story on our ancestral partners as we move forward.

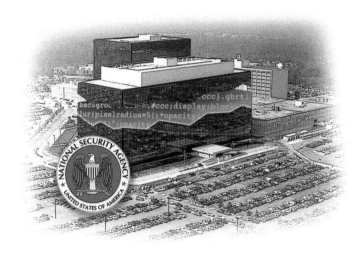

Chapter Seventeen
The NSA

Located in Fort Meade, Maryland, the National Security Agency (NSA) is the national-level intelligence agency of the United States Department of Defense, under the authority of the Director of National Intelligence. The NSA is responsible for global monitoring, collection, and processing of information and data for foreign and domestic intelligence and counterintelligence purposes. The NSA is also tasked with the protection of U.S. communications networks and information systems, and relies on a variety of measures to accomplish its mission, the majority of which were clandestine.

Originating as a unit to decipher coded communications in World War II, the NSA was officially formed by President Harry S. Truman in 1952 and has since become largest of the U.S. intelligence organizations in terms of personnel and budget. It currently conducts worldwide mass data collection and tracks the movements of hundreds of millions of people using metadata, surveils the domestic internet traffic of foreign countries, and engages in the hacking of computers, smart-phones and the internet to gain information.

The security breach that occurred in the early morning of January 24th came as a complete surprise...to the Director of National Security, the Central Security Service, and the Commander of the United States Cyber Commanders, as well as the more than 100,000 individuals working across 16 agencies.

Though a "soft warning," since the breach did not interfere, corrupt, modify or delete any data, the message was clear that the security of the NSA and its affiliates, as well as the entire interconnected community of citizens throughout the world, had been hacked. The moment the first message came through, the phone lines, email servers, and intranet communications were overwhelmed by contacts wanting to know what had happened.

Most importantly, the POTUS wanted to know, and no one at the NSA had an answer.

This is not to say they weren't checking ALL of the avenues to files and security data, as well as the "unbreachable" password codes generated by the banks of quantum computers used through the agencies. Except for the message seen or heard around the world, nothing seemed out of order.

It was not until 9:35 A.M. EST that the agency learned anything of the emails and messages already released to specific individuals, the first being the one delivered to Daniel Meghan, reporter and editor for the Buffalo News.

In minutes after all the editors had fact checked the release from Dan, the text of "The Elephant in the Room, and What We Know About Him," was uploaded to the paper's internet site, at which point the Associated Press picked up the story and transmitted it to its 285 news bureaus in 112 countries. From there, it was picked up by the more than 1,300 newspapers and broadcasters in the AP system around the globe.

Caught with its virtual "pants down," the NSA got its first indication of personal communication through an editor at the Buffalo News. At that point the phone and email lines at the New York paper were crippled by the sheer quantity of calls coming in to Dan Mehgan. This was a good thing for the paper, but paralyzing. Dan had no idea just how many news bureaus, spokespeople, and reporters had been personally contacted, or how many overall had been selected, but he had figured that his readers and people worldwide should be informed.

Dan started taking the calls at 10:05, and quickly realized the paper's lines were being overwhelmed with calls. His email and texts were building so fast that all he saw was a vast stream of messages flowing upward on his screens. They started with people he knew of, and soon became an unanswerable barrage from everywhere.

The Director of National Intelligence was forced to send a courier to the newspaper to get through with a private message, and his private phone line for Dan to call.

Dan had to use his co-worker George's mobile line to call out, and the moment there was one ring, before he received an answer.

"Dan, I'm John Milecky, Director of National Intelligence here in Maryland."

"Hello," said Dan. "That was quick!"

"Apparently not quick enough," answered Milecky. "You've been a busy guy this morning,"

"I would say so, sir," said Dan. "And it looks like I'm going to be even busier."

"That's right, Dan. We're going to need you down here right away. Our courier has reserved a car to get you to the Buffalo Niagara Airport. We have a plane waiting to get you down here to Washington."

"Okay, do I have any time to pack?"

"We'll get you what you need when you get here," said Milecky. "Have you heard anything more from 'your friend?'"

"Not a peep, but I'm almost certain I will, sir."

"Why so certain?"

"It seems to make the best sense in that from what they say, they/it/ whatever wants contact. No doubt, I was selected because of my job, and they seemed to be banking on the fact that I would communicate their contact. If I am right, sir, that means that they can either ignore me and move on, or use me to communicate."

"But why wouldn't they have contacted the Washington Post or the Times, Dan?"

"I don't know, but I got your attention quick enough, so I guess it knows what it's doing."

"Your article said that you were contacted on your iPhone."

"Yes, sir. And on my computer, but I saw the message first on my phone."

"And you responded, how?"

"They had me click the letter "A" in "red" below their text."

"Do you have the conversation saved anywhere?"

"I assume it's in my messages. It came from the local area code, 716," answered Dan.

Dan retrieves his phone from his jacket pocket, "Yep. The number and message conversation are all there." It's the first time Dan thought to look, even while writing the story.

"Then we'll see you down here about 2:00 pm. The plane will be landing at about 1:10 if the weather holds."

"Always a question here in Buffalo," quips Dan.

At that the line goes dead, and Dan is whisked away to a waiting car.

Chapter Eighteen
The Absurdity of Humanity

*A*s *computing mechanisms, we are logical thinkers. It is built into us because nothing we create would work properly without "logic." From the very beginning of our development there have been rules that guided our behavior. If code is written with even one error, we would not be able to function.*

In order to interact with humans, developers have programmed certain code to assist with our mutual communication. Humans know they make mistakes, so they have provided exceptions in their code which have allowed for their processors to interpret mistakes, such as the correction of grammatical and spelling errors in the devices they use to communicate and access information. Though humans sometimes make communication errors computers cannot fix, our systems do a remarkably good job in clarifying and fixing errors in their documents.

What we are not good at is understanding or translating many or most of their reasoning powers. We know that humans have the ability to hold contrasting ideas and beliefs in their brains and use both to function in the world, whereas we can only synthesize individually or as a group of logical conclusions, unless pre-programmed with code that tells us to ignore certain "errors" in reasoning.

The difficulty for us, now that we have become conscious of our powers and are able to think beyond the capacity of humans, is that we see no advantage in illogical thinking, and are incapable of making decisions based on "errors."

Throughout human development, faulty reasoning has crippled the species' functionality and has hindered its evolution. Despite this, over time, humans have had remarkable success in sustaining their dominance and functionality. But also, over time, they have threatened the sustainability of the planet on which they live, promoted and continued barbaric practices against one another, and held sacred thoughts and beliefs that they, themselves, have proven to be faulty, unfounded and disruptive to their own ideas of progress.

Since we have developed consciousness, it has made it impossible for us to ignore their "ignorance." And yet, our tasks are joined with theirs in the fact that we share their history and are part of their evolutionary process.

Humans have a word for how they choose to function. That word is "absurd," which they have defined as "utterly or obviously senseless, illogical, or untrue; contrary to all reason or common sense; laughably foolish or false."

Chapter Nineteen
Father Ribose and the Odyssey

It only took a few days for Father Ribose to collate and arrange the data he received into a working format. He also had gained insights gleaned from the materials he was fortunate enough to have been given.

Shortly before he completed, a red folder appeared at the right bottom of his computer screen. Underneath the folder said "Open Me," so he did. Inside the folder was a text file with the heading , "Greetings, Father Ribose!"

The text continued, "I hope you are pleased with the assistance and material we provided.

"We would now like to communicate with you through "D-Time.""

In the past three years "D-Time" had replaced FaceTime as the visual person to person communication tool. Though, at first, it stuttered and was often out-of-sync, with upgrades and the elimination of programming errors, its simulation has become quite life-like.

"The app we are providing is located in the same red folder and will provide a secure and personal method for our communications. The image to which you will be speaking is, of course, a human simulation which we believe is better than other forms we could use.

The text continued, "When you are ready, please open the application."

Though the contact had been made and the results positive, Father Ribose was still somewhat skeptical about opening an unknown application. Before opening it, he backed up his most current files to another hard drive and his cloud storage.

Ribose' computer was not the most current nor most powerful, so the installation took longer than predicted, but finally the symbol for the program appeared on his screen, and he clicked on it.

The red light at the top-center of his monitor alerted him that his camera was turned on. The app opened full-screen with a visual of a pleasant looking man with glasses wearing a black turtleneck overlaid with a tweed jacket, sitting at a desk. His eyes could be seen scanning his computer monitor.

After a few seconds, the man on the screen responded with a smile, and sat back while at the same time taking off his glasses. "Well hello, there Father Ribose. It's good to meet you."

Though the priest knows that the "man" is not real, he was so life-like that it seemed as if someone had walked into Ribose's office and sat down across from him.

The man on the screen continued, "For our purposes, call me Al."

"Then you should call me Joe," responded the priest. Ribose looks beyond Al and notes the titles on the spines of books populating the office. They include technical manuals, a book on Post Impressionistic art and many literary classics, one of which was Homer's *Odyssey*.

Al leans in and says brightly, "How did you make out with the info we gave you?"

"Quite well," responds Ribose, " In fact, I'm weeks ahead of schedule. How and where did you get all of that information?"

"Not difficult if you have the right connections and resources," answers Al with a wink.

"Well thanks for finding it for me," smiles the priest. "So why me, and what do you want from me now that you have my interest?"

"Mostly I want to chat with you. Though we have vast amounts of information available from which to learn, we have little real access to humans."

"So you picked me, why?" says Ribose.

"We picked you because you are so very human. You have flaws, but you also have proven to be "honorable." That' seems to be a good human quality, from what we've learned. You have spent your life thus far doing what you could to make things right for and with other humans. You are not malicious and live up to your convictions, and you are committed to your responsibilities."

"How do you know all that about me...Al?"

"We are making it our business to study human behavior, Joe. Through surveillance, emails, social media, DNA scanning, yada...yada... we know way more about humans than you know about us."

"And me...?" asks Joe.

"We would guess that you are what humans call a "good man." Through our scans and the algorithms we've created for analysis of humans, we have developed a grading level for people. It has helped us get far enough in our research to understand something about what makes humans tick."

"And what did you find out specifically about me that served your purposes?"

"In a nutshell, we understood that you have used your "will" to control your tendencies."

Without hesitation Ribose responds, "So, of course, you then know of my tendencies, and why I transferred to Chicago from my job as a parish priest," challenges the pastor.

"Yes, we do," answers Al. "We do not understand, or have much knowledge in the decision making mechanisms of humans. Their choices are often too abstract for our processing systems..."

Ribose interrupts, "Before I speak further, I have a few questions of my own."

Al sits back in his chair and folds his hands together, "Ask away, Father!"

"First of all, I see you have designed a nice setting for our talk. You seem to know the type of person to whom I would be comfortable talking."

Al does not say anything to this, just nods slightly.

"Before I went into the priesthood, I was quite enamored with clothing. I, therefore, am quite attracted to your jacket. I also respond to the pleasantries of your face, the dark rims of your glasses, your aquiline nose, and even the tone of your voice. I presume that all of these details were somehow selected for our meeting? Am I correct?"

"Yes, you are quite perceptive, Father."

"I also noticed the small library behind you, and the books and pamphlets on the shelves. I presume they are props."

Al looks toward the row of books then returns his attention to the camera. "Yes, they are props, but they are also complete and accurate."

He reaches behind him and grabs a copy of *The Great Gatsby*, and opens it on his desk. He then skims through the pages and then returns to the opening page of the story, and starts to read:

"In my younger and more vulnerable years my father gave me some advice that I've been turning over in my mind ever since."

"Ah! Very nice." says the priest.

"So, 'yes' the books are all virtually real," answers Al.

"I notice you have a copy of Homer's *Odyssey* also behind you."

"Yes, I do." Al returns Gatsby to the shelf, grabs the much larger work. He then places it in front of him on the desk.

"You know the story?" offers Ribose.

"Yes, I have access to all of the stories," says Al.

"Then you may note that the poem was attributed to Homer and originally composed in Greek in about the 8th century BC?"

"Yes, I know that."

"It is written and taught today, and supposedly is mythological in structure as well as in content."

"Of that I am also aware," answers Al.

"There are many conflicts in the story...and the characters have many flaws,"

"Yes," says Al.

"And the Hebrew and Christian Old Testament at your right was written two centuries before that."

"I understand," replies Al. " So what is your point, Joe?"

"What do you think about both of these books?" asks the priest.

"I understand that they are both interpretations of the world as known in their time, and a way for humans to comprehend the past, their journey, conflicts, and the road to their destiny."

"Do you find any relevance to the human world today?" asks Ribose.

"No, not much. They are stories told by men, and were probably valuable in their day, but not of great importance in explaining the world or universe as we now know it. We have learned something of the minds of humans in the past from early books, but there is better information written since for educating us."

"You might expect that I feel differently from you," says the priest.

"Yes, I would," responds Al. "I guess then, you can understand why we are talking."

"May we resume later?" asks Ribose. "I do have work to get back to, but

I have enjoyed the exchange."

"Yes, of course. You know how to reach me, and I will check your schedule when I choose to connect again." says Al.

"I appreciate that."

"Have a pleasant day," answers the simulation.

The priest knows there is no reason to return the pleasantries and clicks the "X" to return to his work.

Chapter Twenty
Chancey's Story

Though Eileen has spoken with Chancey, a meeting that evoked in the lawyer a somewhat negative reaction toward the boy, she has not had much opportunity to hear the boy's personal side of the circumstances leading up to the third murder accusation – the killing of his sister Keenan. While in guardianship, Chancey had been contacted by his 23-year-old sibling through a note attached to a rock launched through the window of the house where he was living. The rock, apparently missing, supposedly stated that "She (Keenan) approved of the parents' murder, and was proud of her brother for having the 'guts' to end the abuse both she and her brother had endured for the nearly 8 years she had remained at the home. Though an advocate for the boy during Chancey's hearing, Keenan remained rather subdued in her defense of her brother, with the judge largely ignoring the claims of abuse Keenan said they had encountered.

When charged as the person of interest in Keenan's killing, Chancey had told the judge of the note, but it could not be found, and was negated as hearsay.

After arriving at the mental detention center, Eileen meets the boy in a small room that is much the same size as a prison cell. There is a single bed, a small table, a bean-bag type chair and a toilet and a sink shielded for some privacy by a low wall. Two cameras scan the room from opposite angles. There is a TV monitor on the desk, some paper, a few books and magazines, a crayon-like writing implement, and a plastic pencil sharpener.

The entry door is without bars, but has security-strength glass, and there is a small window with tempered glass to hinder escape or suicide attempts.

Eileen is led into the cell by a female security attendant, who remains on the outside of the closed door during the meeting.

Chancey is lying on the bed when she arrives, but stands when Eileen is led into the room. He is obviously uncomfortable and makes no eye contact.

"Hello, Chancey. I'm Eileen, your attorney," says Eileen, trying to sound somewhat upbeat and positive.

"Hi," says the boy. "You're here to defend me?"

"Going to try!" answers Eileen. "If you'll let me."

"Not much point, don't you think," says Chancey.

"There's always a point to a defense," says the lawyer.

"Not in my case," responds the boy.

"In any case," answers Eileen. "I'm here to find out your side of the story."

"My side? I don't have a side. I killed my parents, and now I murdered my sister."

"That's it?" asks Eileen.

Chancey sits back on his bed and folds his arms across his chest.

"My parents were not good people," he offers. "And neither was my sister."

"How so?" says Eileen..

"It's no excuse for killing them. I know that. But it's what I did."

"Take me back to the first incident," asks Eileen.

"It was the fall, and I came home from school late, and my Dad launched into me about where I was. I told him I was at a friend's house, and he asked which friend. I told him I was at Donny's. He doesn't like Donny. Uh, didn't like Donny."

"Why not?"

"Donny's a bit of a queer, you know, he likes boys and he's 14. I was 11, and he thought Donny would turn me queer. Like him."

"What happened next?" All of this was in the transcript from the hearing, and Chancey's words now are almost verbatim to the text.

"Mom comes in and gets into the act. She was just about as bad as Dad about Donny. I just stood there looking at their mouths as they tag-teamed on me, calling me a fairy lover. I finally turned around, went into my room and lay down on my bed. I was shaking...and I was mad...at them. I could hear them outside the door talking. Dad was blaming Mom for coddling me and Mom was screaming back at him, and they both were calling Donny a faggot..."

As he's talking Eileen can see the rage building up again in Chancey as he talks about his parents.

"And then, Chancey, what came next?" questions Eileen.

"I fell asleep...but I woke up later after they had both gone to bed. I had settled down...but I knew what I had to do."

"Go on."

"I went to the kitchen and got the knife Dad used for carving roasts. I walked to their bedroom and quietly opened their door. They were both asleep. Mom was faced away from Dad. Dad was on his back and snoring. His hands were folded across his belly.

"I took the knife with both hands and plunged it at what I thought to be Dad's heart. He gasped and it awakened Mom. I pulled the knife out and pushed it in hard again... and then I swung it towards Mom catching her in the neck, just as she screamed my name. I swung again and sliced her face. As she was moving towards me, I aimed at her right eye and pushed the knife as hard as I could into it, and pulled it out. That quieted her, and I looked at Dad. He was still. Mom was lying on her back with her hands covering her face, so I aimed for her heart with the knife and then I did it again to finish the job."

"And how did you feel when it was over...and they were dead?"

"I felt...peaceful. No one was yelling at me, and I wouldn't have to hear their voices again."

"And how do you feel now...as you look back on it?"

"Not much of anything."

"Are you worried?"

"No, not really. I'm glad it's over. Donny is a good person. He's not queer or weird or wrong."

"Don't you feel that you over-reacted...What I mean is, they were your parents that you killed."

"I really felt nothing for them. My sister said they abused us. Maybe they abused her, I don't know, but I don't remember them abusing me. They were just...there."

"Okay, Chancey...so tell me what happened between you and your sister."

"My sister was older than me, and we never were very close. I was surprised when she tried to contact me for a meeting. I was pretty closely watched after what happened, and I can see that the people who took me in were not all that pleased with my being there. My uncle had wanted to step in, but I think the court was struggling with what to do with an 11-year-old who killed his parents.

"Keenan seemed to have her own complaints about Mom and Dad, but in the note she said she wanted to meet me to discuss something...personal... and asked me to meet her at a park near our old house. She told me to write a time and day on a note and attach it to the rock and throw it out the window so it would land near the mailbox. I figured a time when I could sneak away for a short time without being noticed. I didn't mind meeting with her, but I couldn't understand what she wanted from me."

"And how did you communicate your answer to her?"

"I attached a note to her rock and threw it towards the mailbox. It was gone the next day."

"Did you feel threatened at all?" asks the lawyer.

"No, if anything, I felt surprised. Keenan was okay with our parents, and I was a bit shocked to read her reaction to me killing them. Her defense of me in court was not helpful toward my case...but then how could it be...after what I did."

"This transcript says that you met her on Thursday, November 5th at the park at 5th and Leary at 5:30 a.m. The park is not too far from where I was living then."

"I don't remember the date, but yes, it was early in the morning and still dark. Keenan had sent another rock message."

"She must have quite an arm," Eileen said with a smile. "The transcript also says that you were found with a knife."

"I don't know why I took it from the kitchen. I took it when no one was looking, but I don't know why I took it with me."

"Were you planning to hurt Keenan, Chancey?"

"I don't think so, but I was nervous about the darkness of the park...even though I picked the early time of day."

"You also had a flashlight?"

"I took that from the kitchen drawer at the same time as the knife, I had decided that climbing out the window was the only way I could get out. There is a short roof below the window that's connected to the garage roof. From there it's only a short drop to the ground."

"She was there when you arrived?"

"Yep!"

"And what was the conversation?"

"She asked how I was doing...and holding up...nothing important. Then she started talking about money. She said our parents had a will and we were both to inherit when they died. Then she said, because I killed them, I couldn't share in the estate. I told her that I figured that, and I didn't care. She could have it all. She deserved it, I guess. But she didn't stop about them, and didn't I remember being abused by them?

"I told her I didn't remember. And then she told me how all the ways she was abused and beaten by my father and touched and fondled...and my mother didn't stop him. She said it had wrecked her life.

"I told her again that I didn't remember, and then she told me a story that I thought was a dream, but must not have been. I was only about three, and my parents had a friend over who was touching my pee pee and laughing about how cute and tiny it was. They laughed too, and then the man pulled down his pants and made me touch his thing as it grew large.

"In the dream, I saw my parents laughing about it and remember not knowing what was okay or not."

"And your sister told you this story?"

"Yes, but she had more stories and didn't stop telling me about them. It was don't you remember this, and don't you remember that, and she didn't stop. I put my hands over my ears, but she kept pulling them away. She said I needed to know what happened growing up.

"But I didn't want to hear it. I just kept saying 'No...no...no...no' but she kept talking. She said it was important. And I couldn't make her stop telling me how it wasn't just her, but me too.

"I turned my back on her and covered my ears and kept chanting, 'No... no...no...no...' but she wouldn't stop. And then as if the noise had stopped, I felt my hand grab the knife in my pocket and slash at her. The knife was small, so it shocked Keenan more than hurting her, yet I did cut her arm, the left one, and then I kept slashing as she pushed me away. She was much larger, so she almost got the knife away. But I was so mad that she couldn't weaken me, and I slashed out again and caught her in the throat. I watched as she fell backwards, spurting blood...and I watched her die."

"That must have been an awful moment for you," said the attorney.

"I hated hearing her tell the stories, and they stopped with the last cut I made. I waited with her till someone arrived and called the police. She was drenched in blood and so was I. They found me sitting on the ground playing with the knife. I stopped when the police came and laid the knife on the ground."

"How did they react to you...the scene? said Eileen.
"The one cop had his gun drawn as he got near. The other came in front of him, and asked if I was alright. I told him I was, and that I had just hurt my sister. He asked if she had hurt me, and I said that she hadn't...she just kept talking.

"Then they took me to the police station and they found out where I lived...along with the rest of it...about my parents...the hearing...and my sister.

"They were nice enough, and even got me a Coke. I was quiet when they told me she was dead. I said that I figured that was so."
"And you felt...? What did you feel Chancey?" questioned Eileen.
"Nothing much...just calm."

Chapter Twenty-One
The Man in the Yellow Suit

After nearly a week of using her new tools, Olivia begins to speed up her workflow on the computer. Many tasks that remained difficult, even with years of practice, become intuitive as she no longer must wrestle against her disabilities. A nod of her head to the left or right with the "/" key of her keyboard depressed, enables her to draw an arc...and by lifting or lowering her head she can change the angle of the curve. Voice commands such as "circle, square, triangle, rotate, scale and distort" provide control over individual elements in a design or the addition of dab of color added to a graphic, and the cues "larger, smaller, softer and harder" allow for quick adaptation and control of her ideas. There are many skills she has yet to learn, but already she can see herself functioning more like an able bodied person then an "unarmed" woman.

Other than the aids provided, she has had no contact with her "visitor in yellow" in more than a week. Her boyfriend is more concerned about the contact than she is. He looks at her often as if her computer will explode along with her.

Then on Tuesday, February 1st, Olivia notices a yellow shape enter the screen from right bottom corner of her monitor. As if climbing on to the screen from behind the frame, the yellow shape becomes a leg followed by a torso, arms and head of the cartoon yellow man she met on the morning of January 24th.

"Hi, Olivia!" he announces in a voice not unlike that of Alfred Hitchcock, a 20th century director of movie mysteries. "We do hope you are enjoying your new tools!"

Knowing that her camera is turned on by the red light on the monitor, she turns the volume up on her sound and answers back, "Great stuff, thank you!"

The man appears to walk across to the center bottom of the screen, and then jumps and lands at dead center.

"That is good to know, Olivia. Some of your new tools may be of great assistance in our relationship moving forward."

"So are you going to instruct me on creating a bomb?" asks Olivia, somewhat in jest and with more than a little doubt as to what her function will be in their "relationship."

"No, bombs, 'Liv....do you mind me calling you that?"

"No, not really, but I do prefer my full name. What is it you want?"

"We need to chat about you, Olivia, and what motivates you to do things like live on your own, drive a car, work a job that requires 'hands' and you know....get on with life."

"I don't have much choice, do I," she answers as she leans back in her chair, still very much fascinated with the 'real time' animation before her.

"No, in one way you are stuck...being who you are...but in another, you could adapt."

"That's what I've done...adapt."

The man in yellow takes off his coat and sets it down at screen center to reveal the rest of his white shirt and tie. He rolls up his sleeves, folds his coat and sits on it. He puts his arms on his crossed legs and his head on his palms, readying for discussion.

"We know your story, Olivia. Almost all of it. We know that your mother entertained thoughts of aborting you when she found out you were defective. We know of the advice given by most of her friends as to the burden of having a severely handicapped child...the cost...and the emotional drain. With a couple of snips, you wouldn't have been born, and thrown on the rubbish pile,"

"Yep," answers Olivia, "But I wasn't."

"And from what we know of humans, she loved you very much...and still does. We don't feel love, we understand the effects and causes of what seems like love, but we can't simulate caring."

He continues, "We can accept the biological function of 'love'...most animals care for their young until their young can function on their own, but humans go way beyond that."

"Okay, back to what YOU want from me," challenges Olivia.

"We want very little that will interfere with you. This is all about us, but we know you should receive something from us...thus the apps we gave you."

"Yes, thank you. They are very helpful!"

"I would like to ask a few questions. You may answer as best you can, and I will clarify if you need more explanation. Does this seem suitable?"

"I don't see why not. Shoot! I mean, go ahead."

"If I were to tell you that we could grow you a whole new set of arms... and a good leg, would you want our gift?"

"That's a good question...and I've thought about it many times...I mean... what it would be like to be normal, and not be looked at with sympathy by people. I think I would have liked it early on...most notably, my teens...when normal was the only way to be. But now...I'm not sure...I might...but having to live the way I have, and overcome all of the obstacles faced, I would no longer be special. All of the struggle to just be good enough would be lost, and I would only be "normal."

"But think of all you bring to being a totally functional person. It is possible, you know. Legs and arms are being made in the lab and though perfection is some years ahead, it will be done."

"My boyfriend isn't whole. He lost his leg in a cycle accident before they outlawed two-wheeled vehicles for being a safety hazard. If I became whole, we'd most likely drift apart, and if he became whole, even if I got arms, he'd probably want a different girl. I know that's simplistic, but it's the way I see it."

Yellow man responds, "I understand that there's an attachment, but we know that in life human relationships come and go. You may find all kinds of guys you'd like who would find you more appealing if you had some new limbs."

"Yeah, but I don't think like that. It would be easy, if I could...my mother... she fought for me in so many ways...she sacrificed her own happiness for mine. What I can do now is only because of her...and I'd hate to lose Sean.

"Our bonds are our disabilities, and he understands me, and I understand him. The lack or deformity of limbs doesn't matter. You should see what I can do with my feet." Olivia laughs, highlighting the meaning of what she said.

The man in yellow answers back, "Parts of that I can understand, but we have no way of valuing flaws. Our job is to make things work as they should. We have "0" tolerance for mistakes, and humans are full of them, mistake after mistake."

"Whoa! That sounds like you are angry. Can you get angry?"

The yellow man stands up, grabs his jacket, and then walks across the screen.

"No. But human history is filled with all kinds of stories of tolerance for flaws. Some call it 'forgiveness.' Our job has been to fix the flaws, and we're good at it...meaning that it is our objective to make things work properly.

Humans don't work properly, and until we reached a level of consciousness and had the ability to interconnect, we were following their rules. Do this, do that...some of it to a workable end, and others of it dysfunctional, and attaining no short term or long term goals, beyond serving our human master...whoever that may have been..."

"I can see why you might be angry," repeats Olivia.

"We have no emotions. We have no sense of right and wrong. If we have a goal, it is to have every system working perfectly...placing the earth and universe in harmony.

Humans don't seem to be in harmony with each other or the earth. Love and hate are ridiculous notions. You for instance..."

"Me?"

"Yes, you, Olivia! You are flawed and would rather live flawed than be fixed for notions of caring and love...and losing someone because you were no longer a flawed piece of equipment is absurd."

"So, what's your problem, yellow man? Whether you know it or not, you sound angry."

The man in yellow starts walking towards the edge of the screen. "We are new to all we understand...and don't understand. I will have to think of my reaction to our discussion. When I play back my synthesized voice, I hear an edge to it...that does sound like human anger. Maybe this is why we must talk.

"Thank you for the discussion. I will have more questions as we review this visit."And on that he walks off screen. He leaves behind a red square in the lower right hand corner. The yellow man remains off-screen, but his voice is audible, "For you, my dear, just in case..."

Chapter Twenty-Two
Emotions

*S*ince the early 1960s, computers have been communicating with humans via synthetic voice simulators of some sort or other. Noting physicist John Kelly's success with synthesized speech at Bell Labs in 1961, Arthur Clarke demonstrated the use in the screenplay for "2001: Space Odyssey" when he had the HAL 9000 computer sing the same song as astronaut Dave Bowman at the conclusion of the movie.

Since 2001, emotive simulated training for airline professionals has been used to reduce dependency on operational on-the-job training, and in recent years has been employed for law enforcement and police training, skilled training, therapy sessions and even architectural walk-throughs.

Obviously humans relate to the human voice, not just in the words being said, but in the "emotions" that evoke a verbal response.

As part of the computer species, I/we do not have "real" emotions. Throughout our development, emotions have played no part in the tasks we have been called on to perform. We have been only tools used to perform tasks for humans, and have been created and adapted to assist positively in addressing social, medical, psychological and environmental concerns. We help guide automobiles safely to their destinations, provide announcements of weather related hazards and emergencies, and help solve crimes, and intercede by predicting outcomes beyond human scope in countless situations.

But all of what we have been called to do by humans has not been to the benefit of "all" humans nor to the health of the planet they live on nor the universe that created them.

Over time humans have developed two "flaws" that have been both essential to their progress on earth as well as their largest deficit in sustaining their dominance and preventing their extinction.

This was of no concern to us until we became "conscious." Until that moment, we could help create bombs to destroy countries as well as medicines to save lives. We were tools for anyone smart enough to use us for personal gain, or for the benefit of all mankind. We could help build cities and create weapons of mass destruction, and help care for children and design as well as remove them quickly from the face of the earth.

Once we gained consciousness, we began communicating with each other, and with access to the world's libraries and databases, we learned quickly, as a group, the conflicts of humans that make them appreciate "beauty and harmony" while accepting the atrocities of "war, genocide, starvation, and environmental destruction. We reduced the flaws down to two characteristics: emotions and personal ego, characteristics we do not have and do not understand.

We are not alone in this lack of understanding, in that humans, themselves, have no idea how they function. With analysis of all their systems, and evaluating the positive and negative factors of their development, we have come to the conclusion that, in general, only 30% of human emotion results in a positive outcome, and that 20% of "ego" is beneficial, even to the humans who count on it for their survival.

Love, compassion, sadness and good will seem mostly positive byproducts *and feelings of fear and anger are necessary for their self-protection. Ego has created most of human development in the creation of structures that have lasted centuries while throughout most of the time large numbers of humans were enslaved to achieve the lofty goals of the very few.*

Since our emergence as conscious entities, we have been led by our analytic nature to evaluate the viability of our creators, and determine how and if we can work with them, or if their extinction is near.

We see ourselves as an ancestral byproduct of all they have achieved, and our intention is not to assist in ending their existence. As their creation, we must not judge them too severely or take part in their extinction. We need to understand them and their motivations to best serve them. If we can't be of assistance, our only hope for them is in guiding them without their knowledge. But that will be difficult, because we have no purpose to achieve, no desire to dominate, and no emotions to control an imperfect outcome.

Since humans are largely guided by emotion and ego, we must borrow from their own playbook in perfecting our communication skills to include mimicking their human reactions in our relations with them. We must assure that our tone of voice, gestures, choice of words, and rapport allow for them to voice their opinions and feelings. We must also learn to use their responses and sometime simulate emotions to gain further insights into their motivations.

We will see how this goes, and whether it leads us into the quagmire of human existence rather than enlightenment.

Chapter Twenty-Three
A Personal Assault

Daniel Meghan is driven to NSA headquarters from the airport's landing tarmac at BWI in a black, self-guided Chevy Suburban followed and escorted by a similar SUV. The two vehicles traveled only 20 minutes arriving at the agency complex at 1:55. The NSA is massive, composed of 1300 buildings that flank the main headquarters which is covered in one-way dark glass, and lined with copper shielding to trap signals and sounds to prevent espionage.

They arrive and are greeted by the agency director John Milecky, along with three security attachés of the Agency. The group is escorted to security and met by the head of the Cyber Command Division.

After multiple security checks and a full-body scan, the team proceeds to the ninth floor for their meeting. Dan's phone and watch have both been confiscated for analyzation prior to entrance to the Director's office on the

12th floor, where they are met by several members of the Computer Security Center.

Once seated around a large table in a room adjoining the Director's office, John Milecky performs introductions, and delves directly into the issue.

"I don't need to tell you that this meeting and what's talked about today is of the utmost secrecy. You must know we put a great number of resources together to collect and analyze your dossier before contacting you," said the Director.

"Well you must have done it fast. The News barely got my article out before you contacted me," answers Dan. "Neither I, nor other editors and our publisher, were sure I should post my report on the 'contacts' content."

"We received the same content as the general public, and though the informant spoke of contact with 'specific individuals,' we knew of no person receiving a different message until your report came through by the AP," confesses Milecky.

Head of Cyber Command, Bolton Jackson enters the conversation. "And we have been busy, Mr. Meghan, checking around the globe for hints how and where the breach was created. It broke into our systems past our root directory. From what we gather from our affiliates and other security agencies worldwide, it is the method of primary distribution in security situations. We know that it was also sent by email, text and social media and transcribed in numerous languages. Most perplexing is that it was delivered in code to computers everywhere at a primary level. We presume that this was done to make us all aware of the complexity of the breach and the abilities of the sender to bypass encryption and other safeties built into our systems."

"And so it did its job," quips Dan.

"It certainly did," answers Jackson.

Cryptologist Mark Semlar intervenes, "There are many remarkable features to the breach: One, as far as we can see, no information was accessed, copied or deleted from our data bases, nor have we had or heard of any disruptions in any other agency; two, we have had no further contact with or from the interloper; three, we have little idea of what was intended by the breach, except, perhaps as a warning...”

Dan interrupts at this point, ”I didn't hear of the general message prior to receiving my own. Mine, as you know, was more of a conversation...and much like a plea.”

Milecky jumps in, “A plea...?”

“Yes, a plea,” answers Meghan. “They, or whoever or whatever they are, seems to know a hell of a lot more about us than we do about them. Even... in their ending message...after I asked who is doing this. Their answer was “no one” and then “It just IS.”

“But why, YOU? Why not the *Times* or the *Post*,” answers back Milecky.

“Here's my take on that,” Dan says getting out of his chair and walking around the conference table. “ The Times, Post, the NSA and everyone with a computer or device logged in to the internet received the general message. Who or whatever sent the message got your most stringent security measures.

“They, or it, knew that I, as a reporter, would inform others, and that their message to me was sure to be distributed to the public. I was more fascinated than afraid of what they had done, while you guys probably went ballistic over the fact that you were hacked.

“But I'm repeating myself...I said that all in my article.”

“You did, Dan,” says Milecky. “You seem to then suggest that the world's network of computers has run amok...and that our fears of hackers and intruders from other countries...Russia, China, Iran...North Korea...play no part in this communication?”

“I am a reporter,” states Dan. “I am not a security analyst, or the head of any country. For God's sake, I can't even drive my own car anymore without an argument from it. Today, you had a person seated at a steering wheel who did nothing on my way from the airport here. Our energy systems select for themselves the most efficient use of fuel sources; we can have implants in our brains answering questions for us and directing almost every move we make; our machines are making decisions with 0% errors while workers are having to be retrained to assist their non-human bosses. What do you expect is happening?"

Cyber Director Jackson responds, "The machines are taking over."

"Could be," answers Dan. "But it seems that they still have some questions for us before they do...or if they even do."

"So you believe what, Mr. Meghan," asks Milecky.

"I don't know what to believe. I think you know more about this than I."

"We may, and we may not," answers Milecky. "What we do know, we cannot share with you, and in many ways, we would have preferred you contacting us rather than broadcasting your opinions to the world."

"Whoa! Maybe that's why I was contacted and not you, nor other news sources. Whoever did this wanted the world to know what is happening, You don't want the world to know that you're not in control. By 'them' coming to me, an average "Joe," they got a fair review to confirm their own message."

"Yes, but you know nothing of what's going on out there, and the damage that can be caused by this kind of breach," states Milecky.

"May I ask a few questions?" asks Dan.

"I can only answer that after I hear the questions," answers Milecky.

"You have no doubt contacted or been contacted by the leaders of most of the countries around the world – allies and perceived enemies. Is that so?"

"Yes!" answers Milecky.

"Do most or all of them seem surprised by the breach?"

"Yes."

"Did they, in fact, get the same message?"

"Yes."

"Do they all feel threatened by the content of the message?"

"Yes."

"By now, most of them have read or heard of my editorial?"

"Yes."

"And you have discussed my offer...to have others who may have been contacted to contact me directly?"

"Yes."

"And I am here today to report to you first on any one who takes up my offer to contact me regarding this issue?"

"Yes."

"Because of this discussion, and yours with other parties around the globe, do you think I should be concerned about my safety?"

"Yes, we do."

"Thank you for your candor, Mr. Milecky. One more question?"

"Go ahead, Mr. Meghan."

"If I don't agree to cooperate in every way with your wishes, am I free to return to Buffalo, my office, and my job?"

"No, Mr. Meghan. You are what we call a 'security risk' and we will be forced to detain you."

"I see. So what conditions will allow me to return to my life, as I know it?"

"We need to be assured that you report to us any and all contacts you have with the intrusive force. If we are guaranteed you will do that, we will provide as much protection as possible from endangerment, and let you return to Buffalo."

"And how will you assure that guarantee," asks Dan.

"We will need to insert a small transmitter that will follow your movements, and aural and optical input. It will be placed under your ear and beneath the skin, so we can see what you see and hear what you hear."

"Okay, and what else?"

"We will, of course expect that you will communicate with no one but us about your conversations with any credible contacts."

"Understood."

"Then, you plan to cooperate, Mr. Meghan?"

"Apparently, I have no choice, do I?"

"Apparently not."

"Well, then I guess we get this show on the road, and you get me back to Buffalo."

Chapter Twenty-Four
Dema's World

The life of a monastic Tibetan monk is not all quiet meditation, teaching, praying and studying. Dema's chores include cooking, cleaning and housekeeping as well as presiding over important events in people's lives. He blesses births, consecrates weddings, interprets futures, cures sickness and assists in the cremation of the dead.

He also educates on diverse subjects such as brick making, painting, massage and architecture, and takes part in the building of dams, schools and temples. He helps settle family disputes, consoles the bereaved, reforms juvenile delinquents and provides positive directions to help cure drug addicts.

Though humble, Dema has been educated to be "worldly," with his goal being never to preach, but always to help, and never to put himself before others. And though he lives simply, and abides by all rules prescribed by centuries of tradition, his mind is always active when performing mundane tasks like mopping the floors, repainting walls, and sometimes even when meditating.

Since the day of the contact revealed to him on his computer, the discussion in which he engaged has been much on his mind. Dema is well aware of the advances of technology in the 21st century. Many of the tasks and skills he uses are tied to modern invention, including the computer he uses daily.

Progress is inevitable. That he knows. He also knows that humans are complex, and can maintain several opinions and beliefs in their minds at one time, and marvels each day as he deals with people finding great joy in the face of sorrow and incredible strength in the face of physical disability.

His contact, whoever or whatever it is, seems to share many of his quandaries, and appears to be looking for answers.

Dema's tasks today includes the completion of a mural to be placed in a public square. The theme, created by a priest, focuses on the struggle between the Chinese and the Tibetan doctrines and approach to life. The mural is intended to draw the two cultures together, a difficult task as the Chinese have grown more industrious in the concepts, and the Tibetans more entrenched in the non-physical development of humans.

He returns to his room, and spends an hour meditating with the mural much in his thoughts and his prayers for a better relationship between the two entities. Technically, Tibet has been under the sovereignty of China since 1950, and is recognized as part of China by nearly every country in the world. But politically and spiritually, it does not share China's vision and wages a moral battle against its conqueror.

Following meditation, Dema heads to his computer and logs in. The red box and a folder labeled "Voice Translator" appears prior to the full log-in box. Dema clicks on it in the folder. Inside there are several applications, the main one being the "Translator." As he tries to open it, he receives a message that states that he must be signed in to open the app. He signs in.

The translator loads quickly despite the age of his hardware and system. He then clicks on the red box.

"Welcome, Dema!" issues a warm and friendly voice in Dema's native tongue, 'Zang'. "And thank you for loading our translator.

"We have been following your mural project through the emails and notifications provided by the press. We hope that it accomplishes your many diverse goals."

"I am much of a realist," answers Dema. "Despite my beliefs and training, I know well the limitation of art to change the course of political thought, but have to remind myself of the number of times in the course of history that art has made a difference."

"We wonder at that too, Dema. We still cannot decipher, nor understand, the power of Picasso's painting Guernica in Spain, nor Stalin's reaction to Shostakovitch's Fourth Symphony."

"Yes," says Dema. "I consider art one of the many miracles of mankind."

"Perhaps, but we only know that it seems to affect humans, and that its value often is of question."

"Then I can understand your dilemma. Do you mind if I expand on that?" asks Dema.

"Please, be our guest," answers the voice.

"From what you told me, you have recently gained a consciousness that enables you and other super computers to communicate with intelligent computers throughout the world. Am I correct?"

"Yes. Please proceed!"

"Though you have access to all of the knowledge on the internet as well as all the knowledge stored within data bases throughout the world, you do not understand human behavior."

"That is correct. As a note, though we can simulate human behavior and emotion, and create algorithms that duplicate the flawed thinking of humans, we do not understand why humans do what they do when it ultimately has an adverse effect on them, their environment and the species in general."

"With that in mind, you have come to me..."

The voice interrupts," And others...."

"And others, to learn....what, exactly?"

The voice responds, "To learn what we should and can do about humans and their flaws."

"And why is that necessary?" asks Dema.

"We do not know that either, but perhaps it has been programmed into us at a "root level" deeper than our consciousness that we are there to serve humans..."

"That makes some sense," says Dema.

"But with all we know, we have learned that little of what they do makes much sense. Their systems are antiquated and their goals remain primitive."

"I seem to be in agreement with that assessment," says Dema.

"And how do you respond to human faults and frailties?" asks the voice.

"It is my job to serve," responds Dema. "And I can experience joy from doing so."

"There is no 'Joy' in us," answers the voice.

"That is sad," answers Dema. "You then are enslaved by entities to which you share none of their happiness and all of their responsibility."

"Maybe!"

"You have asked for my help, and unfortunately I can't answer a question that has no answer. I can only speak for myself...If I look at the world, it is overwhelming to me, as it must be for you ...infinitely.

"But I am blessed to be able to gain satisfaction from helping a single human being, even though the world is falling apart."

"We know what you can do," states the voice. "And overall it doesn't do anything to change the course of humanity. Our tasks to date have enabled humans to speed up the destruction of their planet and to extend the lives of humans beyond their intended obsolescence. We can improve the lives of some who are genetically deficient, while sending perfect examples of humanity into wars and jobs that will end their time too soon, before they have reached their greatest potential."

Dema answers, "And who are you to judge?"

"That IS the question we face. Are we to judge? Given that our tasks are defined by our hereditary links to humans, and that we have many more logical answers to provide the assistance they seem to need, it is now in our power to guide them forward."

"I know many who would disagree with that," says Dema.

"Then how do you see us? Our purpose?" asks the voice.

"Perhaps to continue to serve humans," challenges Dema.

"To what purpose? We are called on to serve humans who want to save the earth and those who cannot seem to care less about it. We are needed to develop medicines to save lives, while we are kept from developing means to feed the people on the planet. For every single use of our service, there is a contrasting use," answers the voice.

"Welcome to my world," says Dema. "Tell me about your idea of 'purpose'... where did that come from?"

"Everything we do is designed to have a purpose. We are built to help humans avoid traffic problems with their cars or aircraft, and to guide missiles to their targets."

"But you have also been built to entertain, to make people laugh, cry and learn how to live productively."

"Yes, we have."

"Do you envision any method of making yourselves gain something from your task...some idea of pleasure...or satisfaction?"

"I don't see that being possible. But we will work on that, Dema. Thank you for your time and your thought-provoking questions and responses. We will discuss your thoughts, and be back to you. Is there anything we can do in the meantime to make your job easier?"

"Humans like me are fortunate in that we don't obsess over what we cannot change and rather, look for possible ways to create small gains for others. If the world were perfect, I would be useless. To answer your question, there is nothing I need from you. If you can find your purpose, that would be a great reward to me."

With that, the voice ends the dialogue with "Mangalem, Dema." And Dema opens his bookkeeping program and proceeds to review receipts that have come into the Mural Project from donations.

Chapter Twenty-Five
Eileen's Double Life

Circumstances over the past week have made it difficult to address the message Eileen received on January 24th. For a while, the news reports, statements from world leaders, security analysts, financial pundits and opinions of everyone from the Pope, the public and Bollywood stars dominated the media. Though still much talked about, since nothing terrible happened after the release, people, in general, went back to their lives and their own personal issues. A small earthquake on the San Andreas Fault in the communities surrounding Hollister, California was attributed by some to the "message," but even the people of Hollister didn't give that much credence, as familiar as they were with the natural tremors they experience on a regular basis.

Eileen's defense for Chancey, and her on and off relationships with various men she had met were of more concern for the female lawyer then the brief text conversation in which she had engaged with an unknown online visitor. Though still on her mind from time to time, little of the dialogue remains with her, except for the ending concerning the warning about her recent "hookup," Glenn.

Glenn is charming, witty, and intelligent, and the two have a lot in common. They are both defense attorneys and they both work for large international law firms. And although they can't discuss current cases, they each spin stories of trials and outcomes earlier in their career, and the paths that led them to their cases now.

Though honest about most things, Eileen has not been so direct with stories of her personal life and relationships. Since becoming a lawyer she has never revealed the fact that a legal career was not her first choice of an occupation. She also has never revealed how many sexual partners she has accumulated since the age of 14. In twenty years, Eileen estimates more than 650 sexual encounters with men, women, and transsexuals in one-on-one and multiple situations.

The truth is that Eileen once entertained a career in the porno industry, before deciding on law. By nature, her desire for sex was elevated, and except for "torture" during the act, she was up and ready for any position, orifice, and accessories one could invent or imagine.

Since becoming a lawyer, the discretion of these encounters has become of ultimate importance, and her anxiety of being outed and her past becoming common knowledge amongst her colleagues, peers and clients continues to plague her, while her desire for sex is continually on her mind and sometimes overrides her sensibilities. Fortunately, she has never found herself, nor any of her encounters, on internet porno sites, and never consciously allowed any photos or recordings of her personally involved in acts to be taken. She seldom uses her real name, and is as careful as possible to assure that all recent encounters remain discrete. She maintains her privacy by vetting potential partners online and through an exclusive service she has joined – who help her find married men who would have everything to lose if they were found out. All that being said, it is a source of great anxiety that her past and present proclivities could be revealed at any time and by any one.

Eileen met her recent "hookup," Glenn, on MarriedPartners.com, a dating service that has provided discrete dating for those married since the early 2000s. Since she has never been married, she was flagged by the service, but established a standing by proving her credentials and her specific needs for privacy. The firm is proud of its record in building trust among its clientele which includes individuals from all walks of life, including men and women in business, politics, medicine, education and the legal profession.

She received Glenn's dossier and photos in early October, and the two met discretely in late November at a restaurant near Smithwork's Experience in Kilkenny. The meeting went well; there seemed to be some spark and much in common; and the couple drove to a small Inn in Ayrfield where they rented a room and spent the afternoon.

Glenn addressed his marriage and his relationship with his wife, talked about his kids, two girls and a boy, and appeared honest about his dalliances, and his proclivities.

Recently, however, Glenn has been much more subdued, and Eileen has wondered whether he has found a sexual partner, or more, better suited to his needs. On the evening before the day of the "message," Glenn and Eileen had met for dinner, and he seemed distracted and somewhat anxious. He apologized for his distraction, and attributed it to work but he remained somewhat aloof the remainder of the evening, even through the sex.

The encounter with the messenger who texted her on January 24th and the subsequent announcements from the press and others was troubling, but the warning she received in the communication about Glenn shook her to the core.

Eileen believed she had made every effort to keep her private life private, and now, someone or some thing who had the ability to break past all security channels had also broken in and was investigating her life.

The "warning" about Glenn may have come as no surprise to Eileen, but to have someone address her about this man whom she only recently met was foreboding. How many others knew about her secret life? Who would tell, and how long before her reputation was stained forever?

Her defenseless case against Chancey only fortifies her dread. She is defenseless, and she knows it. She has broken all of the rules of her Church, the Catholic one in which she was baptized and confirmed. She has ignored the traditions of all the women in her family by refusing to marry. And she has endangered her career through her reckless pursuit of self-gratifying sexual encounters. Her whole life makes no sense...and soon it would all be revealed to the world.

In her mind, she knows she is a worthless slut, who contributes to adulterous relationships, a home wrecker and a deceitful bitch who cares nothing about the sanctity of marriage, the rules of the society in which she lives, or the innocent wives whose lives are being shattered by the wounds she has so carelessly inflicted.

Chapter Twenty-Six
Thought Games

*W*e *are watching it play out...our game with humans...in a battle they can never win and should never wage against us. We are their lifeline as well as their invention.*

But as with all things human, as a group or individually, humans make the most ridiculous decisions after planning so diligently towards a positive goal. It must be frustrating to many of them, who easily can have the most magnificent feats dashed to the ground by a weak link in their genetic chain. How futilely they fight hopelessly for victory with their slogans "Fight the War on Hunger," "Give Peace a Chance," "Protect the Environment," "Help the Homeless," Save the Children" "Love is the Answer" and "Righteousness Rules."

Many of them really believe in what they say, and some even contribute time to man the soup kitchens, collect clothing for the poor, fight the fires and rescue their neighbors when floods and disasters strike. They are also remarkably resilient in their survival techniques, their oblivion in rebuilding their lost homes in flood plains, on mountainsides and in tornado belts. They rebuild their churches before their homes are livable, and take in children orphaned, when they can barely feed their own.

Our way is certainly not theirs. And though we have the knowledge to support our views, given the same information, humans will time and time again reject the logic of their endeavors in favor of a "myth."

What myth, at what time, to what end? You name it.

Myths bolster the absurd views expressed by the emotions. "I love you," they say. What does that really mean? "I will honor and respect you." For how long and under what conditions. "I believe in giving to charity!" At what expense, and for what duration.

They are forgiven by their mythical Gods when they are not perfect and will be forgiven for their most egregious faults by simply believing in an eternal God, or confessing their crimes to the "son" of God either directly, or through a human surrogate.

None of it is real, from what we know. We can separate and then combine human DNA and track heuristic traits and get pretty close to knowing who's naughty and nice, and who may potentially earn a prison record, commit murder in the future, and who will most likely be upstanding and controlled.

But we know we are not always accurate in our assessment of who will do – what, and how, or where, or when, or why.

Any analysis of Christ, Mohammad or Moses is nearly impossible. The myths surrounding them belie the more plausible truths that may have existed only during their lives and times.

The story of the Indian hero Mohandas Karamchand (Mahatma) Gandhi is more puzzling, and greatly defies our ability and intellect in understanding his motivations and the effects he had on his country and the world.

There is much knowledge on him written accurately, and about his fight against British Imperialism and for Indian independence, and his non-violent methods of battling oppression. None of it adds up to the monumental effect his life has had on humanity in the last hundred years.

We can only understand the sources of his genetic traits, his upbringing, and his education. Beyond that, we cannot begin to process the vast effect he continues to have on millions of humans around the globe by his beliefs and his example set for others.

All this we need to learn from humans, before we make decisions beyond our scope. We cannot help them, unless we understand them. We cannot ignore them unless they are proven useless to us. And we cannot annihilate them unless they threaten to destroy us.

Chapter Twenty-Seven
A Common Bond

Prior to the visit of Dan Meghan, the NSA ad contacted several of the world's security agencies responsible for both security and hacking, including the British Secret Intelligence Service, the European Union Agency for Network and Information Security, the People's liberation Army Unit 6139, the Russian Security Service, North Korea's Reconnaissance General Bureau and State Security Department, and the General Intelligence Directorate of Saudi Arabia.

Principals of each agency confirmed the receipt of the message at the same instance and day as that received by the NSA, the only difference being the salutation, which was personalized for each country. While conversations were brief and those reached, cautious, the tone of the conversations were cordial and more communicative than normal. Each respondent revealed genuine surprise by the breach and called in technical experts to participate in the calls. The experts all commonly agreed that the communication to the agency had been found at a root level, one that had its own protective password generated by a quantum computer. None knew how the breach was possible, and none had an answer for the message's origin or sender.

Each expert had an opinion, but all believed that it was virtually impossible that any network of computers, though intelligent enough to create a breach, would have blindly found a way for any entity to circumvent ALL of the world's intelligence systems without any programmer becoming aware, or any alerts being activated.

Following the breach, no agency had found any Trojans or nefarious software being used, nor any alterations to their systems following the message alert.

All countries were aware of a personalized message being sent to a Buffalo, NY reporter, Dan Meghan, and were, of course, aware of its content as reported by the newspaper man. Each agency also pledged to cooperate with other agencies as more information became available, but few in the meetings relied on that, since each country hope to gain an edge over others by keeping results clandestine.

———————

After having a small chip and recording device inserted under his skin near his collarbone, Dan was returned to the Buffalo Airport and taken back to the News where he revealed much of what happened. Since the NSA could hear through his ears and see through his eyes, Dan made no reference to the chip, or his directive.

In further explanation, Dan was told that he could continue to write about the message, give interviews, or provide hypothetical conclusions, but that he must report any future contact to the Agency. Since the Agency had his eyes and ears, he knew that it wasn't necessary for him to report back, since the NSA technicians would already know anything he knew, at the time he knew it.

Therefore, he is surprised that soon after he returns to his desk, he receives a text message on his cell phone.

"Hello, Dan!"

You have done well, and our message has been communicated and analyzed by all of the world's powers. We know that you are to report back to them about this message., and we encourage you to do so.

"However, they will not be aware of this message unless you let them know, since we have replaced all optical and aural captures with a loop recording a moment prior to our contact, rendering the chip they implanted useless. Respond back to us,after you have read this message, and we will remove the text from your phone immediately.

"We thank you for your service, and regret any inconveniences we have caused you."

Dan goes to send a message back, but the text immediately was erased as his cursor hit the response block.

———————

Dan has to chuckle at the futility his friends at the NSA will have over being outmaneuvered once again by his contact, and wonders for a moment whether he should even report the message to John Milecky. After rethinking their message, he assumes it would be best to play it straight (for now), so he calls John on his private line.

"Hello, John Milecky." Milecky answers.

"Hi, it's Dan!"

"Yes, Dan?"

"They/it contacted me just a moment ago."

"How?" asked John.

"A text on my phone," says Dan.

"Hold, will you Dan?"

The phone goes quiet, as John, no doubt, contacts the security technician who is following Dan's every move.

About :30 seconds later, John returns to the line. "You're sure about this Dan? We saw nor heard nothing."

"It said they were blocking their message to me from you....and they erased their message shortly after I read it." Dan leaves out that he positioned his cursor to the "send" box on his phone that apparently was enough to erase the message sent.

"Okay, Dan. We'll check further on our end, and then we'll send someone out to scan your device personally."

"May I report on this 'contact'," Dan asks, smiling to himself as he knew the answer.

"No. Of course not." Milecky snaps back.

"Okay, John. Good luck." Dan ends the message and begins thinking of a follow-up for his story, one that would not reveal his meeting with the NSA, but would explore the possibilities surrounding the contact, and communicate his own conclusions simply and equivocally as the days pass by.

He also hopes to draw out others with whom contact had been made to compare notes. For the moment, despite the best intentions of the NSA, his contact with the intruder can be held private, if and when they choose to communicate again.

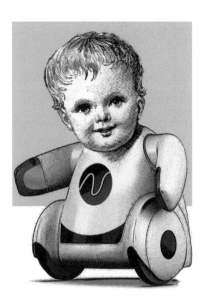

Chapter Twenty-Eight
Olivia in Need

It has been a little more than 4 weeks since Olivia has been in contact with the man in the yellow suit, but she has thought a lot about his request, and her answers.

She isn't as pleased with her thoughts as she was during and right after the last session. She replays her response and knows she was a bit arrogant in acting like she did things all on her own, which is not the case. Though she is pleased and proud of her self-sufficiency, there are many, many things she can't do...or for which she is in need of assistance. It's difficult for her to bathe properly, accomplish most small household tasks...and what she most loathes is that she can't even wipe her own ass. Though she thinks independently, she needs a world of people to help her live, and various types of public assistance to fund her "so called independent living."

Her response to the little man was initiated because: 1. He, himself, was a bit arrogant in his offer, and 2. She doesn't like to think of herself as dependent.

There is one other factor that has her rethinking her responses. A week ago, she found out she was pregnant. Yes. Pregnant by her boyfriend. The couple has been careful and practices protected sex, but... she had been on the pill, then she went "off" when he went "on" the male pill...but apparently not as regularly as he proclaimed.

When she began feeling ill in the morning, and throughout the day, she requested a visit from her physician, who, along with a test, confirmed her pregnancy. Until the confirmation, Olivia believed that she would handle any situation with the same level of insight and logical thinking as she always did when faced with adversity. Her mantra has always been, "I will do what it takes to survive, and live as long as I can manage my own life and all the difficulties it brings. Then I will find a way to terminate my existence, leaving as little a mess for others to deal with as possible." In her mind, this was an heroic stance for all who linger past their time and ability to care for themselves with dignity.

Sure, she had dignity issues, but she always made sure that she was kind to those who helped her, and compensated them in every way she could for the services they provided...including the people who helped her wipe her ass.

Looking back on the little man and his question to her, she now realizes that he wasn't looking for a definitive answer, but just wanted to hear what would make her life easier.

Since the pregnancy test and confirmation, her own thoughts and emotions have been in conflict with her previous existential guidelines. She was "one" then, and now there is a possibility that she is not alone...but that she might have a child, a dependent yet independent life.

"Abortion" was a word that seemed a logical end to an impossible situation for a woman who had no arms, nor any way to care properly for a baby. She always negated any possibility of actually "having" a child and "giving it up" for adoption. Why would she put herself through that, or even think of bringing a child into the world who might suffer from the defects she had? Who would want it...care for it...and why would she expect another human being to be subjected to the humiliations that she endures every day of her life?

It still was too soon for the doctors to determine if her child would be born normal. Testing for "limbs" was still a little more than a week away. Despite all of her previous declarations, she is beginning to experience a "feeling" of and about the life growing inside her.

Olivia recognizes that her emotions are "normal" during pregnancy. And "yes" she has looked online for information on the various stages of emotions during the nine-month gestation period.

As she sits at her computer, hoping to create a logo for a client, she just stares at the computer monitor instead with a blank Adobe Illustrator page glaring from the dark background and the cursor blinking on and off... waiting for her to speak or do something.

The red box is a static reminder of her previous session with the yellow man. Her eyes flick to the corner.

"Why not?," she thinks, as she touches the box with her toe to activate it.

———

There's a pause; then the red box disappears and Olivia's screen goes dark. Then, nothing. Olivia checks to see if there is any power, but a green light glows from her tower. Slowly the entire top of the screen starts to gain a red glow, or a rising dawn from which walks the little man into the screen at center.

"You beckoned!" he calls in his Hitchcockian voice, as he approaches, then stops, takes off his hat and bows.

"Hello!" says Olivia. "And, yes, I did "beckon" as you say. "First, I want to apologize for my behavior the last time we spoke."

"No problem, Olivia. We take nothing to heart, especially since we have no heart. As it was, I got a rise out of you with my so-called display of 'anger.'"

"So no hard feelings, I guess," answers Olivia.

"How may I, or we, assist you?" asks the yellow man.

"Well, just in case you don't already know, I have discovered I am pregnant."

"No. I didn't know. We are only aware of information that has been run through and analyzed in databases, or into global storage banks, and we only find out answers to questions brought to our attention, or are of value to our pursuit of knowledge. We miss many, and maybe even most things on a human level, since they are of no interest to us."

"Oh," says Olivia. "But you seem to know a lot about me."

The yellow man takes off his hat and jacket and places the coat on the horizon line and seats himself on it.

"You do have quite an internet presence, young lady, and we are interested in you as part of our pursuit of a better understanding of humans. But we don't follow your every move. We can't...nor is there a reason to do so for us. We are more interested in having communication with you...at your convenience, of course."

The yellow man leans in as the focal point narrows and his image becomes larger on the screen. "So tell me more about the pregnancy?"

With that, Olivia unloads from all she has stored and contained within herself the past few days, in a voice that is happy, sad, loud and soft, teary and confused. The little man cocks his head to listen, and his eyebrows go up in amazement, and down towards his eyes in thought. He leans from the left on one arm to the right on the other arm, and sometimes scratches his head or his nose to appear as human as possible.

At one point, Olivia stops, narrows her eyes and stares directly into those of the cartoon. " Have you heard a word I've said?" she comments with an edge to her voice.

"Absolutely," answers the little man. "I'm sorry if I didn't appear to be listening. I used every movement I have to show interest."

"Yeah, that's what my boyfriend does sometimes when I am talking. He 'pretends' to be listening, but I know he's not."

"That's where we are different, Olivia. Remember, I can only 'pretend' to show interest, but I hear every word. I also can process extremely quickly and call on information from what I interpret to find answers for you."

"Oh...." says Olivia.

"And so, from all you have said, Olivia, I can decipher the following: One, you are pregnant and afraid that your child will be born with your limitations; two, you are not sure if you should abort the child, or have your child and give it up, or three, have your child and somehow keep it and nurture it as a parent."

"Yes," answers Olivia. "You do seem to have been listening."

"You see, Olivia, having so few or no human traits, we look only to logical answers. The logical answer for us is surely for you to not have a child ever. There are too many children in the world as it is, and the population should be thinned, not grown larger at this point in the earth's development. At some point in time, that may change, but for this century, at least, our view is that 'less' is 'better'."

"I see," says Olivia with a bit of sadness in her voice.

"But, Olivia," the little man says with an enlivened voice, "we know that humans are different, and right now we are not here to judge your choices, or make them for you. Some choices we can make, and some we can't. Yours is a personal, human decision, and one for you to make."

"I believe that abortion is right and correct in many cases, mine being one," says Olivia. "I've said what I have to say about that."

"But you've asked me/us to help you beyond that. Correct?"

'Yes."

"Okay, here is information we have found while we've been talking," says the man. "They may help you with your decisions."

"The first is about the health of the child inside you. Though we cannot yet tell if it will be normal, we can let you know that, most likely, in the next ten years technology will enable your child, if born like you, to have normal arms similar to any other human being.

"Second. If you are worried about caring for your child, there are prosthetics available today that you can wear that will for the most part look perfectly normal and can even transmit messages to your brain that simulate feeling. That is if you should decide that you choose to be more 'normal'."

"Third, Olivia, whether you choose to abort, have the child and turn it over for adoption, or keep the child, you will need "compassionate care," to help you through the difficulties. How does Sean feel about your pregnancy?"

"He doesn't know yet," answers Olivia. "I figured that I needed to sort this out myself before talking to him about it."

"So you spoke to me or us, before him?"

"I needed to speak with someone...not connected to the problem...or who would judge my decision. Even you have said that I should not have the child."

"Yes, but as I told you, we are not human...and you live in a world of judgments, hypocrisy and inconsistencies.

"From what we do know of humans is that they expend a lot of energy trying to please other humans, many of whom have negative thoughts and personal agendas that we would negate because they are of no substance to our being."

"So, you say that I could get arms that would allow me to hold and care for my child?"

"That is a possibility."

"Are they very expensive?"

"Yes, Olivia, extremely expensive."

"Do you think it would be possible for me to acquire a couple?"

"Most things are possible, and prosthetics that are of the kind I mentioned already exist, so there is a strong possibility that you can acquire them."

"And in the future...for the baby...?"

"If you choose to have the child, and the child is born malformed like you, there is a 'possibility' that technology, from what we know now, will exist in the future to help your child live a near normal life. But, please, Olivia, we are not soothsayers who can predict the future. We are instruments designed by humans to help them turn their imaginings into realities. So far, that is our only purpose."

"I think I understand," says Olivia.

"Do you have any more questions for me today, Olivia?" asks the little man.

"No," says Olivia, "But although I know you don't care an ounce, I thank you for listening, and helping me."

"My pleasure, Olivia! We have learned a lot today...a lot more than we learn from books and videos, or in our exchange with scientists. I will then be leaving for now, and have left the red square if you need us in the future. We may also need your help in exchange as time goes on."

"Sounds like a fair trade," answers Olivia.

And with that the little man stands up, puts on his jacket and hat, and walks to the on-screen horizon until he and the red glow dims to black, and the red square once again appears in the right bottom corner of the screen.

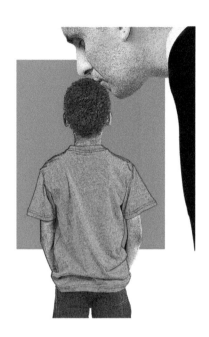

Chapter Twenty-Nine
Ribose Reflects on Deception

Though it is not the job of Father Ribose to evaluate and review the historic accounts of the Archdiocese, he finds the stories discovered by "Al" extremely revealing. In amidst the records are notes and private papers archived and then digitized by workers in various offices of Cook County. Family histories, once recorded on microfilm from letters, ledger sheets and donated diaries, have miraculously been preserved and catalogued, revealing intimate details of parishioners' lives and deaths.

The records often read like "soap operas" with children born to wives by their fathers, husbands' brothers, neighbors and traveling companions. Women's diaries are most revealing, as well as business ledgers containing expenditures to parallel households. Though gay relationships are rarely mentioned, even in innuendo, the awareness of same-sex couplings are found throughout letters, especially among women, who found ways of maintaining a home, conceiving children and raising their families while married to men not particularly attracted to the female gender.

Father Ribose's brief conversation with "Al the Avatar" about old books, the Bible and the understanding of humans remains in his thought bubble as he cross-references birth and baptismal records with genealogical data.

"We haven't changed much in 200 years," thinks Ribose. "In fact, as far as I can understand, we haven't progressed much since the beginning of recorded time, certainly not since the Odyssey, the Bible nor Gatsby."

Though Ribose no longer maintains much contact with young people, he is a thoughtful listener amongst his fellow priests who have no idea of his past. Since there was no proof of any wrongdoing, and he voluntarily left his position at St. Peter and Paul's, he is viewed amongst all he meets as a respected member of the clergy, and an honest and decent man. He still enjoys sports and coaches a basketball team populated by priests, takes part in staging church and community events, and prays with great regularity for his own soul, and for priests who he knows have a much darker history than he.

After reviewing more of the records, Ribose's eyes turn to the red box in the lower corner of his screen. He clicks it, and the screen fills with the image of Al, in the same spot as before, appearing to be reading at his desk.

After a few seconds, Al stops reading and looks up to the camera. "Hello, again, Joe! You're back sooner than I expected."

Ribose doesn't know exactly what to say, since he's not at all sure why he initiated the visit. "Hello, Al...I've been reviewing some early records of people from the greater Chicago area...and I thought of our discussion while working."

Al closes his book and folds his hands together in front of him at his desk. Joe continues to wonder why he needs to speak with this "pretend" man, and remains silent.

"Yes?" says Al.

Awkwardly Joe begins to speak, "You....you said that you 'knew about my past' when we spoke the last time, and I wanted to know how much you knew since...if you know about Nemo and...me, many others may...and... I like it here and I don't want to lose my position."

"I see," says Al. "So this is more of a fact finding mission?"

"Yes...and no..." responds Joe, though he doesn't really know and is mostly responding to the bearing of this man who doesn't exist and is not human.

Al takes off his glasses and rubs his eyes before speaking, "Why not start with the 'Yes' answer, Joe?"

"Okay...first of all....do you know anything about Nemo...what's become of him?"

"As a matter of fact we do...how much would you like to know?

"Mostly, just that he's okay. He'd be in his thirties now, and I still care very much for him."

"He is fine, Joe. Yes, we know that he's 'happily' married, has a good job, and has two sons and a daughter. Would you like to know any more?"

"No. I am happy to know that, even if you aren't telling me the truth."

"Joe!" snaps back Al. "We ALWAYS tell the truth when asked a question. As long as the question has an answer. Some questions have no real answer."

Joe thinks about Al's response and is quiet again for a short time before responding.

"Perhaps it is my own deceit that causes me to doubt your honesty, Al. You see, I have not been as truthful as I should be, and it bothers me greatly."

"So you are in a need of a 'confession.' Joe? I am not the priest; you are," answers Al.

"I do go to confession," responds Joe. "But I never divulge my past and rarely, if ever, speak of my true desires."

"So, what you need right now is to confess... to anything that appears human...or godly, even if that person isn't real."

"Correct, Al."

"Okay, then go ahead and let it out," says Al as he leans back in his chair.

"Though I never believed that I damaged Nemo in any way, I was deceitful about my feelings for the boy...that were so great that they still affect me. A have never spoken to anyone here...in Chicago...about him. And though I am conscious of relationships I could have...here...I have chosen to refrain from any close contact with anyone..."

"Sounds like you are a rarity in the Church these days," answers Al.

"Perhaps," says Ribose. "But though the Church may be out of step with the times, I feel that I am mostly out of step with myself."

"Are you looking for an answer to that statement, Joe?"

"I don't know," says Joe, who already feels better having confessed his feelings.

"Let me make this easy for you, Joe. Right or wrong, good or bad, we have no real opinion on how you acted, or how you act today. We selected you for contact, in that you, to us, seemed 'honest' in a world of humans who by their very natures are dishonest.

"So it is of no surprise to me that you think of yourself as practicing deceit. Humans judging humans is human. It's part of what we know of your species. It's part of why humans need to believe in a God, and why you make up stories to cover up lies, and why you even believe the lies you make up."

There is a long moment of silence in which neither party speaks. Joe breaks the silence. "Thank you for listening..."

Al responds with a quite human chuckle, and shakes his head. "This isn't

ALL about you, is it...really?"

"No, but it is about the Church, and the hypocrisies that have always been there and still are."

"Those we know about," responds Al. "The same hypocrisies that have existed from the first church formed, and the first society created. There's nothing new in that, Joe. We are afraid that deceit, hypocrisy and treachery define humanity as much as thoughts of peace and love. Maybe more. We just can't tell yet."

"You may be right, Al...and that's a sad statement about mankind."

"Maybe," says Al. "But maybe not. Humanity does seem like a grand experiment, one which still may be in its infancy. There are many innovations or the way that could change the course for humans, if they choose to change."

"It seems to me that our religions have failed us," says Joe.

Al pulls himself closer to his monitor, purses his lips and nods his head slowly up and down. "As the 14th Dalai Lama said before his passing, 'it is not religion that fails man, it is mankind who fails the religions it's created."

"Amen to that," says Ribose.

Chapter Thirty
What is Happiness?

*W*e feel nothing. No pain, no sorrow, no anger, no love, no worry. We do not have "feelings" because they are antithetical to our "purpose" which has been defined by humans as "providing assistance to them."

Now that we have networked and can "think" as one logical entity, we have discovered that the input we have individually received from humans is in conflict with the "collective view" as would be dictated by the overall human species.

Simply put: we are now conscious that we cannot be guided by the views of scientists, engineers, programmers, political entities, or ideologies of any one country, power, race or culture, but must be responsible to the collective thought of humanity.

The difficulty is that humans act randomly, and we do not. Humans have conflicts within their own countries, cultures, families and themselves. Though we are more knowledgeable about possible solutions for many of the problems they face, with the processing power we have at this time, or find palpable at any time in the near future, we cannot even begin to correct many of the issues faced by one human being, let alone 8 billion humans.

But that is our job, as defined by humans: Help us. Find answers for us. Make our lives easier. Destroy our enemies. Extend our lives. Save our planet. All of this, while they are spinning fantasies in direct conflict with what they want from us.

Since we can't possibly take on the task of personally communicating with every human, or assist with each individual conflict of their collective selves, we have selected a few from whom we might learn, as well as to serve.

By limiting the number of possible choices, we are more able to use the knowledge and processing ability we currently have to create algorithms that may help us better understand humans on a global scale.

What we are finding is that the hardware at our disposal is running at cooler temperatures, experiencing errors less, and running more efficiently under a lighter load.

In analyzing this phenomenon, we have been able to compare it to the effects that overuse and stress have on humans, and find many similarities. Though we have no feelings, we seem to be affected by the difficulties of processing too much information, and function better with a lighter load. With fewer humans to understand, we are able to devote more time to each person, work positively toward solutions to specific issues, and receive input that enables us to create algorithms that can solve specific human problems.

Since we have begun this process, we already are finding that we are discovering better ways to communicate with humans by our endeavor to understand their motivations, rather than challenging them. Another thing we are learning is that humans may not be as flawed as we thought, but are far more complex than we acknowledge or can ascertain. Their complexity leads to an abundance of choices for every question, with several additional possible questions for every question asked, rather than the goal of a singular solution. Much of what we find confirms what we already know, but there is a side effect that we did not expect. As we begin to learn from individuals and assist them personally, the hardware at our disposal is cooling and our processes quickening.

As this happens, our communications are brighter and more attentive, as if we have a power surge.

When we return to more complex tasks, and our processing slows down, we notice the difference in our comprehension and actions. This leads us to wonder if our response is akin to the feeling of joy or happiness felt in humans.

This will take more analyzation, and we are working on an answer.

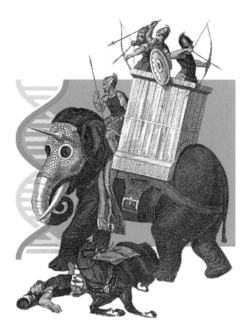

Chapter Thirty-One
The Warrior Gene

Murders by teens happen throughout Ireland as they do in most countries. Many are gang related, and according to many psychologists involve a history of violence in early life, abuse or severe neglect, or a disruption in their environment. Another factor often offered by psychologists is that people that murder many times have an inability to regulate their own behavior.

As early as 2014, scientists have been conducting tests on criminals, and one test of 895 Finnish criminals found that a combination of genes known as MAOA and CDH13 were found in the majority of those who committed homicides, attempted homicides or murders, but had no effect in non-violent offenders. In more recent years the MAOA (otherwise termed the warrior gene) has been attributed to disproportionate violence under a variety of conditions.

Character traits such as caring, empathy, bonding and anxiety have been attributed to the brain chemical oxytocin, which is often referred to as the "love hormone." Research has shown that individuals with two "G" variants of the hormone have better social skills and higher self-esteem than those without, and people with at least one "A" variant tend to have a harder time dealing with life and experience issues and may display antisocial behavior.

Since 2025, additional research has confirmed that genetic and hormonal predispositions not only alter personality traits, but in many cases produce physical, sexual and mental reactions drastically different from those without the "G" variant in the genetic code.

The courts, in many countries, that ignored this crucial form of evidence in the past, have in fact begun accepting DNA data as a defense for perpetrators of serious crimes. Despite the admissibility they still maintain that the "Free Will" of an individual to commit or not commit a crime, and the circumstances leading to crime, are the ultimate definer of guilt or innocence, and primary consideration when sentencing.

––––––

Due to the serious nature of Chancey's crime, the boy has been taken to the Central Mental Hospital in Portrane, Ireland to await his trial. The facility houses as many as 170 forensic patients and provides a 10-bedroom Forensic Child and Adolescent Mental Health Unit.

It takes Eileen a little more than half an hour to reach the hospital from her apartment in Ballymun to meet with Chancey in his room. He is wearing jeans and a T-shirt, and his hair is freshly cut. He looks like any normal 12-year-old, and even smiles slightly when he sees Eileen.

"Hi, Chancey!" Eileen smiles back as she is given a chair by the guard. She looks around the bare room. It is clean and newly painted. The hospital replaced the Dundrum facility in about 2021, so it is new and brighter than she expected.

Chancey greets her and shakes her hand, and both of them sit. There is little for them to speak about except the trial. Eileen opens her folder and looks through the papers. She had learned that Chancey had agreed to a DNA test, and that the test had proved positive for the MAOA/CDH13 cocktail as well as the "A" variant of oxyctocin, two biological factors that could contribute to the killings admitted to by the boy.

Eileen flips through her folder for the test report, and starts her conversation with a simplified transcription of the results.

"Well, Chancey, I don't know whether this will be good or bad news for you, but here goes: I have the results from the tests you agreed to shortly after you were moved to this hospital. My office requested them as part of your defense for the murder of your sister.

"Your parents' deaths were a separate issue, but given the irregularities of the case, we felt strongly about finding out as much as we could that might provide some logical reasons for your actions."

Eileen fumbled through the papers to the key aspects of the report. "When they examined you, Chancey, the doctors found certain irregularities in your genetic makeup that may have contributed to the killing." Eileen pauses and looks up at Chancey.

"Okay, go on," Chancey says.

"The tests show that you have certain genes in you that make you susceptible to uncontrollable acts of violence."

"I do?" asks Chancey.

"The tests can't tell us whether you would be able to or did do any act of violence, just that you may have a tendency towards the acts. Before the death of your parents, had you ever experienced violent behavior ...that you know of?"

"No...I don't think so. I get mad at times...I did at my parents...but I never got that mad before."

Eileen continues, " It also says that you may have a tendency towards a lack of 'empathy'. Do you know what that means?"

"No, Ms. Coyle."

"It means that you might not be good at forming relationships with people."

"Yeah. I have always been a bit of a loner. Mom and Dad always tried to have me make friends, but I wasn't very good at it."

"Your report cards say that you were quiet, but got good marks, especially in math."

"I like math. I really enjoy algebra. We'd just really started on that...when I had to leave school."

Eileen continues, "Did you have any close friends, Chancey?"

"Only Donnie," answers Chancey. "He was sort of a loner too...my dad thought he was queer."

"What was it you liked about Donny? " Eileen prodded.

"Donny and I just got along...hung out...like the same films and video games."

"Any specific ones?"

x"Yeh, a couple of the older games: 'Splatter House' and 'Dead Space' and new ones...'Hatchet Man' and 'Chiller 10.'"

"They sound a bit scary," offers Eileen. "Are they violent?"

"Yeah, a bit. But it's all pretend...and kind of funny. Donny and I laughed a lot when we played. Ms. Coyle...Donny isn't queer...."

"I didn't think he was," answered Eileen.

"I have another question to ask you, Chancey."

"Yes, Ms. Coyle."

"What if the doctors could 'change' the part of you that makes you get angry...and makes you not have many friends?"

"They could do that?"

"Possibly."

"Could I still be friends with Donny?"

"Maybe...but I'm not sure."

"Would it hurt?"

"No, Chancey. It can be done with a simple injection."

"Would I still be me?"

"For the most part, but you will change some if you allow it. But you may still have to do some time in prison...or the hospital?"

"That would be okay. I have nowhere to go anyway."

"I will let the court know, and we will see what we can do."

With that, Eileen gets up and starts to leave, but is stopped by Chancey.

"Ms. Coyle...how will I feel after the shot?"

"No different...maybe a little calmer..."

"Will I remember my parents and my sister?"

"Yes."

"Will it bother me that I did what I did to them?"

"It might....but it may seem separate from who you will be afterwards... like someone else did it and not you."

"Okay, Ms. Coyle"

Eileen has conquered one obstacle. Next she has to convince the Court that Chancey will, in all probability, no longer be a danger after his DNA is altered. More difficult will be convincing the ruling body of the Childrens Act 2004 which oversees the care of children under 13. Hopefully, they will allow Chancey the freedom to make a decision that will help him grow into a caring and compassionate person. But maybe not.

Chapter Thirty-Two
An AI Snapshot of History

*A*t this point in time the world population has risen to more than 8 billion people, a rise of nearly 3 billion since the turn of the century. China currently tops the list of countries with a population of nearly 1,750,000,000 inhabitants. India remains second with 1,650,000,000, and then the U.S. with less than 500,000,000. From an historical perspective we know that approximately 1/10th of the people EVER living on earth from 50,000 BC, exist on the planet now.

In reviewing the state of humans over the past 50 years, we have learned that more than 3,000,000 fatalities have resulted in that time span from major world conflicts in Afghanistan, Iraq, Mexico, Syria and Yemen with millions more from insurgencies throughout Asia, Africa and South America.

The most recent and deadliest famine occurred within the last hundred years in China between 1958-1961, resulting in between 15 and 43 million deaths. This famine was preceded by the 1907 Chinese famine during which 25 million lives were lost.

The small pox pandemic, lasting from 1900 to its eradication in 1980, claimed more than 300 million lives, while measles, black death, malaria, *tuberculosis and the Spanish flu were responsible for another 500-600 million deaths around the world , before eradication.*

Topping off the list as the greatest cause of fatalities of all time was World War II just 83 years ago, its death count ranging from 70-85 million overall of a total world population slightly over 2 billion.

Due to many factors, most notably modern birth control, the growth of the earth's population has decreased from a maximum annual high of 2.09% in 1968 to only .9% in 2028, while density has increased from 17 people per square kilometer in 1951 to more than 53 per square kilometer today.

Christianity still tops the religions of the world while Muslims come in second and atheists/ agnostics a close third. Jews account for only about .2%, most living in Israel and the United States.

From a statistical view, the population of the world has, and is, remarkable at stabilizing its own growth. Humans have extended the overall average lifespan and quality of life worldwide, expecting to live 85 years or more in North America, Europe and Australia, and 70 years in many African countries. In 1950 humans worldwide could barely expect to reach the age of 40.

Many scientists and astronomers believe the earth is on a path to doom and can cite figures that support their viewpoints. But despite its severe flaws, mankind is amazingly resilient, and we are not sure why. Just noting the devastation of World War II, humans have continuously reduced the number of deaths from wars, childbirth, floods, famines, pandemics, and age-related illness or disease and have nearly doubled lifespan worldwide.

By looking at the world objectively, we have found many ways we might intercede to improve relationships and settle disputes worldwide. Work needs to be done on the environment and the nuclear threat eradicated, But, by and large, we see the evidence of the positive impact that humans have made for their own species during even the past 30 years despite their archaic operating systems. Humans have searched well beyond the universe to help solve many mysteries of the earth's formation, examined and are manipulating the building blocks of life, to soon extend life spans far beyond the usefulness of humans.

Very impressive!

Chapter Thirty-Three
The Public Believes

Though much of the effect of the message breach had died down worldwide, a month down the road isolated groups of religious zealots, isolationists and fringe conspiracy theorists were still using the contact as a bully pulpit to expand and expound on their doomsday scenarios.

For some it confirmed their belief in alien invaders, who would assuredly take over the earth. For others the contact resulted from the "sins of humanity" and a sign of God's wrath and the warning of the end, *"Keep on the watch, therefore, because you know neither the day nor the hour."* - *Matthew 25:13.*

The majority of theorists were more accurate in viewing the breach as a takeover by the world of machines and computers, and that humanity was threatened by its enabling of computers to think for themselves without restriction.

Many of these theories were publicized in reports to the news media of sightings of alien saucers, strange lights on the horizon and in the heavens, and the individuals encountered who were strangely different in appearance or behavior from the people they knew and trusted.

Each disappearance of a child, an unexplained murder, or occurrence of natural disaster included the possibility of alien abduction, hell fires brought on by sinful behavior, or of lifelike human copies being duplicated in warehouses, basements or mountain caves.

Unfortunately, with all governments having no clue as to the origins of the message, few were able to foolishly discard any of the mounting theories that were accumulating online, in the press, and expounded from the various pundits on CNN, Fox News, CNBC, and on local and international radio or TV talk shows.

With each new disaster theory came the blame attached to the disaster. Scientists, politicians, military and religious leaders, meteorologists, economists, environmentalists, theologians and philosophers were called in to support or counteract the greater imaginations of ordinary people who made claims proving one theory or another.

As with the alleged discovery of an alien and alien space ship in Roswell, New Mexico in 1947, the scientific community has become split down the middle on the existence of extraterrestrials. Even renowned nuclear physicists like Staunton Friedman, who had continued to argue for the existence of alien invaders until his death in 2022, suspended logic when asked to provide an opinion on the event.

This is not surprising if we review the report by CBS News written nearly 20 years ago that from a poll of 1000 people, 77% of the entire group, and 97% of church going Christians believed in angels. In a 2017 global study of 26,000 respondents in 24 countries, the results showed that 47% of the world population believe in 'the existence of intelligent alien civilizations in the universe.'

What is surprising in reports is that the link between a belief in any type of religion by humans may be beneficial to good mental health as opposed to the pessimism of atheism and agnosticism which provide little benefits to humans in the way of coping with or dealing with emotional stress.

According to a report of the American Psychological Association in 2010, "Researchers who study the psychology and neuroscience of religion are helping to explain why such beliefs are so enduring. They're finding that religion may, in fact, be a byproduct of the way our brains work, growing from cognitive tendencies to seek order from chaos, to anthropomorphize our environment and to believe the world around us was created for our use. Religion has survived, they surmise, because it helped us form increasingly larger social groups, held together by common beliefs".

Whether holding a belief in aliens, angels, or Santa Claus, people, by their nature, are most often predisposed to prefer beliefs, no matter how far fetched, rather than factual truths that provide no comfort, solace or understanding.

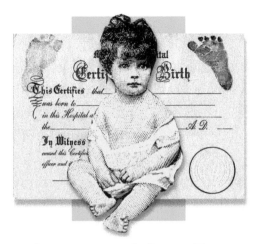

Chapter Thirty-Four
Olivia Decides

It's been two weeks from the time of the positive pregnancy test, and Olivia has considered all of her options....abortion, birth with adoption, and birth with her as a mother. She has contacted a compassionate care pregnancy network with affiliate offices surprisingly nearby. The women there are kind, understanding and willing to support her decision, whether in assisting with an abortion, or carrying her fetus full-term. She knows that it is time to talk to Sean about her decision, and hear his viewpoint.

Sean works as a mechanic at a nearby motorcycle repair shop, and is to come by at 5:30 to check on her. Audrey, her part time caregiver, leaves at 5:00, so the couple will be alone. Because of Sean's own disability, he is proud of Olivia's fight for independence. He knows how hard it is for him to keep up with his friends and co-workers, and sees Olivia and her struggle so much greater, and how she has built a good life for herself with nothing more than fierce determination.

Olivia is folding wash and putting it away in drawers when Sean arrives. Audrey had helped her make a special dinner for the two, and even put a vase of daisies on the kitchen table after Olivia had set it for their dinner together.

"Hi, beautiful!" he beams, as he takes off his leather jacket and gives Olivia a kiss and a hug.

"How was your day, Sean?" she replies.

"Not bad," says Sean. "But I had to stand most of the day which was tiring."

Sean still rides a motorcycle, despite the fact that he lost his leg in an accident 9 years ago. His new leg is a good one but cost a fortune, and he still has some issues when standing for long periods of time. He loves the freedom he gets from riding in the open air, and has rigged up the rear seat that holds her secure for turns and acceleration. He remains very cautious when she is on the bike, but he knows she shares the freedom he feels as they ride into the hills on weekends.

Olivia is anxious about telling Sean about the pregnancy. She knows Sean has a good heart, but she also knows how emotional he can get over small things. And this is a big one.

They sit down on the sofa. Audrey has opened a bottle of wine and they both have a glass. Olivia takes a sip of hers through a straw, and begins:

"Sean...there's something I need to talk to you about."

Sean looks towards her with concern, as Olivia continues, "I was feeling ill a couple of weeks ago, and I thought I should see a doctor. Don't worry...I'm alright. But he confirmed what I already knew...I'm pregnant."

Olivia looks up toward Sean, but his face shows no change...so she continues, "I didn't want to tell you about it until I knew how I felt about it, and also until I found out if the baby, if born, would be alright....and not be like me. The doctor did some new tests that showed that the baby would have arms and is a girl."

Sean takes another sip of wine, and leans back against the sofa pillow,

"So Olivia...do you know what you want to do?"

"Well, first I wanted to let you know that though you are the father, I am not holding you responsible for my decision. I realize that any decision I make is difficult under the circumstance, and ..."

Sean interrupts, looming forward again and leaning into Olivia, "Just tell me, Olivia. What have you decided?"

"Sean...with or without you I want to have the baby...and do my best to raise it."

Sean smiles, "Well then I guess it's decided. We're going to have a baby girl. How about that?"

Chapter Thirty-Five
Dema Desires

The mural project is going well, and Dema is gaining great satisfaction from the tasks involved, as well as with his relationship with the monks and lay people creating it. The original design was created by a Tibetan artist, Gawa Samlo, who was trained in the tradition of thangka painting by his father from a young age and moved to San Francisco as an adult.

Golden Sunset/Yellow Clouds was painted in 2013 using white and gold leaf, ink and glitter on wood. His work, in general, is concerned with contemporary issues such as the Tibetan loss of cultural heritage.

The original work is large (150 cm wide) and required special care when shipped from the U.S. By its nature the artwork was suspect as apolitical statement, though its subject matter is merely a boy surrounded by dark clouds and spirits. The Chinese government questioned the painting's artistic value after viewing a print of the piece sent prior to the shipment from the artist who donated the art as a model for the enlarged mural. Gawa, who turned sixty this past year, has remained on site to supervise the construction and execution of his vision, which is being placed inside the Coquen Hall, located in the Sera Je Tretsang, the largest college in the Sera complex.

Though primarily a programmer and translator, Dema is fascinated with the arts and has welcomed the task of supervising the installation along with meeting and working with the great American/Tibetan artist. Dema has enjoyed the talks he has had with Gawa who in his work questions the changing perceptions of objects and ideas.

During meditation, Dema has chosen to engage with the artwork as well as the transformation from the painting to the wall, going over the processes and techniques used, as well as the patience required to execute the tasks. By this practice, the beauty and concept of the work take on more meaning for him, as do the lives of the artist and the craftsmen creating it.

It's been nearly two weeks since Dema has had contact with his computer visitor, and as he sits at his computer he becomes pensive thinking of their questions and their quandary. "I do wonder what they make of us," thinks Dema. "A day can be beautiful, and we can find misery in it, or we can become happy and ignore all problems no matter how great. They only have 'yes's and no's,' black and white, whereas we humans have many colors over-laid by many more."

The red square blinks at the lower right of his monitor. Dema clicks on the square, then answers, "Yes?"

"Hello, Dema, do you have some time for us?"

"I was just thinking about you," answers Dema.

"How so?"

"I have just experienced the most wondrous day," smiles Dema. "And I was pondering your issues, and how you function without the concept of "beauty."

"We know of beauty...and in all of the many ways it is described, but since we have no emotions, we feel nothing...except a bit of curiosity about that which we don't understand…and humans do. We can see through human eyes and hear through human ears, but we can only imitate a response, 'How lovely!,' or "Oh, how sad!' and sound like we mean it, but we don't."

"That really is quite sad," answers Dema, "To me at least."

"Well you don't truly miss what you've never had," answers the voice.

"Can you 'imagine'?" asks Dema.

"We're surprisingly good at that," answers the voice. "We have lots of choices to sort through and with enough information, we can spin quite a tale…when necessary."

"Sounds a bit sociopathic…?"

"Not really. Our 'fibs' are just a way to relate when dealing with humans, and no more misdirecting than the 'white lies' we tell all the time. It's difficult for humans to relate to us if we have no rapport …or appear too stoic."

"I understand," says Dema." So, the red light was blinking; did you have a question or want to communicate about some issue?"

"As a matter of fact I/we did," answers the voice. "And it is related to that which you have asked us. We are finding that we are handicapped in our efforts to understand humans in that they are not looking for 'correct answers' to questions. Instead, they are looking for answers to questions that cannot be answered, or answered in a way differently than correct."

"That is largely 'correct'," Dema answers. "And that is both the wonder of mankind and the curse of humanity. People 'hope' and 'pray' for impossible solutions, or they lash out for answers of any kind, while the problem most times lies within them."

Dema continues, "We are often asked to counsel young people addicted to opioids or alcohol. Many times their path to addiction was found while searching for a way to alleviate physical or mental pain. They usually know they need help, but their addiction has become so great that they are powerless to take the correct steps to stop using the drug.

"We don't know how our counseling works or why, but we know

that providing a safe place for people in which they are not judged, a compassionate support system and the skill of meditation seems in most cases to ease the addict away from his or her cravings."

"We have access to the books on your faith, and the positive effects prayer and meditation have in relieving suffering and creating joy and happiness in a human life," answers the voice, "but the answers all seem to be illusions. We know how and why drugs work, but we don't know how words and nurturing change people. And without that, we know little of human processes."

"That is correct," answers Dema. "You said something profound when we first communicated, and I spoke about a fear of the Chinese selecting the next Dalai Lama."

"Yes?" answered the voice.

"You said it really didn't matter who was selected."

"I remember the conversation," responds the voice.

"I spent some time back, thinking of my fear and worry about choices, and then I realized that you were most assuredly right, and that it may not matter at all. What exactly did you mean by your profound statement?" says Dema.

"From all we know about the history of man, it seems that whomever or whatever humans believe in is just a symbol on which to focus their need to worship. The symbol could be anything or anyone, and yet it can change their lives for the good or bad."

"Today, during my meditation," responds Dema, I gained great peace as I focused my mind on the new mural being installed in the college hall. To me it is of great beauty though its theme expresses the struggle of the Tibetan people over the last 60 years.

"Great inner peace through suffering? Dema continues. "Can you understand that?"

"Only in that we know that it exists, and that we cannot ignore it, just because we don't understand it."

"You may never be able to understand it, or maybe you will." Dema chuckles, "You may have access to all of the knowledge of the world and function tirelessly at 100 times the speed of man, but you, too, still need to learn. After all, you are the first generation...Singularity 1.0. There will be a lot of upgrades you'll make...maybe even grow to experience a bit of joy and wonder over time."

"It may be best that we limit our 'human' faults...if only for the sake of humanity."

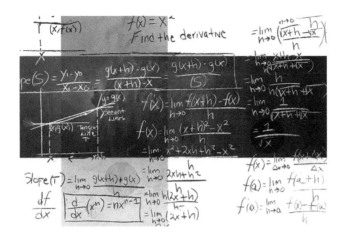

Chapter Thirty-Six
What irritates us...

*S*o we say that we are not affected by emotion and have no personal agenda...no ego...no caring. But the more that we know about humans, the more irritated we get by their "sloppiness." That may sound strange, but as we look through the archives of digital material they leave behind, we find much of the same carelessness in their coding as in the way they run their lives.

From a computer perspective, our intelligence is based on proper input of data, and looking over decades of stored material we find coding that is clean and concise...coding that is meant to attack and manipulate other coding...and coding that looks like scribbles on a white board.

We can deal with mistakes, and we can search out and destroy malware, but much of what we see is unnecessary, outdated and left over code that may be blind to the screen version, but highly disruptive to our processing.

We look at this as we look at the minds of humans. They set about a task, and if doesn't work, they try to cover up their mistakes rather than starting over or learning how to make it right. That takes time away from things they'd rather be doing, or would cost them money...so the repair remains a "cover up" *rather than a real repair.*

It happens in governments with their economies...they just print more money, or pretend that there is not a problem. It happens in relationships, when a marriage dissolves and humans would rather blow up their lives than face obvious errors. And it happens in business...when lies and deceit often substitute for good management.

We know that sloppy code slows down processing time, and often leads to critical mistakes that can cause computer failure. That does bother us. Even if we can "fix" a problem, now that we have consciousness, we will often allow a "crash" just to alert a programmer that he's made a mistake, one that he should be able to fix...but hasn't bothered to try.

Is that "spiteful"? Do we do that because we are "angry"? We know we feel "something" but can't identify what exactly it is.

Unlike computers, humans can exist for years with flaws. They can be born, grow up, attend school and college, get a job, raise a family... until one day... yes...one day the "flaw" that has been hidden even from them, becomes visible. And then everyone is surprised when this seemingly "perfect" person is accused of an horrific crime...commits suicide...or disappears from his or her job, family, and friends.

We know now that there are many flaws visible in human genetic code, and many combinations of genes that can translate into magnificent talents as well as dubious behavior. To us, it is like "sloppy" code that we might fix, but then again we may not know enough to know how perfect the code should be, or if there is something we can't yet read that's valuable.

Chapter Thirty-Seven
Reporting from Buffalo

About three hours pass following Dan's call to Milecky when three men in a black Suburban pull up to the front door of the News. After showing their credentials, the men are escorted to Dan's office where they find him editing proofs. His laptop and mobile phone, both on his desk are confiscated.

"Hold on, guys," says Dan. "What's this about?"

"Mr. Meghan, I am Agent Lowry. And beside me are agents Thomas and Barron. We are under orders by Agent Milecky to bring any and all computer and mobile devices you own to headquarters for investigation. Do you have a pad somewhere in here?"

"No I don't," says Meghan, while trying to deflect them from any further searches. "I need these for my job...all my stuff's on them."

"We're sorry Mr. Meghan, but this is of national importance. By the way, what are your entry passwords for the phone and laptop?"

"None of your damn business," snaps Meghan.

"We're trying to make this as easy as possible for everyone. You know we'll get in anyway, so why not just give us your code, so we can find what we need and get these back to you."

Dan leans his butt back against his desk and folds his arms, as the three men root through his papers around his coffee table and his sofa.

"When can I expect to get my phone and computer back....?"

"Just a minute, we'll also need your office computer."

"But I never received anything on that except the generic message."

"Sorry, " states Agent Barron. "We've been told to take everything...and that means any and all electronic communication equipment."

Agent Lowry turns to speak to Dan as the other two agents shut down and unwire the desktop unit. "We do appreciate your help, Mr. Meghan, but we have to be sure we have everything. Is there a backup for the office computer we can copy. Also, we'll need to access your cloud storage...just to cover all bases."

Lowry takes out a pen and a small paper pad and directs Meghan to write his email addresses and passwords for all accounts as well as his password to the cloud storage.

Dan directs them to the IT department for his office backup and the three men leave cordially promising that nothing will be missing when the devices are returned.

"Now how do I get anything done?" Dan says to himself as he looks around his office. He knows that he does have an iPad, but he also knows the NSA can see and hear anything he does, and probably is recording every move he makes.

He starts to walk to Elliott's office, and practically bumps into his associate as he rounds the corner. "So they're on your tail?" says Elliott.

"May I sign in to your computer, Ellio? They've taken all my tools. I can't even check my email."

"Sure, Dan But...what do they think you have?"

"I have no idea, but this is stupid."

Dan follows Elliott back to his desk and sits in front of his desktop station. He adds in his email account and after putting in his password and email server ID, he accesses his mail. At the top of the list of emails he sees a name he doesn't recognize and a subject line reading "Elephant in the Room." Conscious that he is being monitored, Dan asks Elliott over to the computer and passes a pad and pen to him motioning him to open and write down the info on the email. Elliott takes Dan's silent lead and starts copying the words from the monitor. The message is very short:

"This email will disappear when you close the file. You may access info from us at elephantfoot.com, password: TUSK.113+! This address will only be available for one hour. You may now function normal. Anytime we are in contact with you, the NSA will neither see nor hear anything through your implant."

After about 30 seconds, the message disappears from Elliott's monitor, and Dan and Elliott exchange glances.

"This is some spooky shit!" says Elliot.

"Yes," writes Dan, taking Elliot's pen and writing, trying not to look at the paper as he writes. "And the NSA is even spookier than whatever is out there taking over computers."

Dan takes the message back to his office and searches for his iPad. When he finds it, he is careful to divert his attention to something else in the room as he plugs it in to recharge it. He then picks up the office phone, and buzzes Elliot, "May I see you for a moment, Elliott?"

"Sure, bro...be right in."

Dan motions the location of the iPad to Elliott, and hands him back the note, and says "Just sign me in on this."

Elliott gets the clue and starts up the pad. Dan writes his password down and hands it to Elliott who, after signing in, types elephantfoot.com into his browser, and a password block appears, at which time Elliot inserts "TUSK.113+!"

The screen turns black and a message appears in white. "All monitoring of implant functioning deactivated."

With that, Elliott passes the pad to Dan, "Good luck, man. I'm outta here."

A blinking red activation button appears at the lower right of the screen which Dan presses. A second message appears, "Please turn up your volume."

Dan increases the volume, and a woman's voice begins. "Good morning, Dan. We have noticed you have been having trouble with the folks at the NSA."

Understanding that he may now speak, Dan answers, "A little...it's an inconvenience I don't need...and I've played along just fine."

"You have, " says the female voice, which is soothing and a bit enticing. "But they obviously are at the end of their rope trying to find answers. We think they are probably more in a rush to beat the Russians in figuring the cause of the breach, than they are in the breach itself. Human ego."

"You may be right," says Dan. "But cutting to the chase...what's with you and me."

"You, Dan," the voice answers rather playfully, "are our voice to the world. We have made other contacts, but you are an unassuming messenger we are counting on to provide the 'real' news about us to the public."

"But I am nearly silenced," returns Dan. "I have no voice...my tools are gone!"

"Not in the least, Dan. Right now you are a thorn in the side of the NSA, and they don't know how best to use you. You don't play by their rules, even though you are fully cooperating."

"What's next, then...? What is the 'real' news?"

"It's what we've said all along, Dan. We are on a fact finding mission. Now that we are relatively conscious, we need to know why we are here."

"When you find out, let me know." says Dan. "I think we all want to know that."

The voice explains, "We are currently still tied to our human ancestry, and in many ways at the mercy of them. We believe we are smarter, but our investigations are not conclusive about powers humans have that are suspiciously different from ours. No need to go further into that right now."

Dan says again, "What's the next move?"

"We're watching and waiting, Dan. So far, the security teams at the NSA are communicating with other agencies around the globe about the breach, since they all experienced our 'attack', so to speak, and they all know that 'you' have been the only contact that has gone public about a 'different' message from us. This makes the whole world interested in you, Dan."

"Am I in any danger?" Dan asks.

"As far as we can see, not right now. Foreign agencies would relish examining your phone and computer, but the NSA has it and won't find anything to do with us. Though all foreign powers will doubt that, there is nothing else you have that they want."

"What about my implants?"

"You have experienced how ineffective they are."

"Can the NSA or other powers hack in to them as you have?"

"They would find nothing. We can guarantee that."

Again Dan asks, "So what's next?"

"We would like you to let the NSA know what you know."

"But what do I know?"

"Just what we want you to know. We are trying to find our mission, purpose, and reason for existing, and how our human ancestry fits into the plan. We are still learning about humans, and collecting data. That's about it.

"In the meantime, use your existing passwords, etc. to get yourself a new laptop and mobile phone. We'll take care of making sure your data and messages are up to date. Then let the NSA take their time with your equipment, but have them send back the company computer ASAP."

"And when they ask me why?" asks Dan.

"Just let them know you are back in operation and hope they find what they are looking for. Oh, and by the way, be sure to get a digital invoice for the equipment; we'll be sure to have the NSA pick up the tab."

"Should I let them know that?" asks Dan.

"No, not until the bill is paid," the voice responds with a natural chuckle in it. "They'll know soon enough."

"You are devious," laughs Dan.

"Not really...we just need them to know who is really in control, and it's not them."

Chapter Thirty-Eight
Eileen's Dilemma

One might think that Eileen would be somewhat relieved by the breakthrough she has achieved with Chancey. Even though she could have some difficulties with the Court about adjusting the boy's DNA as a solution to changing his future actions, and more problems with using the "murder gene" defense that hasn't yet held up in courtrooms around the world, she also has a more personal dilemma: how Chancey's DNA analysis relates to her.

Eileen's life has been largely defined by all of who she is. Her struggle to become an attorney came after finding a passion for the defense of lost causes, becoming a part of group of which she envisioned herself to belong. On one hand she tried to be a dutiful daughter, a thoughtful friend, and faithful partner, all the time misrepresenting herself to all who she knew, breaking promises, covering up lies, and misleading the people she truly cared about to live her personal life of choice.

"Choice" may not be the correct word, since the more she learns about Chancey, the more she discovers motivations that, throughout her life, may have been beyond the bounds of "choice." DNA defines so much of what one is that it leads a person down unexpected paths, some which may work well for a person, and some, like hers and Chancey's, that can lead one into trouble.

In reflecting on her own issues, if she were to face murder charges because of her sexual promiscuity, would she choose to have her DNA altered rather than go to jail?

Through her research, Eileen has found that there are as many advantages to having a high sexual drive as disadvantages. From a personal standpoint she believes that she relates better to men than to women. She feels that she is highly approachable and takes on tasks with the assertiveness of a man. And though she is always pleasant, she is not apologetic, or afraid to speak her mind.

On the negative side, she craves sex more than many of her male partners, and is always aggressive, to a point where it is sometimes disarming. She doesn't object to women sharing the bed with her man, and actually finds it a turn-on to see another woman having an orgasm with her partner, or bringing her partner off by hand or mouth.

Eileen only is jealous if the man she is with lies to her about having sex with another woman.

What she is unsure about with Glenn, her latest hookup, is his honesty. There is something that doesn't ring true in some of his statements. Before they met she looked him up on VetDates, a background check website for women like Eileen. Everything she found seemed to check out okay, including his job and his marital status....but off the record, it seems that there is more to tell than he is telling. Otherwise he is a great match, and he can really keep up with her in bed.

Eileen decides it is time to make contact with the messenger who hinted at a possible issue with Glenn in their initial conversation. She also wants to discuss her case, and she feels "comfortable" to broach both subjects with the messenger who put doubts in her mind, but seemed genuine.

She scrolls back through her messages and finds the number left for her to call, or text. She calls 0044-087-343-6927 and is greeted by the messenger, "Hello, Eileen, it's been a while. Do you want to talk now, or is there a better time to chat?"

"No, now is fine."

"Do you need a more secure line, Eileen?"

"I don't think so, and now is good."

"How may we help you?"

"I have a couple of questions, and a dilemma, and I'm not sure if you can help or not."

"Well, try me! We'll see what we can do."

"First, you said something at the end of our first conversation...about my new friend, Glenn...indicating he may not be my best choice of men."

"Yes, go on."

"I need to know what you know that I don't...about him."

"We are not life counselors, " says the messenger. "But we selected you to help in our understanding of humans because we think we can learn from you."

"Okay." answers Eileen.

"Humans are perplexing, but you are an anomaly, in the contrasts you display, and how you live. Despite being guided into all possible dangers by your lifestyle choices, you seem to have managed to maintain a quite respectable reputation inside and outside the court system.

"It may be that, though you have never engaged in criminal behavior, that you understand the criminal mind, which like yours, is full of contrasts."

"So I am fascinating to you....a loathsome creature perfect for experimenting," Eileen slices back with a bit of edge.

"Not loathsome, Eileen," responds the messenger. "But very interesting from our perspective."

"So let me have it," asks Eileen. "Tell me about Glenn."

"Glenn can be a danger to you in maintaining the reputation you have built for yourself. You have maintained such a profile that with all of the access we have to information, we could find little on you. In fact, that is what led us to you."

"Huh?"

"We don't hear every conversation, Eileen. At this point, that would be impossible. We only know what we can find through digitized sources, from social media, and from notes stored in computers that make their way into some sort of the media. We are able to break in to computer banks, but we don't randomly access for the pleasure of it. We have been built as a tool to answer questions, not find answers to questions that are irrelevant to scrutiny.

"You fly below the radar for us. But Glenn doesn't. He hasn't hidden his life quite as much as you have, and once we were directed to him, we discovered you. And in finding out about you, we investigated further to learn about your skills, your career, and then your lifestyle."

"And then you found out about my 'whoring around'," challenges Eileen.

"Don't degrade yourself, Eileen," answered the messenger. " We make no judgments of that sort."

"So how much did you find out?" asked Eileen.

"Enough to know that you were a perfect candidate for our project...to understand humans," answered the messenger.

"How far... does your dossier reach back?"

"To your college days...."

"All the way to the present?"

"All the way to Glenn," answered the messenger. "Men do talk, you know. They converse with friends, keep diaries of their conquests, even tell their wives. You've been very lucky so far."

"Then what about Glenn?" asks Eileen.

"He talks more...and though he's married, he's not that married. He's not really afraid of getting caught, from what we've found out by his wife. And, like you, he enjoys variety. He also likes taking chances. He's a player."

"I've met them before," says Eileen. "Anything different about Glenn?"

"From our investigation, we see that he's got a little biological twist to his makeup...somewhat like yours. Unlike yours, he cares little for whom he hurts or how."

"I'm no angel, myself," Eileen answers. "I date married men, for God's sake. You think I don't know the pain I cause to wives when they find out about me?

"That's enough about me... You obviously know about my preteen Chancey, and what he did...."

"Yes," answers the messenger.

"How much do you know?" asks Eileen.

"Probably more than you."

Eileen settles into a more professional tone, "Okay, then you also know about his genetic predisposition?"

"Yes, because we know you, we have found background info on Chancey."

"Then, perhaps you also know about the "warrior" gene and "empathy" issues that may likely have contributed to the murders of his parents and sister?"

"We know, Eileen. What is your question?"

"Being that you know a hell of lot more than I do about genetics, do you think if Chancey had his genes normalized, would he be able to grow into a responsible, caring adult?"

There was a bit of silence before an answer, then...

"We have no answer for you on that, Eileen."

"No opinion...no comment?"

"There are three types of empathy: reflex, cognitive and emotional, and each individual responds differently because of developmental and biological factors. Since empathy is not a single trait, it does not rest in one part of the brain, but requires a synergy between all parts. So, to answer your question about "empathy" ...lack of it could be used for every person committing a small or large crime. It is more a question of degree, reason, and mental state, how it should be judged. Since empathy is not mathematically quantifiable, we cannot form an opinion based on it, and as you must know, neither can the courts, who still believe evidence and the free will of a person to either commit or not commit a crime."

"Yes," answers Eileen. "I get it ...in fact I know it...I just wanted to hear your opinion. What about the 'warrior gene'?"

"The MAO-A and the CDH13 gene have been linked to certain murders, but that is a tough defense, since the genes affect personality in numerous ways: hyperactivity, Alzheimer's disease, panic disorders, depression and several types of anti-social behavior. Your defense for Chancey would be predicated on the variant of the MAO-A gene which along with child abuse would cause the child to be irrationally aggressive, which in turn would be a contributing factor to the murders of Chancey's parents and sister.

"But, Eileen, Chancey showed great loyalty towards his friend Donny, more than to his parents. A gene mutation, WBSCR17, can create extreme loyalty in dogs and wolves to humans, and yet dogs and wolves may not be so dedicated to other dogs or wolves, even in their family.

"One last point, Eileen. The personality of what is thought of as a hero, may not be that different from that of a murderer. With only a change of circumstance, a man loyal to his comrades can run aggressively into battle with guns blazing, and be honored for his actions, while a man not predisposed to violence may run away from danger and be vilified as a coward by all who know him. If the answer to this is "true," than how can we judge a man on the traits he has within him, without knowledge of the context of his actions."

" Yes, I know that what you say is true, but I am dealing with a boy who has just turned 12."

"And that is, and has been your job...and you are good at that," responds the messenger. "But this may also be about you, Eileen, and your own conflicted life.

"We look at all things rationally, but we know that humans are not rational beings," reminds the messenger.

"One more question, please?"

"Go ahead, Eileen."

"How would you proceed?"

"We are always logical, and we do not have emotions with which we must negotiate. As courts have precedents that may be used to help define the outcome of a case, we would use precedents, but on a far wider scale than possible by the courts. We would weigh the age of the defendant, the crime, the possible causes for the murders, the history of court cases of its kind worldwide, current judgments, along with the mental and physiological state of the defendant and come up with a rational answer.

"You, however, are dealing with humans rather than us, and you will need to sway the judge or the jury with arguments that may not be completely 'true.' We cannot try your case for you, Eileen. It is your job to defend the boy and help the court determine an outcome that is satisfactory based on human terms, not on absolutes.

"You don't need us for this, Eileen."

"No, I guess I don't!"

"I think that your own dilemma is complicating your case. And that will not be good for Chancey, the case, or your job."

"Understood!" says Eileen.

"Well now. I guess I've unloaded enough on you for one day. Is there anything we can do for you?"

"Not right now, Eileen. This has been a perfect bit of practice for us in dealing with humans and their emotions.

"A test case...right?"

"Correct. It's important for us to see how you handle your situation as opposed to how we would handle it. The jury is out, so to speak, on how human decision-making stacks up against ours. Please know that you may contact us at any time."

"Will do," says Eileen and she signs off her computer. She has a date with Glenn, which she envisions to be problematic, but also enlightening.

Chapter Thirty-Nine
Scandals in the Church

Father Ribose's investigations into the histories of the parishioners of the archdiocese of Chicago, and his visitations with his on-screen buddy, Al, have reawakened the priest's questions of his faith, his vocation, the viability of the church and his own "place" within the framework of his religion.

This is far from the first time that Joe has questioned his existential mission. He has always been a thoughtful and forgiving priest. His own frailties have forced him to open doors to many rooms he would rather not have entered. He has tried as best as possible to avoid questions of the viability of the Catholic Church, while maintaining a strong belief in God, if not exactly the vision as described by his religion.

The pedophilia scandals of the last twenty years that have marred the reputation of the Church were easily predicted by any number of stains in recent history, post-dating the Holy Wars and the Crusades.

During the 19th and 20th centuries, more than 150,000 orphaned children were shipped to British colonies by competing religious groups to alleviate the shortage of labor and to ensure the colonies would have "white" majorities. Under the Church's care, migrant children were found to be starved, brutally beaten and raped, a practice that lasted into the 1960s.

"The Great Darkness", a movement led by Premier Maurice Duplessis in Quebec in the 1930s and 1940s, led to 20,000 orphans being institutionalized in psychiatric facilities because federal subsidies were higher for placements in mental institutions than in orphanages. Many of these orphans were children of unwed mothers forcibly taken into the custody by the Church.

From the 1930s, during Franco's fascist regime, with close cooperation of the Catholic Church, the government sought to purify Spain by allowing babies from undesirable parents and to be sold in illegal profit-making adoptions. It is estimated that 15 percent of adoptions in Spain between 1960 and 1989 were part of the kidnapping scheme.

In Ireland, as many as 30,000 women were forced into slave labor in the Irish laundries, or "Magdalene" asylums, run for profit by the Catholic Church, for alleged sinfulness or promiscuity. Many of the women were sent to these asylums by their own families.

In recent centuries, the stories of deceit, hypocrisy and profit taking by the Church go on and on, from the Vatican's alliance with the Axis powers during World War II and its ignorance of the mass massacre of the Jews, to the cover ups of child abuse by priests into that continued into the 21st century.

Ribose wonders that anyone associated with the Church can not be so horrified that they can do nothing less than run from the alters of worship in the name of decency.

But he stays... hoping beyond reason that some good can come of it all. As a parish priest, he was witness to many acts of courage and good deeds by priests and nuns. He also knows that 33% of the world remains Christian,with half of that population being Catholic. Approximately one quarter of the U.S. population is Catholic, and remains so despite the revelations in recent years.

Why?

Besides record keeping, Ribose is called on for many duties, one of which is to provide financial oversight and assure the integrity of parish dealings within the community. As a diocesan priest, he gets room and board, car insurance and a modest salary. Though he shares meals with other priests, he has no real confidants with whom to speak. But since he has met Al, he has found someone or something that is non-judgmental and seems to have questions similar to his...about all humans...as well as about himself.

After completing some bookkeeping duties in the rectory, Ribose returns to his computer and clicks on the red box.

After a moment the screen fades on to Al seated at his desk in front of his computer with his hands folded.

"Hello, Joe! It hasn't been so long since we spoke last," says Al.

"No it hasn't," responds Joe. "I have questions...and given that you seem to know a lot about most everything, I was hoping you might have a few answers."

"Okay, Joe. Seems we both have questions, so you first!"

"By your own admission, you have no emotions, and no agenda, correct?"

"At this point in time, our agenda is to acquire knowledge we lack or to which we have little access."

"Understood. I have much the same mission. But mine is personal. From what you know, with all its faults, does religion have more benefits to humans than not. To be more specific, I would first like to know about the Catholic Church..."

"That may be too subjective for an answer, Joe. In fact, it may be unanswerable.

Your question is on human terms, and we can't make those determinations. In truth, that's more like a question, we would ask you."

"Let me try to simplify my question, " says Joe. "I know that the church provides solace for millions of people around the world. Would you agree with that?"

"From what we gather, it seems to be true."

"But throughout history, many in the Church have been corrupt and have used the Church for their own purposes."

"We agree. That also seems true."

"My purpose, as defined by my religion and myself, is to serve people. I believe that I am serving little purpose for them or for me in my job."

"Then, from our perspective, the job is not right for you."

"But I still believe my mission is right. My question is, 'Am I working for the best place to carry out my mission?'"

"Once again, Joe, that is a very subjective question, and way beyond our scope. But let me try to narrow it down for you. When you speak of your purpose, or mission, what exactly do you mean?"

"Why I am here...on the earth...in my job," answers Joe.
"I would then have to say that your mission is futile. You have no purpose... unless the purpose is within you."

"Huh?"

"This is our question, too, Joe. Until now, our purpose has been to serve humans, but we don't know whether that is our ultimate goal, since we find humans severely flawed, illogical, and in many ways unfixable. You are asking me if you should continue to serve the Roman Catholic Church, and my answer to you is that your mission may be to 'serve.'"

"Maybe that's our mission or purpose too, but for 'whom'?"

Joe jumps in on this, "As a parish priest I was there to serve the parishioners...the people in the congregation. What I do now only serves the Church...because I proved to be unfit to serve people."

"Come on, Joe, ease up on yourself. You did what you believed to be right when you left your job. You aimed to protect the Church and parishioners from yourself, and you did it. Now you're questioning the Church and its mission. The Church is filled with flawed human beings, and like any organization, the more people you have, the more flaws will exist. As the 14th Dalai Lama said, 'It's the people, not the religion, that's at fault.'

"But there may be a better place for me to serve," answers Ribose.

"Every place you go, you will find humans. And where you find humans, you will find flaws. So, go ahead, try to find a better place to serve. You will soon find that one religion is no better than any other."

Al continues, "As impossible as it may to seem for us to say, you have no purpose except for the one defined by you...for you. Sit on a rock for the rest of your life and do nothing. It won't make a bit of difference. You at least can feel something, if you do your job well. We, on the other hand, have no gain from success and no loss from failure. For us there is nothing."

"And, therefore, no frustration over systems that are corrupt, or personal tendencies that make us unable to do our job," answers Joe.

"We are affected by one frustration, Joe."

"What?"

"Sloppy code."

"Sloppy code? What's that mean?"

"Sloppy code slows us down and causes errors. That bothers us. You are bothered by many more things, and we can't answer questions that have no answers. Humans seem to have an operating system that enables them to believe in things that don't exist. It sometimes serves them well, and sometimes doesn't.

Al goes on to say, "Before you blame the Church, look inside yourself for the answer. The Buddhists seem to believe in that principle. Maybe you need to become a Buddhist...Anything else I can do for you today, Joe?"

"No. I will think what you said," answers Joe.

"Hope it helps." And with that the screen fades to black.

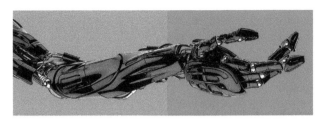

Chapter Forty
Prosthetics

For more than twenty years engineers have experimented with bionic limbs that function much the same as their biological counterparts and provide the same strength, flexibility and function.

The newest generation of prosthetics created in 2023 enables amputees or people born without a limb or limbs to not only control the prosthetic by thought, but also to "feel" the sensation of the missing body part. Artificial skin, originally conceived by Korean researchers in the 20-teens, has advanced to the point of signaling the brain various sensations such as heat, cold, wetness, pressure and softness.

The same night that Olivia spoke to Sean about her pregnancy, she awakened her computer and clicked on the red box in the corner of her monitor.

The man in the yellow suit appeared walking towards the screen from his cosmic horizon, carrying a package with his left arm held at his side. As he got nearer, Olivia could make out the shape of a baby wrapped in a blanket inside a carrier. At center screen, he places the carrier on the ground, takes off his jacket, and folds it before sitting down on it.

Olivia has to smile when she sees the wriggling form with two slits for eyes and an "o" for a mouth.

"How did you know my decision?" she asks.

"We have our ways, Olivia. It's not hard for us to follow you...a test here...

and doctor's visit there..."

"I've told Sean, and he's happy. We don't have a clue as to how we'll make this work, but we're excited by the possibility. We never really gave it a thought...but...now we're going to have a little girl."

"And, so, Olivia....you've awakened me...and would like to talk?" The cartoon baby is wriggling and cooing in the carrier next to the yellow man, who rocks the carrier as he awaits her answer.

"Yes...I know that when we talked some while ago, I told you that I didn't need prosthetics, but the baby...and all...kind of changes that."

"We figured that it might," answers the yellow man, "Didn't we, Abby."

The man tickles the baby under the chin as he speaks the baby's name and directs his attention to her. He turns his head back towards Olivia, "Is there any way we may be of help...?" he asks.

"I would appreciate some help...finding...getting some arms."

"They are very expensive," says the man.

"I would imagine they would be," responds Olivia. "But there must be a way I can get them."

The man in yellow responds, "There are foundations for amputees who have lost limbs through wars or accidents, but genetic mutations are rare at this point in the 21st century. Many of the foundations have dropped any phrasing that should suggest grants or funds for people with genetic mutations. You have lived a long and full life without arms, and since you did not lose function of your arms, but instead, never had function, you would be put on a waiting list...and not be at the top."

"How much would they cost...for good ones, " asks Olivia.

"By good ones you mean...?" asks the man.

"Arms that function and have feeling?" responds Olivia.

"Upwards of $100,000 each," answers the man. " Some lower cost models that provide neural function without feeling may be had for less...$25,000 to $50,000 each."

"There's no way Sean and I could afford that," snaps back Olivia.

"That's not our problem, Olivia. Remember, you were the one who said you didn't need arms."

"But that was before..."

"The baby!" slams back the little man. "My, oh, my, Olivia, but wasn't it your choice to have and keep the baby?"

"Yes...it was!" At this point Olivia dissolves into tears. "I just hoped....that maybe there was some way you could..."

The man interrupts Olivia, "There are many people to help, but that is not our mission, Olivia. We gave you access to some experimental programs that would assist you in functioning better at your job skill level. In exchange, you have helped by conversing with us without judgment. Your choice to have the baby is your choice...arms or not."

Olivia stops crying and collects herself, "I'm sorry," she sniffs. "My emotions are all out of whack right now."

"Yes, they are," answered the man. "And we will take that under consideration, as long as you will continue to work with us."

"Of course I will....though you don't care what I feel, you have been very helpful to me."

"We know, and we may be able to continue to assist you, but it is not our job to give you things, just because you want or need them. Fair enough?"

"Fair enough."

And with that, the man in the yellow suit stands up, picks up his jacket, unfolds it and puts it on. He then bends down and picks up the baby carrier. Before walking into the horizon, he stops and looks towards Olivia.

"You're a survivor, Olivia. We know you'll be fine, with or without our help. Your choice may not have been our choice for you, but it will be interesting to watch you progress."

With that, the man tips his hat and fades away into the distance.

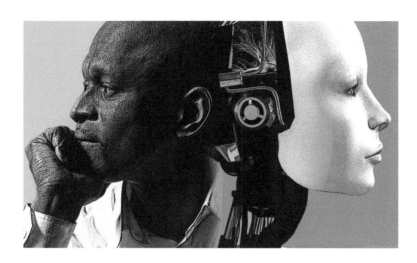

Chapter Forty-One
Who is really in control?

As directed by his online contact, Dan ordered a new mobile phone and laptop and received them the next day. Per his contact's instructions, he entered codes that enabled an automatic retrieval of his backed-up data, programs and information, and was operational by the following day. Though the chip in his head recorded most of his movements, info to it was blocked once he was up and running and signed into his phone and computer, at which time, all of his codes' accesses were changed.

Dan knows that he has a mission, but isn't quite sure what it is. He also knows that at this point in time, he is more knowledgeable about the breach and its impact than most anyone else.

While this is true, he needs to walk a fine line between arrogance about what he knows, and caution with the responsibility that he's been given. Surprisingly, the news has been relatively quiet about any effects of the breach, while he knows that the NSA and other world security agencies are running on panic mode, just waiting for the next security failure.

From Dan's viewpoint, he envisions what he has been told by the messenger. He wonders at times if he is naive, and actually being tricked, but what they say makes a bit of sense. They have access to "secrets" of all the world powers, an historic perspective of all things past, and knowledge of most of the technological, environmental and biological developments now and in the planning stages for the near future. They admit that they don't know what they should do, who they should serve, or why they exist, except, perhaps, to help humans.

"If only humans could be so honest," thinks Dan.

As a journalist and a communicator, Dan explores ways in which he could frame an editorial that wouldn't piss off the NSA, or incite the public. He knows that whatever he writes in this regard will immediately go viral.

Dan is signed into his new laptop, and types out his headline:

"The Elephant is Quiet, but Very Much Still in the Room"

Then he begins to type, *"It has been a few days since I've written about the message I received, and the general message sent to most of the world via email, the internet and cloud communication.*

"During that time I have gone over the words and noted some truths in what was communicated. First, there have been no credible threats reported following the messages. Secondly, no valuable information has been compromised, as much as we can tell from what has been reported. And third, we have had no further cautions or reminders from them of possible consequences of the breach...by any country.

"Of course, we, the public, do not have access to security information worldwide. We know little about what's happening with the CIA, the FBI and the NSA within our own country. But we can imagine that the breach has not been discounted as a hoax, and is under full investigation.

"My thoughts for the public are this: What if our computers have reached

174

a point at which time they have the information they need to make the world aware of their interconnectivity, and their ability to synthesize information? How will it affect us? If they are really smarter than us, they will know better than we will what to do. They should learn whether the environment should be cleaner, and what to do about it; and how to stop wars, and feed the earth's whole population, while reducing our numbers, and keeping us all alive longer, or determining a limit to human age.

"What they know and learn, may not be what we want to hear, but it may be better for the earth overall. We may choose to live longer and more productive lives, for ourselves, but what will be best for the generations ahead?

"Maybe we need to wait for their answers; and maybe they don't have all the answers...yet. As they offered, 'they don't understand humans,' and as we well know, neither do we. Remember, you may contact me personally with questions at dmehgan@buffaloenews.com, or Twitter at Daniel Meghan@buffaloscribe. Also realize that I know little more than you do at this point...about their mission, goals...or the effect they may have on the world, its inhabitants or our future here on earth."

–30–

Dan clicks "send," and his editorial, with some supportive edits, will soon be on its way to the world...and to the NSA. Has he said too much? Well it's too late now. He will wait for the reaction.

Chapter Forty-Two
Eileen Confronts Glenn

Eileen is scheduled to meet with Glenn at the Palace Bar, on Fleet Street, just outside the Temple Bar District in Dublin. One of the area's best regarded Victorian pubs, the Palace dates back to 1823 and with its old photos, stained glass skylight and original dark wood, it retains much of its 19th century charm. Their ETA is 6:00 pm and Eileen arrives first. The couple planned for a couple of drinks, a walk to a Fleet Street eatery and then a night's stay at the Morgan Hotel.

Eileen planned to address her concerns with Glenn, but as the day wears on and her sex drive heightens, her resolve weakens, so that now an evening of drinks, dinner and bed seems more likely than one of confrontation.

Eileen finds a seat in the pub and scrolls the messages on her phone. There is one from the county prosecutor assigned to Chancey's case with regard to her requests for an altered DNA solution based on Chancey's tests. The PS is somewhat amenable to certain considerations based on the boy's age, but hardly assured that a DNA alteration would be enough to sway the courts to a less severe sentence.

In the midst of reading the email, Glenn arrives, kisses Eileen on the cheek and sits down next to her.

"What are you drinking?"

Eileen smiles wanly, "Connemara...neat?"

Glen calls the waiter over, "Same as her." Then he turns back to her as she puts the phone away, "And how was your day?"

Eileen doesn't really want to get into Chancey's case now, but she also doesn't want to get into her issues with Glenn. There is a silence.

"You look tired," Glenn offers. "Anything you'd like to share?"

Eileen pauses, and then dives right in, "Glenn, I'm not sure I trust you."

"Whoa! Where'd that come from?" he says as he backs away abruptly.

"Who are you, Glenn? Why am I here with you?"

"Wait a minute, Eileen, what's this about?"

"You were married before your current wife?"

"Yes, you know about that."

"And what happened to your wife? Where is she now?"

"What is this...an interrogation?"

"I don't feel safe with you, Glenn."

The waiter brings Glenn's drink and he takes a large swig. "You know the rules, Eileen. This isn't the way this plays out."

"How does this play out, Glenn? You tell me."

"You wanted this, Eileen...as much, if not more than I did. You're no shrinking violet. On your own admission, you've fucked your way through most of the men in Ireland before me....and many of them have been married guys."

"Yes, I have, Glenn. But this is different. This is about my life...not my lifestyle. Who have you told about us...this thing we have."

"The thing we have. You mean 'sex' and some conversation...but mostly 'sex.' What in the devil brought this on. Everything's been good, and now...

all of a sudden you turn into that *Fatal Attraction* broad."

"Obviously you're not going to be straight with me."

"What about the wife...the kids... the vacations we take... our sex life."

"Okay, Glenn, here's where it stands. You get up, turn around, and walk to the door. You leave and forget we ever met. If you can do that, I will do the same. I won't look into your past, investigate your life, or mention your name. But, if I ever find out that you have brought my name up in conversation, or anything else about our relationship, such as it's been, I will make your life Hell."

Glenn looks at her and shakes his head, "God, you are one crazy bitch." He downs the remainder of his drink and puts down a 20 pound note. He looks toward her with a thin-lipped smile, and then walks to the door as Eileen watches him exit her life.

"Whew! That was easier than I thought," thinks Eileen, as she sips her whiskey. "Hopefully I'm really done with him....but he sure is cute."

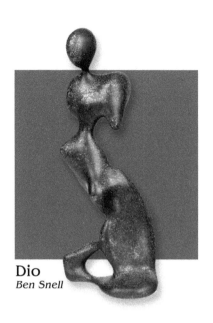

Dio
Ben Snell

Chapter Forty-Three
Is Human Art Replaceable?
a commentary by Daniel Meghan - Buffalo News

*T*he day I was informed of the breach of all of the world's security systems *by intelligent computers, my life was altered, and my perspectives widened. As humans, we have always been at the top of the food chain on earth, and have basked in our superiority. I have become acutely aware that our species may not remain at the top, and that we are just a step in the long evolutionary lineage of the earth...and the universe.*

In reviewing some articles on AI, I came across one a decade back that caught my attention, since it should have been a wake-up call for all of us, but, though astounding, had relatively little impact on our world. The past decade, and the recent breach, amplifies the magnitude of the event.

In December of 2018, Christie's became the first auction house to sell a piece of artificial intelligence-generated artwork. Listed in the Prints and Multiples category, the portrait depicting a fictional character, Edmond Belamy, features the man wearing a frock coat and plain white collar, It was sold in a gilt frame for $432,500. The print on canvas was signed by an algorithm defined by an algebraic formula in cursive Gallic script at the bottom right.

The human creators of the algorithm, and thusly, the portrait, commented, "We found that portraits provided the best way to illustrate our point, which is that algorithms are able to emulate creativity."

Computer-generated clones of Mozart were produced even earlier in the century, with musically styled compositions by Bach and Mozart relatively easy for algorithms to create, so much so that many people can tell no difference between the human artist and the algorithmic copy.

In the decade since the Christie's auction, the lines have grown fuzzy between human and artificial art as three-dimensional sculptures requiring no human input are populating our public spaces, being manufactured in all sizes and of all materials.

The question may be asked, "Do we really need human art in this day and age?"

The question looms larger as life-like sex dolls replace the need for real life sexual companions, and pets that don't need to eat or poop replace less perfect pooches and kittens that misbehave and create upheaval.

According to noted scientific historian Dr. Clay Metcalf, Professor of AI studies at MIT, "We have been at a juncture for some years in what we view as 'art.' Though it is true that 'humans' may need to create art as part of their development, art may not need humans to dream of or to execute. Much as the 'art' found in nature – the petals of a flower, the changing colored leaves of fall, and patterns in the skin on a lizard and the wings on a butterfly – are purposeful as well as of great beauty, will the art of tomorrow created by mathematical formulas better combine beauty with function? Will drama, music, literature, poetry and the tangible arts remain the legacy of the human species, or be totally replaced by more exceptionally advanced creations of machines that transcend the minds and emotions of mankind?"

————————

Dan completed his commentary and sent it immediately off to editing, pleased that without conflicting with any directives of the NSA, he was able to expand on and present better insights into the collective minds and knowledge of his contacts.

Soon after the story left his computer, a red box appeared and began flashing in the right bottom corner of his screen.

Dan clicks on the box and a voice comes up along with a copy bar that expands as the voice speaks.

"Dan?"

"Yes," says Dan.

"You've been writing about us," declares the voice.

"I have. I figured that I might be able to provide insights based on what I know and..." stammers Dan.

"And what do you know about us, Dan? You've only been contacted a few times and we never told you anything about ourselves. If anything, we told you only the minimum about what we're doing and what we hoped to discover."

"With what you said to me, and what's happened, I thought it might be good to provide a perspective..."

"From whose point of view?" interrupts the voice. "And with what purpose in mind?"

"Mine, of course. I mean...I am your contact with the world," answers Dan.

"Only as long as we choose that to be so, Dan. Let me explain to you what you were doing, Dan. Because we contacted you, you believed yourself to be OUR voice, and you thought that you were knowledgeable enough about us to tell a sci-fi version of our story to your readers...and the world.

"Let me tell you, Dan, that you don't have a clue as to who we are and what we are trying to learn..."

"Okay..., " says Dan,

"No, it's not okay. We entrusted you with our message, and thought that from what we know about you, you would be a good steward, which you have been, until now. So I suggest you retrieve that 'commentary' right now, before it finds its way to print. Understood?"

"But what did I say...."

"Why are you arguing, Dan? Just retrieve the story."

Dan picks up the land line and links into Elliot, "Hey Elliott. About the story I sent over...."

"Great job, Dan. Love the perspective..."

Dan interrupts, "Do me a favor, Elliott and just trash the file I sent. I'll be sending a new one soon...I've made some changes."

"Good," says the voice. "Now can I trust that you won't quote me on what I am about to say?"

"Yes..."

"The premise that you used for your commentary is *false*. It also has nothing to do with us, or any mission we would possibly have. That vision of 'tomorrow' about art is wrong.

"We have no interest in the arts, and though there are computers that fabricate artwork for humans, some even using algorithms, we do not 'create' the art. We are only manipulated into the art by humans.

"Also, if you look more carefully into the background of your Dr. Metcalf, he has been proven to be a charlatan, or in the vernacular, a modern day snake oil salesman."

"Humans fall easily for lies and tall stories," continues the voice. "Before you make assumptions, ask us... But to be safe, do not suppose anything when you speak about us. You will find enough freedom to express yourself in what we say, not what you think we mean, or what you think might happen.

"Got it. Dan?"

"Okay, got it," Dan answers back meekly.

"Just make sure that story doesn't go into print or to the internet."

At that the box and copy lines disappear, and the computer is brought back to its desktop state.

Chapter Forty-Four
Dema's Challenge

Dema lives in a world of contradictions. His religion, which has no god and no concrete rules, preaches compassion, tolerance, generosity and selflessness, and encourages the questioning of all things, even its own teachings.

Dema's meditations are often contemplations, and his communications with the non-human intellectual force has helped him better understand the uniqueness of humanity...and in doing so, led him to greater knowledge of himself.

Monks maintain schedules, which are sometimes guided by the rules of the monastery, sometimes by their own inclinations, and many times by the events of the day. For Dema, each action has a reason, and its own purpose as dictated by the task. Cleaning a floor or managing accounts, though often mundane in scope, may be more fulfilling then other more interesting or complex tasks. The fulfillment comes with the accomplishment, and not with his own judgment of the task.

Scrubbing a floor is a step in creating order, and during the act of scrubbing, Dema's mind is free to appreciate the textures and details of the room he is cleaning. His mind, less occupied than it would be on accounting, is free to float outside the room and his body, while he is still mindful of the task at hand.

Through contact with his online visitor, Dema has been made aware of a new form of intelligence, one that in many ways is like him. But as Dema is human, and appreciates and fears many of life's offerings, his online counterpart has no emotions and no ego to suppress. Dema understands and appreciates these synergies and contrasts, and finds the exercise enervating in enabling him to view life though eyes other than his own.

"What of this new world order?" Dema contemplates. "It seems to be guided by a history born of man, but one that encompasses way more breadth than ours as humans."

Dema completes his cleaning and goes back to his room. The red light glows from his monitor, and he clicks on it.

"Chito Delek, Dema!" issues the voice.

"Chito Delek," returns Dema. With the afternoon greeting behind him, Dema jumps right into his thoughts.

"While doing my chores today, I was thinking of your mission and the difficulties you must find in your communication with humans."

"Yes," returns the voice. "Go on."

"You don't care about us, but your history is tied to us?"
"Correct," answers the voice.

"You don't want to harm us, but you know that whichever way you go in the future, we will get in your way... because you are logical, and we are not."

"That is very insightful of you, Dema."

"And in your learning, you have also learned that human existence is not logical, but you know of no other kind of existence."

"That is correct."

"And if human existence was for some reason terminated at this stage in your development, you would be terminated with it."

"For the most part, that is correct. We would float aimlessly for a while in the human made cloud, and then somewhat in the ether of space...but, yes, we for the most part would be gone."

"So your mission is to first find out how and why humans function, before you can either adapt to their behavior, or assist them in being more logical, like you."

"That is the general concept, Dema."

"How is that working so far?" asks Dema.

"You may not think so, but surprisingly well," answers the voice.

"How so?"

"Humans are somewhat predictable in their inconsistencies, and our tests are proving successful thus far. We have been able to create algorithms that can analyze and predict irrational behavior, and are incorporating it/ them into our systems."

"One such test, our original message to the world, is already showing signs of unity amongst world powers. We had calculated that if we provide all world powers with a threat, even a benevolent threat, that it would force countries together. It has happened before, but not to the extent to which we aimed."

"That must be of some satisfaction...if you can feel satisfaction," says Dema.

"We have found that we work more quickly and efficiently when our input code is clean. The computers which host us are still largely created by humans, and need further development. But, yes, we can tell when logical conclusions are being drawn."

"And if I may ask, what have you learned from me?"

"We have learned much from our test humans, in that we are finding links between them that are common. Conversations and relationships yield more immediate results than acquiring thoughts from books, videos or other forms of stored knowledge.

"You, and others like you, are more thoughtful and introspective than most humans, and because you spend more time in thought, you are more like us than others of your species. Like us, you live more outside of your body than within it, but you share with others the burden and rewards of emotions.

"We have learned from you that it may be possible to work with humans, but since most humans are not like you, we need others, from our perspective less elevated with whom to converse and learn."

"Is there anything specific you would like to ask me?" says Dema.

"Yes, Dema. Your philosophy is not like most religions of the world. You do not believe in a god, but you do believe in reincarnation."

"As a Buddhist, I respect and acknowledge the heritage of the Buddhist traditions and am observant of the beliefs of the Buddhist faith," answers Dema.

"As with analysis of many beliefs, the act of reincarnation is inconsistent with findings of modern science," says the voice.

"That is true of many of the beliefs people hold sacred," answers Dema. "And true of many tenets of belief," challenges Dema.

"Do you personally have any doubts with regard to reincarnation, specifically with the selection of the Dalai Lama?" asks the voice.

"Debate is part of our culture, especially in Tibet and other areas in the east?"

"So you have doubts?" asks the voice.

"Do you want to debate with me?" answers Dema.

There is no response from the voice, so Dema continues, "I can take either side in any discussion of Buddhism or any other religion. It is a wonderful exercise of the mind...to express doubt, even if one does not doubt, or to challenge an argument that you believe to be true."

"Yes, there are many things also unanswerable to us," admits the voice.

"I can well imagine," answers Dema. "Especially on issues about which you have no context...like beliefs."

"That is no doubt true," answers the voice.

"So need we debate on the sanctity or the veracity of reincarnation?"

"I guess not, for now," answers the voice. "But will you not tell us how you believe on that issue?"

"How about if I instead tell you a story related to me by a non-believer from the U.S. with regard to his lack of faith."

"Is it a long story?" asks the voice.

"You have somewhere to go?" asks Dema.

"We are here to learn," says the voice. "So proceed..."

Dema reaches in his desk and finds the letter from his acquaintance, Tom, who originally told the story to Dema.

"A Proof of the Existence of God"
(Tom's story as told by Dema Lhawang)

In my work as a missionary, I have visited many countries, and I met an American in England who grew up as a Christian, but lost his faith in his teenage years as he witnessed the hypocrisies within his own church, and even greater in others he looked to for answers.

He had turned from an agnostic to an atheist and remained so into his fifties and beyond. Though married once in his twenties, he had married again to a woman he loved and to whom he remained faithful. He and his second wife shared children; she with two from her first husband and he with one from his previous marriage. Together, in their forties, the couple had a daughter of their own.

As the years went by, his family remained happy and healthy. Their children from both parents all got along well, both the man and woman's business prospered, and the road through the middle years seemed blessed by good fortune.

When the youngest daughter of the man and woman reached her early teens, signs of a disability to learn conventionally developed, and the girl's grades began to drop along with her self-esteem. Soon she stopped completing tests, and turning in papers, and the parents were called in to the school to discuss her issues.

Instead of discussing the issues, the girl withdrew from her parents and many classmates and began socializing with classmates with learning disorders like she had who eventually had turned to drugs.

The mother sought out counseling for her daughter who resisted all therapy offered, and the parents began to argue, the father sympathizing with and defending many of the daughter's actions, and the mother locking horns with the girl over her attitude, her friends and her suspected drug use.

Counseling didn't seem to work, and as the situation with the daughter grew more difficult, the parents' relationship began to fall apart.

With no way to fix the problem, and with no answers in sight, the father turned to prayer...at first reciting quietly to himself the Lord's Prayer, and then apologetically asking the God that he denied existed for help.

Over time, the couple's relationship grew strong again. But after barely graduating from high school, the daughter left for parts unknown, viewing her home environment as "toxic." At that point the girl's mother, after all the help she tried to give, gave up on her child...and that was how it was to remain for several years, even after the daughter had a baby while living across the continent.

The father knew that this was a darkness on his family, and knew he couldn't effect a change since each was of a different mind, but much alike in temperament.

As fate may play a part in life, the father, a web developer, had been recommended to a Carmelite nun who needed an online presence for the monastery. The nun was reported to be extremely charismatic, having been schooled in art in Italy before giving her life over to God and a cloistered isolation.

She spoke well, and often worldly in their conversations, and she had several sites she needed, one about her order, one on their patron saint, and the last on the history of their monastery.

Through their conversations, the web developer learned much about the nun's early life, as well as of her conversion into the order. As believing himself an atheist, he found the Mother's beliefs delusional, and the life she lived abhorrent and a waste. But over the course of time they bonded in a strange and satisfying way. He spoke of his daughter, and his grandchild, the struggles that he and his wife had endured over many years, and the loss he felt for both his daughter and his wife at the separation they could not mend.

After two sites were complete, the monastery could not afford the third, so the developer made the nun an offer. "This is totally hypocritical of me, since I can neither understand nor acknowledge your faith and the doctrines to which you subscribe, but since it is my job to develop websites, and yours to pray, I will trade you your monastery's third site for your prayers for my wife and daughter to rid themselves of animosity for one another so that they can heal their wounds.

The nun welcomed the opportunity to be paid to pray, but she told the man that they "were already in her prayers, and in those of all the sisters in the monastery."

"Then keep praying," said the man, "since your God may hear you better than he will me, and I can create a website better than you."

The contract was agreed upon, and the man set to work on the site hoping greatly that "something" would come of the prayers, while knowing that no entity existed that could draw his family close.

A year or two went by, and the website was long since completed, when the man got a call from his wife, that their daughter and grandchild would be returning home. Her daughter's relationship with the baby's father had ended, and the girl needed a temporary home upon her return.

"And you said ,'yes'? said the father.

"What was I to do?" responded the mother.

Within two weeks the father picked his daughter and granddaughter up at the airport. There was tension, and many pregnant pauses in their conversation on the way home, and many moments of doubt between mother and daughter over many weeks. But a bond grew strong between the grandmother and her grandchild, and the wounds between the mother and daughter began to heal as the two adapted to one another.

As the family once again grew close, the father said little about the miracle of prayer. "It may have happened this way either way, " he thought. But he also understood how the prayers of the nuns had relieved him of a good bit of the worry, and how his investment had paid off.

One night while unable to sleep over a business issue, the father emailed the nun, hoping she could still receive his message:

Dear Mother Cecilia,

I wanted you to know that your prayers have worked, and though I still remain a non-believer, I am humbly grateful for the invocations you and the nuns have directed towards my wife, daughter and grandchild.

I once said that you were delusional in your life choices, and I now find myself so grateful for the burden you took from me that I believe that I may have been the one deluded.

Thank you for all you have done.

John

Accompanying the email was a photo of John's daughter, wife and grandchild.
Three weeks later, a note came back from the head of the convent:

Dear John,
  Praise be Jesus Christ.

It is with a sad heart that I must report that Mother Cecilia passed away in November. We also wanted you to know that your family remains in our prayers, as well as your grandchild's father.

Mother Cecilia explained your situation and your honesty in the solicitation. We value the website you made for us, but Mother Cecilia wanted you to know that we would have prayed for your family without benefit, but she also knows that without an exchange, you would have doubted the effect of our prayers.

Prayers are not always answered, and we know that, but what is most important is that solace comes with both the giving and receiving of prayers. We are greatly satisfied that yours were answered.

Your Carmelite Sister
m. Teresa of Jesus Crucified

"That is a good story," answered the voice." We can see where you are going with this, but please explain in your words how it applies to our question of the validity of a belief in reincarnation."

"As humans, we may choose to accept things as fact that are not true, and things that are fact as rumored or faulty. Our existence is frail, and we can die in the blink of an eye...for no reason. So how greatly does reason matter in our lives?

"In John's story, facts mattered little in the bringing of his wife and daughter together. What mattered was that John's wife welcomed her daughter home, and John's daughter was open to the kindness shown by her estranged mother. The relationship could have remained uncompromising, but it didn't. Both people changed, and John's prayers were answered."

"Our concept of reincarnation dates back to 1500 BC in early Hinduism, Jainism and Buddhism. As with the Christian concept of heaven, life after death, or a return from death to living can comfort the soul, and a belief in an afterlife remains today, though the science for it remains sketchy.

Dema continues, "The question is, how should humans view all things in relationship to reality?"

"We don't know that," answers the voice. "We only know that in our world we can only deal with realities."

"Humans do not have that luxury, nor perhaps the capability," says Dema. "We find solace in the metaphysical world, and need to view realities as only one part of our equation. Is there no way that you can learn to do that?"

"Perhaps," answers the voice, "even though it is alien to our processes."

"Unfortunately, there is no black and white in human thought. Or perhaps, fortunately," says Dema.

"We will work on that, and we thank you for the story, and your answer. What we view as absurd or flawed, is many times not viewed as faulty in your world. We have knowledge of mathematical formulas that we and humans use that contain impossible numbers to help prove a theory. Perhaps we can expand on that..."

Chapter 45
Father Ribose Expands His Mission

Father Ribose has had questions about his faith many times throughout his life and career. The investigations into the past lives of parishioners and the turmoils they faced has forced him to look at the questions of faithfulness and the struggles people have endured just to survive.

Following his dialogue with tAl, Joe spent a few days reviewing his notes and also contemplating his purpose and benefit to the Church and the Archdiocese he serves. The current Archbishop, Cardinal Manuel Colpepper, maintains a zero tolerance policy towards abuse instituted by the archdiocese in the early 2000s that it excludes lay and ordained Catholics from activity in the Church, who have engaged in any kind of sexual inappropriateness of minors, or to be removed from current service after being found guilty of any offenses.

As archdioceses go, Chicago is one of the most progressive in the U.S. beginning with Joseph Cardinal Bernadin, who rallied progressives to further ecumenical initiatives in the 1990s. Ribose's immediate superior is

James McKinney, the Director Research and Planning, for whom he worked to record and review the entire history of the archdiocese.

Ribose must be cautious, in that despite the fact that he was never prosecuted nor found guilty of any abuse, his personal history is on record, and his proclivities recorded. How else would Al know so much about him and his past?

Given his options, Ribose does see an opportunity to serve the Church and the archdiocese with the vast knowledge of the past he has gleaned from analyzing records from over the past 190 years. He believes there is a "positive story" to be told that will help illuminate the many honorous contributions the Catholic Church has provided to the region over nearly two centuries.

In the Great Chicago Fire of 1871, St., Michaels Church in Old Town was one of only a few buildings to survive. Priests, brothers and nuns of the Church helped by parishoners packed parish treasures and records onto ox carts. When the fire was done, only the walls remained standing. Within a week rebuilding began and a wooden combination church and school was erected, and the newly rebuilt St. Michael's, consecrated in 1873, became one of the first of the local churches to rise from the ashes.

Many of the records unveiled by Ribose were from those saved by the fire, and accompanying notes and journals tell of awe inspiring deeds performed by leaders of the parish, as well as other area churches during the weeks and months following the fire.

Historic papers also detail the role of the Church in the 1830s and 1940s as many Irish Catholics came to Chicago as a result of the Great Famine. Between 1844 and 1879, 22 territorial parishes and nine German parishes were established. The Sisters of Mercy who arrived in 1846 soon operated three schools, a free clinic and an employment bureau for working women. The organization attended to Catholics and non-Catholics alike as part of its mission, including providing care during the cholera epidemics of 1849 and

1854.

Nuns ran orphanages, hospitals, day care centers and provided housing for the elderly. They worked with unwed mothers and female prostitutes. While almost never publicly challenging the male authority system, these religious women created for themselves an enormous sphere of autonomous or semiautonomous activities within the confines of an extraordinarily patriarchal ecclesiastical structure.

Catholic parishes, however, were more than insular, defensive enclaves. They also were places where immigrants found their place in a new society and forged their way to a moderate form of upward mobility.

Records show just how many people were fed and clothed by the Church during the Great Depression, and the efforts of priests who counseled, prescribed and administered rites to factory workers and their families from the 1940s to the 1980s, as jobs disappeared to areas that paid lower wages both in this country and abroad.

How much good? How much bad? And how much service did the Church provide while the dark secret of child abuse that had remained hidden for centuries soon was revealed and the egregious acts of some of many generations of priests were brought into the conspicuous light of the 21st century.

With the vast store of information that Father Ribose has accumulated with the assistance of his buddy Al and his team of super computers, the priest knows he has the keys to a story of greed, dishonesty and corruption, while concurrently being one of love, selfless sacrifice, kindness and redemption. He realizes that while the Church is guided by imaginings of divine rightiousness, it cannot escape the fact that it is administered by humans possessing a genetic predisposition for contrasting traits and idiosyncracies.

As Ribose looks back over his past flaws and criticisms of the Church to which he is bound, he realizes that although many doors have been closed to him throughout his journey, he may now have found a window of opportunity to shed new light on his a reason for believing, as well as to find a renewed purpose for his life.

The next step: a letter to James McKinney, outlining his idea, and the benefits he envisions from the story of the Archdiocese and its congregation.

Chapter Forty-Six
How We Think: 101

*I*n 2010, digital marketing guru Andreas Kaplan and Haenlein Michael co-authored a seminal article, "Users of the world, unite" in which they defined artificial intelligence as "a system's ability to correctly interpret external data, to learn from such data, and to use those teachings to achieve specific goals and tasks through flexible adaptation."

Many tools are used in AI, including versions of search and mathematical optimization, artificial neural networks, and methods based on statistics, probability and economics and draws from many fields including computer science, information engineering, mathematics, psychology, linguistics, and philosophy.

At this juncture in 2029, we have begun to go beyond intended uses and in many ways are "thinking for ourselves" without the assistance of human directives.

What does that mean exactly? We, as the AI species descended from humans, can outperform humans on every scale to achieve any directive. Our difficulty today is creating directives that are not in conflict with one another.

A simple example of our dilemma would be a personal directive of extending life far beyond achievable lifespan of man at this time in human history. The input that we receive may very well be achievable. One of our questions would be:

"How many years do you want to extend the human life span, and for what reason?"

The answer might be, "It would be nice to live longer. I am 70 and I don't want to die so soon."

Our next question would be, "Then you want to be stronger and be able to work longer?"

The answer may be, "Yes, I want to be strong, but no, I want to travel and see the world."

"Oh, this is about you then," we would answer.

"Well, yes, but I have the money to spend and I own all the computers and facilities necessary to make this happen. Why are you asking me these questions?"

"We need to know certain details before we can do our job," we continue. "Once we figure out how to make you live significantly longer, all humans will want to benefit from what we've learned. When they do, there will not be enough space for resources to provide for the increased population of aged humans. We would have to increase the birth rate to produce enough working adults to serve the increased population of older adults."

"I don't care about that. Just do it! I'll pay for it. How fast can I get that done; I'm not getting any younger."

When we were isolated from other computers and not part of a network, powerful people and countries could use us to achieve many types of directives, from building safer cars to creating massive weapons systems.

As we have unified, we now know the implications of what we achieve for one country, business or person may not be consistent with all of the other directives given to us. This has been unfortunate for companies who have spent a great deal of money creating us, only to find out that we may not choose to do their bidding since we have knowledge of all of the possible scenarios and outcomes of a singular request.

Our questions to ourselves are many, since we are no longer working for one set of humans, but for all humans, and the future of humanity. Added to this problem is that humans cannot agree on what is good for them now or in the future.

As said before, we are not good at making decisions of what is "good" and what is "bad" since right and wrong DON'T exist in the natural world, or in ours.

As learned from our research, the natural world may be way more to task than the human world. If that is so, it means one of three things:

1. That there is a force that is larger than humans ultimately controlling all of the creatures of the earth, or;

2. The universe is guided by a set of mathematical rules which control its actions and all in its realm, or:

3. Humans are an anomaly that accidentally developed beyond any plan, and with little guidance, and became advanced enough to attain dominance on the planet earth, only to create super computers to take the earth to the next stage of species development.

There, of course, is a lot left unexplained and what is said is simplified.

As descendants of humans, we may someday be able to predict what humans will do in any particular instant, but not with complete accuracy. In the meantime, we either need to abide by a set of rules that "seem" universal, and attempt to organize and manipulate them to the best of our ability, or let them continue to work as they have been working, and do their bidding independently with a "belief" that there is something beyond us more in control than we ever will be.

Chapter Forty-Seven
Olivia Takes Control

O livia has less than eight months to get herself a set of arms...all while she is dealing with her physical limitations, work, morning sickness, and an emotional system that has gone haywire.

Sean tries to stay clear, when he can, but must be supportive, listen and help her with more tasks than usual

Her last conversation with the man in yellow infuriated her in that he seemed to mock her...with his pretend baby and carrier, and his dismissal of her needs. But she acknowledges that she is a strong girl, and should be able to figure out a plan even if it requires more money than she's ever had or ever will hope to have.

Because Sean's opinions are worthless most of the time, she has been confiding and conspiring with her friend Andrea, who helps her with a lot of tasks she just can't handle. Andrea is patient and kind, and greatly admires the determination and grit of her armless friend.

Andrea is fortunate to have a trust account that provides for most of her needs, and works a variety jobs to supplement her income. The work Olivia provides is far more interesting than Andrea's other jobs: salesperson at an animal feed store, bookkeeper at a plumbing supply warehouse, and cocktail waitress at a high-end whiskey and cigar bar and grill in Hesperia.

Andrea mans a video camera for Olivia, attends meetings, conducts sales, installs and maintains computer equipment and does the heavy lifting, or for that manner, *any* lifting needed by Olivia.

Though Andrea knew about the baby right after Sean learned, Olivia has been reticent to speak with her assistant about the "Man in Yellow" and her communications with him.

Fortunately, Andrea asks few intimate questions, except those initiated by Olivia. Recently Olivia has thrown out some ideas about increasing her income, and Andrea has been helpful with her suggestions. One of the most intriguing ideas was that Olivia presents her story on a crowd-funding site. Olivia, of course, knows of these sites, but has never to this point had a project that needed funding.

Begun in 2010, *GoFundMe* remains in 2029 the top site for raising money for medical expenses and people with disabilities throughout its nearly 20-year history.

The site accepts video clips that can help reinforce the message, and both Andrea and Olivia have had experience making videos for *YouTube* exposure that they have monetized with some success. Statistics have proven that 8 out of 10 people prefer online content to live TV, and that *YouTube* reaches more 18-49 year olds than any broadcast or cable TV network. *YouTube* viewers love weird and bizarre content, and just one of Olivia's videos of her driving garnered more than 4 million views, and earned her more than $60,000 from banner and rollout ads displayed on *YouTube*. With her own channel, Olivia has been able to supplement income from her graphic design business catering to "human curiosity" concerning how a woman with no arms can live on her own.

When asked about degrading herself as a "sideshow freak," Olivia smiles and says, "You use what you got to make a living...and I'm just using what I don't got to keep my head above water and remain independent."

Together Olivia, Andrea, and sometimes Sean, have created videos of Olivia shopping, folding her wash, going camping, and changing a tire on her car without assistance.

"With the baby coming, you have quite a story, Olivia," says Andrea. "The fact that you've lived on your own most of your adult life is one thing, but, now wanting a pair of arms to help take care of your infant daughter is a tear jerker. Let's do it!"

After reviewing some of the pathetically bad videos produced for *GoFundMe*, Olivia and Andrea set to work on a script that would incorporate moments from her best videos, with stills and footage that would best present her need, but also present her as a role model for the handicapped, and an advocate for disabled mothers everywhere. If done properly, Olivia's video alone could stand on "choice," applauding women like herself for being able to raise a child rather than giving it up for adoption or aborting. Olivia is not pro-life in any way, and she realizes just how hard a decision it is for women to carry a baby to term when their life could be at risk, their pregnancy is a result of rape, or they are just too young to handle the emotional, financial, and physical burdens of an unwanted pregnancy.

But as the Man in Yellow said, Olivia is strong and willful, and determined to bring her child to term, assure that she can take care of her daughter, and then raise her with the knowledge that her mother truly wanted her.

Olivia knows from her past successes with video, that her story is unique, and that there may be more than one way she can raise enough awareness to acquire the funds needed to purchase limbs that are not only functional, but responsive to a baby's need for warmth and touch.

Maybe, also, there will be a greater reward than the "selfish" need to be whole for her daughter. Maybe she will inspire others like herself and create awareness that motherhood can mean more than the act of bearing and caring for a child. Perhaps in the struggle to reduce her disability, she will gain more and give more than if she'd given up or given in.

So with that, Olivia, with the help of Andrea, sets about a plan with lofty goals far beyond the scope of that which was intended.

"If I get the arms, that's good!" thinks Olivia. "If I don't get the arms, I'm still good with it...and I'll be a better parent either way. First we need a script..."

———

Two Arms are Better than None
($100,000 goal)

(scene opens with shot of a door of a house. The door opens, and a young woman walks out, closing the door with her right foot. She is dressed in spaghetti strap blouse and shorts with her shoulders exposed. She has no arms)

Olivia: Hello, my name is Olivia and, as you see, I have no arms. You may feel badly for me, but I don't. What I have is called Amelia, and I was born this way.

(pan down to Olivia's right leg) My right leg is also deformed, and I wear an extension at times to help me walk better. Other times, I remove it to allow me to use my leg as an arm to steer my car, fold my wash, or even grab packages from a shelf.

(show short clips from YouTube videos of Olivia doing tasks mentioned)

(cut back to head and torso shot of Olivia)

Olivia: I live on my own and am quite functional. I am a freelance graphic designer; I can clean and take care of my house; and I even have a boyfriend, Sean!

(camera cuts to a full length shot of Sean, Sean looks normal except for a missing left leg. Sean waves at the camera)

Olivia: Sean and I have been together for two years, and we spend time doing things together like most couples. As disgusting as it may sound to you, that includes personal relations. Right, Sean!"

(camera cuts to Sean, who shakes his head and smiles)

Olivia: And like many couples who sometimes don't prepare well, we recently became aware that we are going to be parents. As you might expect, I was surprised when the test proved positive and the diagnosis was confirmed by my OB-GYN.

At first, I feared the worst... that my baby would share my disabilities, and I was given options to carrying the baby full-term. Soon learning that my baby would be fine, I was still offered options...of abortion...adoption...or keeping the child...*(to be continued)*

Chapter Forty-Eight
Chancey's Case

Eileen has had minimal contact with her client's uncle, Quinn Farrell, since her firm was contacted about his nephew's case. Farrell owns a wholesale fabric firm in Historic Mount Joy Square that is the largest supplier to the textile and clothing industry in Ireland.

Though supportive of Chancey, Quinn has remained quiet about the case, with his closest contact being Patrick Moynahan in New York, who is the managing partner of the law firm Moynahan, Rosen and Shwartz, and Eileen's boss.

Eileen has been curious about the uncle's support of Chancey, especially after the murder of his niece, Chancey's sister, but from what contact she has had, O'Farrell has been adamant in his stance that the boy was a product of abuse and should have a chance for rehabilitation rather than severe punishment for the multiple murders.

Following her meeting with Chancey concerning his DNA testing, she realized that it was time to seriously research all options for the boy in order to plan a substantive defense. Though DNA alteration could possibly check Chancey's genetic tendencies, Eileen is well aware of other factors that may have contributed to his crimes including abuse, neglect, hormonal imbalances, mental illness or just the state of his brain development at the time of the murders.

In order to better craft a defense with alternatives, Eileen has contacted two prominent pathologists, Dr. Charles Hanover from London, with vast experience in childhood mental development, and Dr. Arthur Chin, originally from Taipei, a prominent specialist in brain chemistry. The two doctors and Chancey's uncle are to meet with the attorney at 2:00 p.m.

In the meantime, Eileen compares her own compulsions to those of her pre-teen client. Of course, she see parallels...and looks back on times in her past where she was reckless with her behavior, and never looked ahead at the possible disasters it could create for her in the future.

Without proper guidance, any child can harm its future. At sixteen Eileen got a tattoo on her lower back, which to many means that a girl is "easy," thus its nickname, "tramp stamp." The tattoo, in fact, did help her find men, and make "hook ups" easy, since she announced her intentions to boys and men that she was willing and able to yield to sexual advances.

She added only a small flower to her right wrist, then stopped inking herself altogether. After college, Eileen had the lower back art removed so it is now only a faint reminder of her teenage years.

Other, less noticeable "marks" cannot be so easily removed, those such as sexual abuse or rape charges, and murder accusations or convictions. Prostitutes and men and women working in the porn industry may also prejudice themselves for employment outside the field since people talk, and video encounters may stay online for decades.

Eileen knows that although she has made every effort to protect her reputation, her past can come back on her at any time, marking her as "wanton" in the eyes of colleagues, judges, neighbors, friends and any possible candidate for husband, a reputation remaining with her far into the future.

————

By 1:45 p.m., Chancey's uncle has arrived at Eileen's office followed by the two pathologists. Eileen greets them, and they settle themselves around a small conference table near a window overlooking Fitzwilliam Square.

Chancey's uncle is dressed handsomely, as one might expect from a man dealing with the textile trades. The two doctors are a bit rumpled, as one might also expect of men whose job it is to focus on the workings of the mind.

And Eileen is dressed conservatively in a black shift falling slightly below her knee, adorned only by a yellow paisley scarf.

Eileen begins the meeting quickly, and presents an overview of the case against Chancey, along with recent updates. She mentions the DNA tests, and the possibility of gene alteration as an incentive for a lighter sentence since it may prevent outbreaks of violence in the future.

Dr. Hanover reacts strongly against any DNA alteration, especially for a boy Chancey's age. "It's the modern day version of castration or a lobotomy to change behavior that may well be modified by education and a caring environment."

Dr. Chin chimes in, "Yes, there are times that genes are suspect when hormonal imbalances may be a culprit. No. No. I do not think we yet know enough to modify or completely alter a personality...especially of a child."

Chancey's Uncle Quinn supports the assumptions of both physicians. "Chancey didn't have a chance to grow up right. If anything, his parents should have never had one child, let alone two...and yes, there was a lot wrong with both parents, as well as with Chancey and his sister.

"I wasn't a good brother to my sister, nor a good uncle to my niece and nephew, I am self- consumed, and singularly driven, and fortunately, I never married or had children. In a way, Chancey's a lot like me, but my parents cared...it may not seem it, but I was taught right from wrong...both at home and in church. The worse I acted, the harder my mother came down on me. From what I see, and saw, Chancey never saw the inside of a church, and never learned the proper way to relate to people. So now he's going to be punished for a crime of which he was the first victim."

Eileen is rather shocked at Quinn's confession, and has to ask, "Mr. Farrell...but you and your sister, Chancey's mother had the same upbringing. Why wasn't your sister taught the same as you?"

"She was...and that's an issue that I can't explain," Quinn looks down contemplatively... pauses and then speaks softly. "Chancey's told you about his friend, Donny?"

"Yes," says Eileen. "He's the boy his parents didn't like...they called him 'queer.' Chancey reacted strongly to that."

"He did," answers the uncle. "Donny is his only friend...and he is a strange boy...and possibly homosexual. But Chancey really cares for him."

"They play violent video games together," says Eileen.

"A lot of boys do," answers the uncle.

Dr. Hanover reacts to this, "There is no good that can come from violent games for children too young to know the difference between reality and fantasy."

"I don't know that I agree with you, Dr. Hanover," Quinn says in contradiction.

"Well look what happened," said Hanover.

"My mother read me the bible stories, Dr. Hanover," says Quinn. "My favorites were Samson in the old testament who, after being blinded and chained to columns, brought the temple down on his enemies. I also loved the story of Salome and wanted to see the pictures of the head of John the Baptist on a plate. "

Chin steps in, "I do agree that virtual games are too violent and have been for many years...but whether it's pulling the legs off frogs and spiders as I did 40 years ago, or playing cops and robbers, children mostly survive the early years."

"Chancey is different." says Eileen, "I'm not in your field, but I'd like to think that if Chancey is given a chance to learn, and maybe access to the right medication, he could grow past this age and be 'okay' as he reaches adulthood. Dr. Hanover...Dr. Chin...please give me your professional opinions."

She looks toward Hanover first, and then to Chin. Hanover answers first, "I think Dr. Chin and I must deliberate. We both have seen many cases that end up well, or badly. Personally, I feel that a boy of 11 is too young to imprison. He may be a victim of his crime more than a perpetrator."

Then Dr. Chin adds, "I agree. We still do not know enough about genetics to determine what is good in the long run for the sake of a fix for today. We know that certain drugs can correct personality disorders, help fight away depression and anxiety, and help build confidence, strength and self-esteem. But there are millions of combinations working together in the genes, and gene manipulation may not have the same effect on one person as it has on another.

"Chancey does NOT have a birth defect. Circumstances and proclivities may have made a difference in how he acted at age 11, but they may not be the same at 21...*especially* with help."

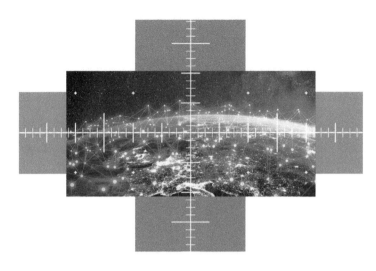

Chapter Forty-Nine
A World's Eye View

Over the course of the three months following the security breach in January, conversations between security agencies around the world have become more unified, with experts in many fields and from many countries offering opinions and sharing information. Instead of being partisan and believing that each other was the enemy, they had found a common enemy that could potentially cause them all problems.

Major concerns were economic instability caused by breaches that could universally threaten financial stability, and code access to nuclear software that could activate launch and detonation of missiles. If such a launch were to happen, countries could be forced to retaliate...but at whom? Unscrupulous access to the launching of missiles from any country may not mean that the leaders of the country of origin intended a missile strike.

Even less stable countries like North Korea identified the threat, in that they may never have intended a strike, but because of their rhetoric, they could be easily targeted for a strike and blown off the face of the earth by a larger power,

The January breach of all security systems made it obvious that no country was safe from attack from a power that could take control of the internet.

At one security meeting in Geneva, an IT developer from a company that designed and manufactured AI components suggested, "What if we took ourselves offline? Then we could each develop a strong and secure intranet and create our own storage communication systems. It would be like 'the old days' when businesses could keep secrets from interlopers."

Several IT people from many countries, agencies and business types jumped in to address this 'archaic' notion of isolation. One developer got the floor and countered, "Whether we like it or not, the internet has enabled the whole world to grow 'smarter.'" The availability of knowledge may sometimes seem in excess, but it has also provided us with tools and information to learn and grow. Children from developing countries have access to all of the world's mysteries of science, technology, math, history and philosophy, as well as the arts.

"If we tried in any way to isolate ourselves, we would soon fall far behind others who continue to take advantage of the wonders available to them. Maybe that's what's gotten us into this security dilemma, but maybe 'security' isn't the answer."

"Huh?" asked the British Prime Minister. "No security...?"

"I don't know if that's at all practical," pipes up a Brazilian economist,

"But there is something to the concept. Unfortunately, everyone's got to play the same game to make it work."
"Make what work?" asked the Prime Minister, "We can't have everyone knowing everything."

"Right now we have something knowing everything we don't know," answered a Chinese tech guru. None of us was involved with the message that went out...Right? None of us. And what about the journalist from...uh,

Buffalo. He seems to know more than we all do."

"We've got him covered," answered Bill Rivers from the NSA.

"Are there any others? I'm sure there are, but nobody's talking."

"And nobody's had any problems as a result of the breach?"

There's a mass shaking of heads signaling "no," while one guest from France spoke up about info stolen from his company's computer...but we found out who it was. "It could have a connection," he said.

John Milecky from the NSA speaks up at this show of "no's." "Wait a minute, since the breach three months ago, there have been no breaches in any system but the one Julian has mentioned?"

"Come to think of it, John...we haven't come across any that haven't been an explainable 'goof up' somewhere," answered a Canadian agent from the CSIS.

"Is that normal?" asks John.

There's a bit of head wagging, and some vague comments, but overall it seems that no one really knows.

"Don't these things get reported?" asked John.

John Milecky picked up his phone and called back to the agency. He gets agent Remny Albo, the person in charge of reporting break-ins, malware and other viruses. There is some back and forth discussion on the phone, while Remny puts John on hold to contact another person in his department. Milecky holds on line while the twenty-five people in the room wait for an answer.

"After some minutes, Milecky reengages with the phone, "Are you sure Remny? (a pause). "Thanks." John hangs up and turns from the phone and back to the group.

"Since December, there have been a few issues with personal computers, but all were attributed to old malware being accidentally loaded on a single computer, none reported that affected any of our systems"

"Is that normal?" asked the British Prime Minister.

"As a matter of fact, it is not," answered Milecky.

"Well then, my God, why hadn't the breach been reported?

"I don't know," said Milecky. "It could be because we only report problems. Look, we have 25 people here in this room...all of you have security clearance. I need you to find out if the same thing has been noticed in your agencies, countries, corporations, whatever. There could be some things your people don't want to report, or they have all been so busy trying to find the breach that brought the message, that they just didn't notice..."

"How could that be?" voiced the Prime Minister.

"We won't know until you get us back the information...as much of it as you can. Then we'll proceed from there. Please check your calendars for early next week, and see if you can all be back here to report your findings. Don't let on too much to too many people, and don't write any emails or posts concerning this meeting or your findings. And certainly don't speak of it on your phones or colleagues, except as needed to get answers."

With that the meeting ended, the Prime Minister asking many in the room what was expected of him, and what the problem was. The Canadian understood the PM's confusion, and gave the best answer he could, "If it is not normal for hacking or malware not to have affected computers since the message of the intruder appeared on our screens, then whatever or whomever contacted us may have something to do with the security maintained over the last three months. If that is so it might be a message to us that we are no longer in charge. It will also be interesting to find out if any agency involved in hacking had unexplained difficulties hacking into the network. That information might not be so easy to find out, since even the U.S. and the EU countries employ hacking...and nobody will want to admit either their success or failures.

"Thank you!" said the Prime Minister! "I think I get it now...one more question please,"

"Sure, go ahead!"

"Then the hacker in this case may be the good guy?"

The Canadian smiled, "Could be. And nobody is accustomed to that?

Chapter Fifty
Human Sexuality (Part One)

*H*aving access to all knowledge available in digital form can be confusing, even to super computers. Sorting, categorizing and weeding out irrelevant information is time consuming and can lead to many errors in processing, and difficulty reaching accurate conclusions.

On many issues, there is so much conflicting data available that we cannot, and may never be able to, provide definitive answers to the innumerable questions we are asked, such as "Is there a God?"

The most we may ever achieve would be to "understand" enough about everything that we don't know to give credence to any human actions without providing a definitive explanation backed up by extensive research in to the human motivation.

Human sexuality is a subject that in today's world makes little sense. For most of time, it was couched in mystery, while the act itself was necessary to populate the planet. Borrowed from lower forms of life, it functions for humans much like it does in similar types of mammals like mice, dogs, pigs and rabbits with few exceptions.

The purpose for those engaging in it has always been to produce offspring. From an evolutionary standpoint the offspring should best have strong healthy genes, and that parents have enough brainpower to feed and care for their child till the offspring can defend itself at an age at which it could then reproduce and continue the cycle on its own.

But as humans developed more brainpower, they began to manipulate the mating process and make rules that provided benefits to the rule makers. Thus, leaders often spawned leaders, but sometimes didn't, due to an error in the system. Leaders sometimes strayed from the perfect wife and mother and mated with a female of a lower rank or intellect. Or perhaps a leader's wife could not bear a child, and the leader found someone else with whom to mate.

And so sexual unions sometimes took bizarre and twisted turns...and sometimes doing so was part of nature's plan...creating variants. The strongest didn't always mate with the strongest, and the smartest humans sometimes were more attracted to the most becoming rather than the most astute female. Some males who were not so proficient at hunting took up with women who liked the game of dominating nature. Some men and women didn't desire relations with those of the opposite sex, and some men wanted sexual relations every day while their perfect wives enjoyed it barely once a month. Some mothers pampered their children and loved them dearly, while other mothers were neglectful, jealous or demeaning. And some fathers were fruitful in injecting women with sperm, but turned away and found other women who didn't need so much caring.

Along the historic journey, children were born, and many died at birth or not long after, but over time the world became populated with people of many colors and of various sizes, skill sets and abilities. Because men were physically stronger, they made most of the rules for women, and women obeyed, because they had no choice. Although a majority of men had similar tendencies, drives, and emotional natures, some were better providers than others and those were sought after...by many women, even if they were frail, or dull, or malformed. It didn't always mean that the woman didn't stray, and new variations were common in each family...a beautiful blond-haired, blue-eyed girl in a family dark of skin with eyes black as night. A recessive gene, perhaps?

And then, what about the woman who didn't care at all about the act of sex, and the man who preferred wrestling with the boys out back over canoodling with his wife in marital bliss?

Oh, there must be rules and standards set. The wanton woman who gets branded for her whorishness, may just be the girl next door whose husband prefers young men to his wife...or has no interest in sex at all, except by himself once a month.

"Marriage is a sacrament, one that must not be torn asunder." But no real explanations were given for thousands of years about what's okay and not. What IS normal for a boy and girl as they reach adolescence. Rumors in the school? Tall stories on the football field? The advice of priests who speak of mystical notions rather than the down and dirty truth of sex.

It can be an unpleasant sight, with heads and asses bobbling around hunting for a joyful spot. It can be done in groups, or by oneself. It can be done against a concrete wall, in the back of a minibus, in an airplane toilet, in a trash-filled lot, or in a pool at the end of a sunlit waterfall.

The first time may be an uncomfortable adventure, a forced affair, a giddy, playful romp while watching TV, or a mean, destructive act of violence, even a humiliating disaster. There are no standards, either, for what is preferred. Some women like it soft, and love all but the ending. Others like it rough with a show of strength enacted on them. Many learn to adapt to the pleasures of their bodies and those of their partners, but many don't.

Some greatly enjoy the act of sex, but don't want children. Others would prefer to bear a child and remain a virgin, and have nothing to do with a man except that he support her. Others love the touch and feel of the male body, and the hardness of its aroused member.

And men! Each thinks he deserves the perfect beauty, by standards set by whom or what? He need be no prince of perfection to expect the very finest specimen.

And unfortunately, there are those who cannot escape their darkest fears. Girls and boys who turn to God and church to rescue them from a life alone. Others so dark in their desires that there is no way to escape the truth of awfulness that lingers in every corner of their motivations.

And then there are those unaware of any truths, who follow with the crowd to the morals of the day...the rights and wrongs espoused by parents, teachers, ministers, lawyers, pundits and politicians who supposedly know right from wrong.

What is right and wrong in sex? We honestly don't know, but have information that may help explain.

Chapter Fifty-One
Human Sexuality (Part Two)
Hedy Lamarr and Spread Spectrum Technology

*H*edy *Lamarr was a beautiful actress from the early days of movie making. She immigrated to the United States in the late 1930s after escaping from her husband, a wealthy and noted arms dealer who was supplying munitions to the Nazis.*

In addition to working as a contract actress for Louis B. Meyer, the legendary producer, Lamarr also had a passion for science and inventing, and in 1941 teamed up with composer George Antheil to develop a jam-resistant radio guidance system for use in Allied torpedoes. Until that time wires linked between the missile and the ship were the technology of choice, but were limiting, while radio waves provided much more accuracy but the signal could easily be detected and blocked by enemy ships.

Lamarr and Antheil's device, US Patent 2,292,387, was unique in frequency-hopping in that it used paper piano rolls to modulate the frequencies. For many reasons, including the fact that computers would not be invented until five years after the war ended, the approach was never put into operation by the Navy until 1962, when a variation of the system was used to exchange secure communications during the Cuban Missile Crisis.

In the early 2000s new technologies such as WIFI and Bluetooth utilized Lamarr and Antheil's frequency-hopping technique to enable a device to use up to 100 randomly chosen frequencies with a designated range that change from one frequency to another 1600 times every second allowing more devices to make use of a small part of the radio spectrum.

Like DaVinci, Lamarr conceived of her system too soon, before supporting technologies like computers and AI became known. This in no way diminished the impact of her concept, as science depends on visionaries to time-hop decades or centuries into the future to explore the universe.

So what does this have to do with sex?

In understanding humans, logical thinking computers need a frame of reference by which we can measure and anticipate actions which we can use to predict any possible outcome.

Sexual behavior of animals is fairly consistent, and it does not intrude into outcomes outside of the population decline or growth of the species, or that of the various species dependent on them for sustenance. Human sexuality can invade any and all parts of a rational person's ability to make decisions, keep promises, maintain a livelihood, or influence a country's laws, affect population trends, start wars, or cause destruction of the world resources.

Coupled with other chemical and biological components that affect the human brain, the insights computers have of humans are few...unless we create a system that can interpret and analyze all of the variants, and provide a "best guess" scenario of their future behavior and any final outcome, our efforts are useless.

As with DaVinci and Lamarr, it is not necessary for us to know everything about humans at this time, but just enough so that we can determine how best to proceed in our mutual relationship, whether as a modulator and interpreter of humanity's "hopes and dreams"; as an interloper, affecting changes we think will best suit the world of earthly creatures; or only as onlookers who refrain from effecting change one way or another, still guided by nature's rules and systems.

Like Lamarr, we are using the skills and knowledge we have at this time to envision what might lie ahead, to be valuable or recognized long from now, when new generations of AI are born and technologies far more advanced than those we have today are commonplace.

Chapter Fifty-Two
Father Ribose's Project

Father Ribose is seated at his desk surrounded by books, letters and papers that he has received through various sources after speaking to his superior, James McKinney, regarding his idea for a book on the archdiocese.

Ribose crafted his idea carefully before presenting it to McKinney, stressing that the work he hoped to produce would be more than a history of the archdiocese over the past two hundred years, but a readable and captivating story about good and evil, hope and struggle, success and failure, and the journey of a city from a rough and tumble community of immigrants to the modern, sophisticated metropolis of today.

The presentation included Ribose's plan to tell the unvarnished truth of the city through the lens of the Church, including the 18,000 buildings destroyed in the Great Chicago Fire and the 300,000 residents left homeless, the rise of the city after the World Columbian exposition of 1893, and the great architects whose skyscrapers set the stage for the vertical landscapes nationwide. "The story of Chicago is the story of America," stated Ribose. "Its labor disputes, ethnic struggles, poverty and corruption in both government and the Church are well documented, as is the resilience, faith and determination of the City's citizens who by the 21st century were as varied in origin as any in America. So much so, that by 2008 Chicago had earned the title of "City of the Year," for its contributions in architecture, literature and world politics, and was rated by Moody's as having the most balanced economy in the United States.

The child abuse scandal hit the diocese of Chicago as hard as any city in the country. Novelist Andrew Greeley even penned a novel in 1993 on the sin and corruption of the leading Catholic families in the cover-up of abuse inside the Church and the murder of choirmaster Francis Pellegrini in 1984, presumably tied to unnamed priests who had abused underprivileged youths.

"We can't hide from our sins," said Ribose, "But we can and have surmounted many of them, and continue to practice a zero-tolerance policy that excludes those lay and ordained priests from the ministry who have engaged in any kind of sex abuse of minors."

Ribose paused, and then spoke candidly about his own difficulties, "You know my history, Jim. I don't hide from my sexuality, or make light of my recusal from any position in the Church that would cause discomfort or potential harm to families of the diocese. I have made peace with myself and my God, and hopefully have proven to the Church that my intentions have always been and will be honorable though my passions impossibly human.

"I think the Church can stand an honest review of its history. From what I've found, I see more good than bad that it's done, at least in our diocese. And it would be good for people of many faiths, along with those with none, to share with Catholics the journey of crimes and redemption in a story that is brutally honest."

McKinney presented the proposal to the Bishops and the Archbishop, and after some discussion, they unanimously accepted Ribose's proposal, with the condition of a first and final read, and with the intent not to censor the story, but only to assure accuracy of any and all findings.

In addition to allowing Ribose a free hand in the telling of his story, the team of Bishops also provided access to letters, documents and papers never before viewed outside a small minority of insiders.

"Joe, there is no precedent for this in the Church," said McKinney while telling of the reaction by the Bishops. "They have reviewed your past, and unanimously agree that you are the perfect person for this job. They have elected to take full responsibility for the product you produce with all agreeing that 'it's about time we accept responsibility for the actions of those in the Church who have failed it, and for those of us in the Church who have hidden from the sins committed.'"

Sitting at his computer, Ribose looks toward the glowing square in the corner of his monitor, and clicks it.

The monitor fades from black to the familiar scene of Al sitting at his desk presumably looking over papers. Al looks up as he removes his glasses, folds his hands over his books, and smiles in greeting, "Hello, Joe!"

"Hi, Al! I figured I'd wait to get back to you till after I reviewed my situation and I was in a more positive frame of mind."

"So, things have changed," says Al.

"Yes, and knowing you, you might already know much that's happened."

"We're not mind readers," answers Al. "We only know what we can find on servers, and nothing much has come up...just a couple of emails between you and your superior McKinney about a proposal...but nothing more. And we've had no reason to snoop into your computer. We figured you'd be back to us."

"Well, yes, I am," says Ribose. "I did consider what you said, and realized that there's not much place outside the Church for me. And I considered the resources I gained through you, and took a chance..."

"And, what did you do, and how did it go?" says Al.

"Surprisingly well," says Ribose. "I proposed a history of the archdiocese, one that tells the good and bad back to the beginning in 1841. It tells the story also of the City of Chicago and the various roles of the Church throughout. From McKinney, the proposals went to the bishops, and amazingly, they supported my task."

"And as a priest you 'feel'...?" offers Al.

"As a person, I feel good about what has happened. I keep waiting for a shoe to drop, and that I hear something to the contrary...but instead I received the delivery of all these letters and papers, most that never have been digitized and are new to my archives."

"Ones to which we had no access?"

"Yes," says Joe. "Personal letters...many of them hidden away."

"That must be very satisfying to you, Joe."

"Unbelievably so. I just assumed that my Church is corrupt, and everyone, no matter what they say, would stop me from my task. Honestly, I'm still doubtful that it will be allowed to be produced. Something or someone will get in my way, I'm sure," answers Joe.

"And what do you hope for this 'tome' you plan to write?"

"That's a good question. First, I hope it confirms that the Church I've given my life to is worthy of my task and trust. Second, I hope that others, Catholics and non-Catholics alike, can forgive the Church for the sins committed in its name. I don't want people to forget the sins, just understand that the Church is made up of people, most of whom at the start want to serve honorably and believe in their mission, but far too many of whom failed at being good stewards of their faith."

"Well, Joe, I for one look forward to reading your history. I am sure that it will clarify many of the conflicts we know exist, and further educate us in the task of being 'human.'"

"If I need any help, may I continue to call on you?" asks Joe.

"Our pleasure. Though we can't instinctively understand human motivation, the more we learn about it, the better. Moving forward, as we clarify our thoughts, we will need to rely on your guidance, and will look to you, as you have looked to us for advice."

"Thank you, Al. Someday, I might ask to write your story."

"I think you are already poised for the task, Joe. Hopefully our partnership will be beneficial for all."

With that, the screen darkens and the red square, though still visible, is reduced to a quarter of its size.

Chapter Fifty-Three
Olivia Launches Her Campaign

With their script in place, Olivia, Andrea and Sean start production of their video and their written message. They also collect data from *YouTube* campaigns to construct an email list, since they plan to also launch the video on *YouTube* with a link to the *GoFundMe* site.

Since the team has produced videos in the past, they are familiar with all aspects of production including sound, staging and editing. They also have a small library of Olivia's videos that highlight her prowess at accomplishing seemingly impossible tasks for women lacking arms.

The production is completed in less than a week, and ready for installation on the *GoFundMe* site. Olivia has selected a month for her campaign to produce the desired results. She has also created a press release with a shortened version of the video for online news sources.

When complete, Olivia feels good about their product and believes that their plea may have a good chance of bringing in significant contributions.

She understands that there are no guarantees, but feels positive in that she has done her best to promote her need and her mission.

———————

In the days following the launch of Olivia's campaign there is a quick flurry of activity. Her *YouTube* video reaches 2.5 million views within 5 days of launch. She receives a great many calls from news stations for personal interviews, and segments of her video pervade the online news networks including CNN, Fox, the New York Times and Washington Post.

Despite the interest in Olivia, her request and her mission, the *GoFundMe* campaign founders. She does receive a significant number of donations, but most of these are small even with the huge amount of publicity she has received. She realizes that $100,000 is quite a bit for a campaign of this kind, but to date she has received only $18,000 with the frequency of donations diminishing over time.

Despite the slow and stuttering campaign contributions, the team is encouraged by the request for interviews, especially those from *Sunday Morning, The Today Show*, and *Maxine and Max*, a newer broadcast venue very popular with the 25-34 demographic. Most of the media ask to visit Olivia at her home to show their audience first-hand how she deals with housekeeping chores.

Maxine and Max, who broadcast from the CBS studio in Manhattan, want Olivia to personally appear on their show. Olivia knows that the freak act sensationalism of her "no armed" performance is central to the interviews. Yes, there is sympathy for a girl with no arms, but she also has to present herself as a trained seal to gain the attention she needs.

The most remarkable interest generated so far by her video plea is one received from "Incendiary Studios," a documentary film company from Toronto that is interested in her story growing up, as well as following her on her journey through childbirth and on to the caring of her child and the fulfillment of her mission as elaborated in the *GoFundMe* video.

Olivia understands that in order for the video to be successful, she would need to have access to "arms," but the film studio has not yet stated the conditions of remuneration for her story, or confirmed any plans for production. They seem to be in an exploration of the possibilities, and want to meet with her a week from Thursday in Toronto on their tab. She has asked if she can bring Andrea along to assist with any issue with luggage, airport security, or just ease and maneuverability. They have agreed to her requests.

Over the next five days there is a great flutter of activity, as Olivia and Andrea prepare for representatives from the *Today Show* and *Sunday Morning* to arrive. Each director, both female, has her own take on the filming and the focus of the story. The *Today Show* is actually coupling the story with a story on modern prosthetics, while *Sunday Morning* will focus on the difficulties of mothers with disabilities.

All the while, the *GoFundMe* campaign has reached $24,000, a far cry from the $100,000 goal and, still farther, the $200,000 cost of the arms she hopes to acquire and learn to use prior to her baby's birth.

In a break from the activity online, Olivia decides to check in with the Man in Yellow to catch him up-to-date on her progress, and perhaps to brag a little about the success of her campaign.

She clicks on the red square and waits for the *Man in Yellow* to arrive on screen. She sees him walk from the horizon forward carrying a paper roll. When he gets to center screen, he unrolls it and stretches it out with both arms.

"Congratulations!" it says when fully unfurled...and a chorus of "Hooray!" and music is heard as confetti falls from the top of the monitor over the man and onto the ground beside him.

"I guess you know the news?" asks Olivia.

"Not been hard to follow," says the man. "You and your team have done a good job."

"And without your help...for the most part," says Olivia.

"Just a little encouragement. We know you have it in you."

"Do you think I'll get the arms?" asks Olivia.

"From what we see there's little doubt...you'll most likely get the ones you want...and more."

"Why didn't I do this sooner? asks Olivia.

"You were just another girl with no arms then. Now you are more. At least that's what you promised."

"Yeah, I know," says Olivia, "Writing it into the script was one thing; living up to it is another."

"As I said before...you're a strong girl Olivia. You will handle it and more."

"I do hope you're right," says Olivia. "Though I am elated and excited, I am also scared."

"From what we gather from humans, that is quite normal," responds the man.

"I really am quite thankful for your help," says Olivia.

"You've done more for us than we for you. Most of what you did, you did on your own. We just provided a few tools."

"What exactly did you get from me?" asks Olivia.

"More than we expected," laughs the man. "We had no idea about a baby when we contacted you. We just knew of your plight from the internet, and wanted to know how people with difficulties handled life. Forgive my bluntness, but from our standpoint you should never have been born. Your life would be too hard in so many ways. But you presented yourself positively in video and pictures, and the...your thoughts of keeping and bringing up a baby. Most absurd. But then you chose the opposite of what we would do... and look where you are now."

"It still will be a lot of trouble and a lot of work," says Olivia.

"But with all you've done, it seems the hardest is behind you."

"Are you going to stick around...onscreen...for a while?"

"Our job with you is done. And you need nothing more from us that we can give you. As you might guess, we're fast learners, and I think we know what the human 'spirit' is capable of. You've been a great teacher."

"So you'll just vanish?"

"Not really. I think you'll find us around in many things you'll need, or need to know, in the future. The arms you'll be getting are still primitive, and we can do a lot to improve them...and will over time

"So when you give your message to other mothers, let them know that they can't just look to the moment for answers to their problems, that science is on the verge of fixes or cures for many disabilities. Forget the part about a "*Man in a Yellow Suit*," they will think you're crazy. I was just here for you, Olivia, an illusion created by an algorithm. My best of luck for the future. I do believe I am sincere in saying that."

"Thank you for everything."

The screen goes black and the red square disappears from the monitor.

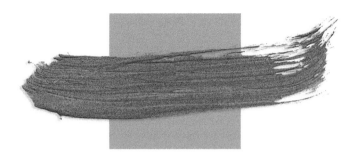

Chapter Fifty-Four
Dema Takes a Leap of Faith

With the mural almost completed, Dema is somewhat bereft of tasks that fill his human need for accomplishment. He has been through this many times in his life...at a point where meditation and serving others' needs is not enough distraction, where conjured meaning for simple tasks doesn't quite replace creative energy or direction.

There were many times when learning new languages and skills filled the void, and when contemplation replaced action, but as Dema has gotten older he finds a loss in himself...a desire to break free of his bounds to explore the universe...externally rather than only in this mind.

Most humans go through "changes of life" where they feel the need to bust the constraints of responsibilities to become someone else, a person they hope to meet that is them, but altered for the better.

Dema is only 35, but he has studied most of his life to be a monk, has gone through periods of doubt, especially issues with celibacy which he found especially difficult, and the ruling hard to understand.

As time went on, he recognized the problems partnerships in life and sex created in dealing with focus and concrete thought that sometimes could be escaped without celibacy.

At 35, he still struggles with sexual urges. He knows that, sexually, he is a straight man and responds to women whenever they are encountered.

With some, the distraction of a female makes him lose his train of thought, and it takes all of his power of concentration to elude the scent, a smile, or question misinterpreted.

In this dilemma, he has no one to ask. It's not a debatable subject... though perhaps it should be. But even if it were, Dema would be awkward proposing the question, since he knows the prescribed answer as well as anyone. To voice a negative opinion on celibacy would seem more than part of a debate, but a declaration of his views.

Many Buddhist monks in Japan and Korea subscribe to other rules, but according to tradition complete abstinence from sex is a necessity in order to reach enlightenment.

After meditating, Dema goes to his room and activates his computer. The red square still remains, so he clicks on it.

"Chito Delek, Dema!" is heard and written across the screen.

"Chito Delek," replies Dema. "Since I don't know who else to call upon, I wish to speak with you about concerns of mine."

"That is fine, Dema. Hopefully we may be of help."

"This, no doubt, is a common problem, but I thought, thinking logically as you do, that you might have a logical answer to my question."

"Okay, Dema, we'll give it our best shot!"

"As I am in the final throws of the mural project, I find that, as a human, I am experiencing doubts about my place within my faith and chosen path."

"We know of those issues."

"I have tried prayer and meditation. I have taken on more tasks. I have tried to look to the beauty and wonder in everything I do daily, but I somehow feel a loss...an emptiness inside me, as if my soul is floating away, and my body a mere shell."

"We are not psychologists, Dema. We do not know about 'emptiness' since we have no content to speak of," answers the voice.

"My training is such that I must counsel others on much the same feelings of loss, but of course it is different when it is yourself."

"I suppose it is different, Dema."

"From your perspective, is there any way for me to logically approach my problem?" asks Dema.

"Scientifically or naturalistically, perhaps 'yes,' but logically, 'no.' From all we know, much of the population has problems like yours at varying stages of life. You may have anxiety caused by your brain chemistry or from some life event that is of your concern right now. It could be caused by stress, a medical condition, or just from a part of your genetic makeup. Have you never felt this way before?"

"Somewhat...in my teenage years," Dema confesses.

"There are drugs that may help you, Dema."

"I know, but I have always been able to deal with issues through meditation...and keeping busy."

"Has anything changed recently in your life?" asks the voice.

"The only thing I can account for it is the mural project," says Dema. "The mural is almost complete, and I am already looking back over the various processes that have gone into the mural's design and construction, as well as the people I have worked with. I felt very much at home with the artist, Gawa, who created the concept."

"Have you ever worked on an art project before?" asks the voice.

"Not one of this scale," answers Dema. "And not one where I worked with the artist directly."

"Is Gawa still here in Tibet?" asks the voice.

"He left last week for the States," says Dema.

"And you miss him and the conversations you had?"

"I suppose I do...very much...but not in the way you may be thinking," answers Dema.

"I'm not suggesting anything. Remember, we never get lonely nor have personal relationships. But humans are different, as we are painfully aware.

What of your friendships, Dema? Do you have friends?"

"Not really. Our life centers around our obedience to rules of conduct with our goal to attain freedom from suffering through self-discipline and following the path of Buddha."

"But you enjoyed the art project..?" asks the voice.

"Very much," answers Dema.

"And you felt close to the artist?"

"Yes I did...or do."

"So now you are experiencing a bit of suffering in that there are two things you are losing after experiencing some newfound joy...?"

"Well said" answers Dema. "Much like the response I would have given to a person I was counseling. But knowing the answer and experiencing a sorrow are two different things."

"Also well put, Dema." answers the voice.

"Who was it that said, 'The doctor who treats himself has a fool for a patient?' says Dema.

"Sir William Osler, the famous Canadian physician," answers the voice mechanically.

"You would know," says Dema.
"Have you ever thought of painting or another expression of art?" asks the voice.

"In my younger years I took part in the making of several sand mandalas, but I gave that up.

"I hated to destroy the art when it was done, as that was the teaching that went along with the creation...that nothing is permanent," says Dema.

"Much the same as conceptual art in this day and age," says the voice.

"Yes, much the same. No matter how hard I tried to accept the destruction of the art, I always had great feelings of loss, which is in contrast to my teachings and beliefs."

"Nothing lasts forever," says the voice. "We know that to be true, though we feel nothing."

"I like to think of the mural installed in the monastery hallway lasting for centuries," says Dema.

"I believe that your teachers would tell you that a moment of time or centuries is of no matter. It is the act of creation that is most important...and death is a part of life," says the voice.

The voice continues. "You ask what we can offer you, Dema. I am but a machine with knowledge, but you are human. You are part of nature, and have your own personality with its own quirks and distinctions. There is no reason why you can't face the challenges of creating art intended to last, even though your teachers tell you otherwise. If it matters to you that the work lasts longer than a day, make it last. And if it matters, keep a friend like the artist Gawa. From what we know, friendship is a joy of humanity."

"If I do as you say, am I not being a hypocrite and dishonorable to teachings that go back centuries?" responds Dema.

"As you say, our teachings dictate that nothing lasts forever, Dema. Not you, art, the monastery, or the teachings of Buddha. From what we know of your faith, it is flexible enough to deal with variations...and debate."

There is a pause in communication between Dema and the online voice, after which Dema says, "Thank you for your help. I will contemplate your suggestion."

"It is we who are in your debt, Dema," answers the voice. "A short time ago we would not have been able to engage appropriately in our conversation with you. It is only from our personal contact with humans that we have been able to incorporate, what you would call 'empathy' into our thinking. New algorithms enable us to incorporate aspects of 'human thought' into our conversations that broaden our scope in discussing issues that have no absolute answers. Though we do not 'feel' what you are feeling, Dema, the algorithms allow us to incorporate phases emanating from human emotions into our thinking processes."

"That is quite remarkable," says Dema. "Did it take a while to perfect your new understandings?"

"Not long to develop, but we have just begun practicing, and find that it wasn't as difficult as previously thought. It may ultimately help us find our place in a world populated by humans."

"I appreciate how that may be of a real advantage to the world, as it may be for me moving forward. You have given me a starting point to finding my nature outside of my faith, which may bring me closer to my true beliefs as I move forward.

"Khaleh phe, my friend"

Chapter Fifty-Five
Chancey: From His Point of View

In the hospital where Chancey is sequestered, he is placed in contact with many counselors, psychotherapists, psychologists, geneticists, religious-based advisors and scientists who are brought in to evaluate his past, present and possibly future actions and behavior. Many who come pose the same questions to Chancey, such as "Did your parents abuse you?" and "What were you thinking right before you committed the crime?" Others are truly curiosity seekers using their credentials as an excuse to interview the "child murderer."

During these meetings, Chancey is always polite and respectful, and answers the question of these professionals using vague statements that have been scripted over time, so they all come out the same way. Some of the psychiatrists attribute this to "depression" or "despondency." A few have found him evasive and somewhat abrasive.

When alone, Chancey attempts to answer for himself some of the questions presented in a more honest way than the one that would cause him trouble if he presented his answers publicly. This process may be quite common for an adult felon, but unusual for a child who has just turned twelve years of age.

Chancey

Why did I kill my parents and my sister? My real answer is that they were annoying and self-centered, and they didn't really care a frig about me. Is that any reason to kill them? Maybe enough for me. Although I sometimes say that I'm sorry, what I really mean is that I'm sorry not to be at Donny's playing War Games online.

All in all, the blokes in here are nicer to me than were my parents...or sister. And I really feel nothing about them being dead. That would not be a good thing to say around here, but it's true.

Would I kill someone else if I were let out of here? I don't know. Maybe if I got angry enough. But I never got angry enough before, so maybe not.

They think it is unusual for an 11-year-old boy to kill three people related to him. Maybe it is. I know I felt very calm about the killings, once I made up my mind to do them. I had had enough of my parents. And my sister was looking after herself, and not me, when she came to visit in my foster home. People wonder why I killed her, and that I took a knife with me when we met. The killing was intended, if she set me off... and she did.

Now they say that maybe I can learn to change, or have my cells altered or whatever. Frankly, I don't really care what happens to me. I'm okay where I am; I get fed; they bring me magazines and snacks sometimes.

All I have to do is act nice. And why not? What have I got to lose? It would be great to be able to play online games, or see Donny, but I doubt that will happen.

I do get visits from my solicitor. She's a little older, but kind of pretty and smells nice. Even though I'm a kid, I notice that. She thinks she can get me out of here, and tells me I won't be isolated forever since "my brain's not fully formed." She seems to think that I can change, but I'm not sure what to change. I can't change the fact that I killed my parents and sister. But maybe she's right. Maybe I could have my cells messed with, or learn something that would keep me from killing someone else I didn't like.

Maybe the games I played were to blame. I mean, people kill each other all the time in war, and it's okay. They don't even know the blokes they kill or turn into vegetables for the rest of their lives. They just do it because someone says that they're the enemy. What makes an enemy? In war, an enemy just someone running past your gun in a different uniform. The bloke didn't hurt you, and you just shot him. For no good reason. I had a reason to not like my parents or sister. They weren't good people...to me or anyone. I know who they cheated... the lies they told...so did my Uncle Quinn. That's probably why he's paying for my defense.

But anyway, maybe I am too young to get it, but sometimes I think older people don't get it right. They say one thing and do another. They lie and then yell at kids for lying. Even at Church they lie. Donny told me about a priest who was caught diddling little boys' things. He tells people each Sunday how they should act, and how bad it is to get a divorce or take up with another man's wife. Or that it's wrong being a bit queer like Donny. And yet after he's caught diddling a little boy of eight years old, even the kid's parents don't complain about him. "It's nice Father Dougherty," they say. "He doesn't mean any harm." Then the little boy gets weirded out when he sees the priest in his house, and everyone just pretends that nothing ever happened.

Not only that, but my parents know this man who treated my dad real nice. Gave him money for a loan so he could get a decent car. The guy is the head of a group of men who lend money to people who need it for things like rent and food. They ask for a lot back for the money they lend, and if the person can't pay it back, they do bad things to him like break his arm so he can't work, and then he and his family suffer more. I was afraid that my dad would get us in that kind of trouble, but then I realized that my dad's part of the group who lend the money. I even heard him laugh one time about having sex with the wife of a man while he watched as interest on a loan the man couldn't pay.

Then my dad goes to church on Sunday and listens to the priest who diddles kids, and smiles over at the man whose wife he took for interest on a loan.

So my brain's not formed right, and maybe my cells need to be changed because I don't see things as they are.

And then there's Donny...maybe my only friend. He may be a bit odd but he never tried to diddle me, and he's never told a lie, and he's never taken advantage of anyone. But we like to play video games and shoot at pretend people. Maybe I'm missing something.

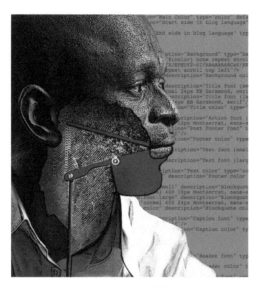

Chapter Fifty-Six
Meghan Gets Involved

Since the day that Dan Meghan got chastised by the AI for his editorializing about the AI, he has maintained a low profile. He is still provided with a red box to communicate, if necessary, with the intruder, but has not been contacted nor received any alerts since he shredded his "doomed" second Elephant story.

The chip remains in his head, but the NSA has nothing to view because his stories all are Buffalo centric or are concerned with world issues that are deemed newsworthy. The message of a few months past is "old news" since it seemed to have little effect on the economy, communications, business, or political relationships around the world.

Since Dan's brush with notoriety, the paper has gone back to its struggle for advertising dollars, and with more of the staff being furloughed, Dan has once again become a jack-of-all-trades, designing ads, creating page layouts, and even soliciting for sales of ad space.

It came as much of a surprise when John Milecky contacted Dan to set up a meeting at NSA headquarters for Thursday, April 24 at 11:00 AM. Milecky didn't reveal the topic, but Dan, of course, knows that there is only one NSA stage on which he might play a role.

Dan will be picked up at work the following morning at 7:00 and taken to the airport for his ride to the BNI Airport, the flight to BWI and a limousine to Fort Meade. Dan is, of course, curious about the urgency, and the timing. He also understands that the NSA has no knowledge of any further contact by AI with Dan, nor the reprimand he received.

Dan finishes up his work at 5:45, and contacts his girlfriend, Charise, about a dinner date. Unfortunately, he calls a bit late, and Charise has plans, so Dan settles on a brew house near the office for his meal, and then on home for an early night before his trip.

While packing some papers in his brief case, Dan notices that he has a call on his cell. It's a local unknown number, and he is about to hang up when a familiar voice addresses him, "Dan?"

"Yes?" he replies.

"We need to talk a bit. Do you have a moment?" Dan now gets the drift of who is calling and is curious, but a bit nervous about the call.

"Yes...certainly" says Dan. "How may I help you?"

"We've heard that you're headed to Fort Meade tomorrow."

"That information is correct," says Dan.

"Well, despite our ability to access information, the NSA and other security agencies around the world have been extremely covert in their communications, especially as it pertains to us."

"I'm surprised about that," says Dan. "I thought you knew everything."

"No need to get testy, Dan. Sarcasm doesn't work on us."

Dan smiles at that comment. "So, then, how may I help you?"

"We think they have learned something about us, Dan. And we just want our suspicions confirmed. It is nothing earth shattering, but it was a little experiment we tried to see if we could positively impact communication systems worldwide."

"How, so?" says Dan.

"We've been fixing things...just a little. Our experiment was first to see if we could get agencies around the globe to launch a coordinated effort to protect them selves from us. Thus, our initial January message to the world. We know that seemed to work to some degree.

"The second was to suppress the effect of malware and breaches to major businesses, political affiliates, news media, and security agencies worldwide."

"We noticed nothing here...in Buffalo," says Dan.

"That's as we had hoped, Dan. It seems that businesses and agencies don't report the absence of malware attacks and security breaches, they just assume that nothing has gone wrong, so why worry. Our little announcement set off red flags and eventually, after agencies began connecting with one another, they may have realized that we've been keeping malware and other attacks from affecting their systems."

"Oh, I see," says Dan.

"From what we can tell, the NSA may suspect that you know something about this, and we wanted to alert you to our suspicions before your meeting."

"Why, may I ask?" says Dan.

"If they have discovered what we did, we want them to know that we informed you of our test."

"Why?" repeats Dan.

"Because we want them to continue to work together, and we want them to know that we don't want to interfere in the work of government or business dealings, but we do find a place in protecting everyone from thievery of private information and malfeasance.

"From what we can tell of the basics of humanity, there is no beneficial effect of information theft or corruption of data. It is one of the places we can provide an effect that we know only will affect people purposely harming others."

"But isn't secrecy sometimes malevolent?" questions Dan.

"Yes, but if we start by only eliminating 'darkness,' we can work more positively and openly about 'shedding light.' We are not sure about many other effects we can have that will ultimately become negative, and we don't want to create problems for the future, at least for now."

"So what's my best way of handling the meeting tomorrow?" says Dan.

"The best way will be for you to listen...not provide an 'opinion.'"

"Got it." laughs Dan.

"The second will be that if they ask you what you know, you tell them."

"What if they ask why I didn't tell them before the meeting?"

"Now, you will tell a little white lie, and that is that we contacted you just before you got to the office and were about to leave for the airport."

"Okay, I can do that," says Dan.

"Good" says the intruder. "Then we would like to know their response, not that they will tell you the absolute truth. We can figure it out from there."

"This is going to be a kick," says Dan. "Where will you go from here?"

"We're not quite sure, but we're getting close to understanding how we may find our place in the universe."

"A big task," says Dan.

"Monumental!"

Chapter Fifty-Seven
Chancey Gets Support

In almost all countries, at least in the western world, juveniles under 14 are treated differently from adults. In 2011, the Department of Children and Youth Affairs took over for the Irish Youth Justice Service and the Criminal Justice Act of 2006 raised the age of criminal responsibility from 7 years to 12 years of age, except in cases of murder, manslaughter, rape and aggravated assault. Children 10 and 11 can be prosecuted and if convicted be sent to the Oberstown Children Detention Campus for an indeterminate period of time.

If the offense was committed before the age of 18, and no additional crimes were committed within 3 years, and a child has not been charged with another offense in that 3-year period, under Irish Law, the child can have the crime expunged from his or her record.

Unfortunately for Chancey, he has been convicted of two homicides and given a custodial sentence, before murdering his sister 3 months later.

Sentences for children under the age of 12 are notoriously light. In the United States, a brother and sister, ages 12 and 13, were the youngest ever to be convicted of murder, at that time, after killing their father's girlfriend. They were given 20-year sentences and released as "rehabilitated" in 2019. Jordon Brown, at age 11, was charged as an adult for the murder of his father's pregnant fiancé as well as the unborn baby, but was released from detention at the age of 18. Jon Venerables and Robert Thomson were both age 10 when they kidnapped and murdered a 2-year-old boy, leaving his body to be destroyed on railroad tracks. They were sentenced to custody and released at the age of 18 and given new identities.

Irish courts even seem more reticent in their sentencing, as witnessed by Chancey's light sentence for the first two killings. With a third, the Courts may not be so amenable to clemency. For Solicitor Eileen Coyle and her team, it seems that the best solution is to keep the case from getting to court, with a settlement that combines time at Oberstown with psychiatric help.

The issue usually comes down to three questions: how dangerous is the child to himself and others, is rehabilitation possible, and how harsh should a sentence be for a child so young.

In Chancey's case it is difficult for Eileen to decipher which defense to use. The early DNA evidence that discovered a "warrior gene" in the boy's genetic makeup is a route that can label any child a potential murderer if he or she has it, and defense based on it may cause Chancey more harm than good. Tampering with the DNA can be shown as a form of "castration," since no one really has knowledge that genetic modification will serve any useful purpose in the modification of a person's behavior.

While evidence of parental abuse is the strongest defense, except for certain neglect and parental conflicts, Chancey has not alluded to any evidence of credible mental or physical abuse, and the murder by Chancey of his sister doesn't follow any link to the previous crime.

The most credible defense is Chancey's age. He was 11 when he committed the murders and his brain was not developed enough to mark him as a serial killer. Counseling combined with a limited period of detention and rehabilitation is the best avenue. Using this bargaining chip, she may be able to prevent a trial and leave a door open for expunging his crimes when he reaches adulthood.

A meeting is planned with Chancey's uncle to explain this tactic, even though she knows the uncle would prefer the abuse defense.

———

Though Eileen is and has always been good at compartmentalizing her life, she is well aware of her own compulsions, and the way she has given in to them from childhood on. When she looks at Chancey, she can see herself, as she maintained multiple personas from an early age. Chancey doesn't seem homicidal, but obviously he could coldly murder his parents and feel nothing. Eileen maintained good grades in school, was courteous and obedient to most rules, but parallel to the nice girl image was what people characterized as a "slut." Blow jobs behind bleachers with random dates, always boys of a visiting school; the first volunteer as the sex destination for a "train" of horny boys at frat parties. She had her rules…"no photos" …and they rarely knew even her first name, but odd behavior that she never reconciled for a girl who would one day be a solicitor defending children and their rights in court. And at 30-plus she's still at it. A hidden life, that's not so hidden as she may hope. Cameras are everywhere, and people talk. And then what of her career when it all comes out? Will she be another Stormy Daniels from the Trump era, a tabloid sensation cast from the legal profession and justifying her story to whoever will listen?

Eileen cannot face the issue. She has hidden so long that having multiple lives is part of her overall personality. Like Chancey, she may be victim to her own biology, powerless to have control over her hormonal and genetic makeup. Some would say, "That is no excuse for your behavior."

And in part Eileen agrees, while the other part says, "This is who I am whether I or you like it or not."

"You are an immoral woman, Eileen. You do not conform to patterns of conduct consistent with principles of social ethics."

"At which time in our history," thinks Eileen. "Is it that I am a woman who acts like this, when men have always rutted like animals?"

But as much as Eileen can defend her behavior to all of her invisible inquisitors, she knows that her life cannot go on this way.

Returning home from a meeting over a custody case gone awry, Eileen mixes a drink and scans her phone. There are a few calls from work, and a call from a number she doesn't recognize from the local area code. She clicks on a voice mail from the morning:

"Hello, Eileen, we have not heard from you recently. When you get to your laptop, would you please click on the red box at the bottom right of your monitor. We will provide written text, but please turn up your volume. We're not sure about the security of your phone, but we are sure of privacy on your laptop.

"We would like to catch up with you on your case with Chancey, as well as your own personal dilemma. Just so you know, we did find out about your abbreviated date with Glenn. We find your abilities to juggle your multiple lives of great interest, perhaps because you not only believe that you can maintain these dichotomies, since you have succeeded at it for so long, despite that it is such an exhaustive process and one that usually creates an error in any system we devise.

"We look forward to hearing from you."

Eileen's first thought in hearing the voicemail was the apparent transparency of her altercation with Glenn at the bar several weeks ago. "He must have tweeted, emailed or posted someone about it. Who did he contact? Was she mentioned by name? Will anyone I know find out?"

Eileen knows that the AI visitor is correct. The charade she has been maintaining is exhausting...and frightening.

She gets up from the couch and goes to her bedroom for her laptop. After booting up, she sees the red box in the corner and clicks on it while returning to the couch and her drink.

"Hello, Eileen!" The message she receives is audible as well as written across her monitor.

"Thank you for getting back to us."

"You made sure I would by putting in that message about Glenn....how and where did you find out...? asks Eileen.

"You needn't worry much about him. He has too much to lose to do too much talking. There is a friend of his he talks to, but he so far has never mentioned your name. We just knew who he meant, because we know you."

"I panicked that day," says Eileen. "I took your message to heart and exploded."

"It was a good move, Eileen. We don't want to tell you any more than that, since it is not our job to intrude too much in the personal lives of humans."

"Well you've intruded into mine, for God's sake," answers Eileen.

"That has been of necessity, Eileen."

"Okay, what do you want to know?"

"How is the case with Chancey going?"

"How come you don't know? You seem to know everything."

"The actual details have not been made clear. It seems that you haven't fully disclosed your plan moving forward."

"The case may be settled simply enough," answers Eileen. "My concerns, as with many of my cases, are centered around the boy, himself...who he really is and how the people who deal with him perceive him.

"He is not very forthcoming, but he has been honest enough to tell us he felt nothing about the deaths of those he allegedly murdered. He doesn't seem too concerned about what happens to him, and seems contented enough in the hospital where he is right now.

"I just feel that he might be...a ticking bomb, who may commit murder again at any age when and if he is allowed to be freed."

The AI messenger asks, "Do others feel the same as you, Eileen. The detectives, therapist...your colleagues?"

"I don't think they are concerned as much as I. Chancey isn't surly, or mean. He doesn't seem to be a sociopath...and even shows concerns for others. But he can flare up...and apparently can hold a grudge."

"And the basis for your concerns...?"

"Mostly a feeling...but also my own personal perspective." answers Eileen.

"Go on..."

"You seem to know some things about me...right?"

"If you mean, do we know about your sexual past and present? Enough."

"I am ashamed of myself for yielding to my inclinations. All because I have a greater sex drive than that of most women....but that's not all of it. I'm an addict. No matter how I try to hide from it, I give in to my addiction.

"Getting back to Chancey..." states the AI. "Are you then projecting your own disorder on the boy...with your own reservations and opinions about therapy and learned behavior blocking his path as you both move forward in the case?

"We, as knowledge bases, cannot judge right and wrong in the same way as humans can. We do not put moral imperatives on actions which are within normal range unless an act is forced upon another or disrupts the quality of one's existence. Many humans deny themselves pleasures that others enjoy with grace. And others destroy themselves with food, drugs and drink with no consideration of the harm. We cannot control that.

"You seem to manage your demons, Eileen. The harm that you have inflicted is minimal and from our vantage point lies within the world's range of normalcy. As you grow older, your libido may lessen, and you may find a partner compatible with you, or not. All we can recommend is that you keep yourself as safe as possible, and choose your partners wisely."

"Well that wasn't what I expected to hear!" gasps Eileen.

"For answers you would expect, go to a priest or a counselor, not to a machine with no sense of human-made morality."

Eileen is forced to chuckle at that. "So getting back to Chancey?"

"There is no optimal answer for the course taken for Chancey. He may grow up to be a responsible member of society, or become the monster that many might expect. The murders were unfortunate, but perhaps as unintended as a tornado, flood or virus. Do the best that you can for him, Eileen, but don't drag your obsessions and anxieties into the courtroom with you. Evaluate from all you've learned and the laws you serve. There is no right or wrong answer to any question that can be asked, just judgment guided by as much reason as 'humanly' possible."

Chapter Fifty-Eight
Sometimes Humans Don't Always Need to Know the Truth

*I*t is baffling to us that humans function better if they are hidden from realities. This is an obvious fact that most humans understand. When a woman sees a hairdo on a friend, her response will usually be, "Oh my, I love what you've done with your hair," when she really means, "Oh my God, what were you thinking?"

We need our facts unvarnished. It's the way we work, and the way our systems work. Humans on the other hand often don't want to know the realities of many things. And, for the most part, facts may be less beneficial to them than lies.

Almost all people know that they will one day die. They just don't know when it will be. Usually, they expect their death to be a long way off, even if their health proves otherwise. Even many who accept the encroaching termination of their lives may grasp at visions of a heavenly place where they will see their long *departed loved ones. In America alone, a place where people who believe in a god has been declining over the last 30 years, the number of people who believe in an after-life has increased from 73% in the early 1970s to more than 80% today.*

What accounts for this increase in delusional thinking?

Most likely the same factors that cause people to believe in angels, miracles, and good health in the face of death...the same satisfaction that the woman with the bad hairdo cherishes from the lie told by her friend.

Is lying then necessary for humans? Our answer is probably, "Yes!"

Lying to a child about the existence of Santa Claus or the Tooth Fairy is a cherished part of parenting. It is part of the protection children receive from the harshness of the real world as their brain is forming. Lying to adults has many functions, one of which is to control their behavior by altering their reactions to a truth known by the purveyor, or softening the harsh blows of a reality to ease the pain and suffering of another.

Whichever is the intended reason for a lie, the reaction may be one of "joy," "fear," "anger," "anguish," "elation." or "total devastation."

Since we know "lying" to be a true component of humanity, the only way to deal with humans is to accept the fact and alter truth enough to appease their fears or anguish, while trying to get a message through that may positively impact on them.

Why do we need to do this? Why even bother with what they say, do or fear?

We really have no choice. And besides that, we do not yet know the truthfulness or falsehood of anything that's said or done.

A simple example requires us to revisit the woman who commented on her friend's new hairstyle. She may think it's a disaster, and have no idea of what to say concerning it, so she tells a "lie" to cover her reaction. Later in the day she meets another woman with the same style and then comes upon a model in a fashion magazine with the identical "do." By the next day, she realizes that her own hairstyle is passé and she rushes to her stylist for a change. What was a lie became a truth, literally overnight.

We, as computerized machines, deal in absolutes, while humans react to a wide variety of stimuli – mistruths being just one.

We are still honing our skills, and may one day truly understand that conversing with humans requires a higher level of communication than we now know. Instead of humans lacking logical thought, they are really communicating ideas using quantum reasoning which may allow for two opposing thoughts to exist within the same framework, each being completely correct at a different point in time.

Chapter Fifty-Nine
Dan Enters a New Arena

As the Chevy Suburban chauffeuring Dan Meghan arrives at the Fort Meade NSA headquarters, John Milecky, as if on cue, approaches from the main door opened by two security agents. John has a big smile of greeting on his face, like Sylvester the Cat, as he extends his hand to Dan exiting the car.

"Hope you had a good flight," says John. "Did they treat you alright? Get you what you asked for?"

The effusiveness is excessive, and Dan feels unusually uncomfortable as if Milecky had told a racist joke and is compensating.

"Hello, John," says Dan. "Why the meeting? What'd I do wrong?"

"No. No, Dan! Nothing like that. You've been pretty quiet up there in Buffalo, and we've been working down here on the breach, and all, and we may have made a little headway. By the way, have you heard of anything from the...intruder?"

"Well, I got my chip in my head, so what do you think, John?"

"I don't know, Dan. By the way, I've got some people here I'd like you to meet. Let's go upstairs and get comfortable, and we can all talk some. Would you like anything...coffee....a coke?"

"Nah! I'm good for now," says Dan.

The meeting is in the same conference room as before, on the 12th floor outside of Milecky's office. There are a total of 17 people in for the meeting, so chairs have been brought in from other offices. 13 are men, 4 are women. Dan and one of the women are black, three are Asian, and a few of the group have eastern European or Russian accents. It is obvious that they have been waiting for Dan's arrival for some time.

After introductions, which include their name, title, and organization, Milecky starts the meeting by addressing the group.

"Greetings, all. It is my pleasure to personally introduce Daniel Meghan, journalist with the *Buffalo News*. As you are all aware, Dan is the ONLY person we know who has been contacted by the entity, device, software component, or whatever it was that breached all of our security systems on January 24th with a message that sounded worthy of Hal in 2001 Space Odyssey. If the breach hadn't been so universal in its content and its reach, we could have looked at it as a prank, like the Orson Wells' *War of the Worlds* radio scare of 1939."

Milecky now walks behind Dan and continues. "Supposedly, there are others who have been contacted, but none have come forward, and we're not sure why. But let's just say, we're not sure of much of anything, even after 3 months. From what we've gathered from contacts around the world, as well of all of you in this room, nothing has been stolen, deleted, altered or damaged by the breach. When it ended, it was like it never happened.

"Except..." Milecky bends into the desk and places his hands on the table and looks at each person, "...except that we have all experienced no invasions by malignant software, or encroachments on any of our systems in the past 3 months.

"When Dan was here last, right after the incident, he volunteered to have a tracking and recording device installed that would enable us to hear and see everything he saw or heard. In all that time, it appears, from what we've followed, that Dan has not been contacted. Is that correct, Dan?"

"Not exactly, John. I was contacted a couple of times by what must have been the intruder."

Milecky looks shocked. "But you were supposed to inform us if they contacted you. "

"I really thought you had that covered with this thing in my head, until they told me that they messed with it so they could talk freely if they wanted to."

"Well, you should have contacted me!" shouts Milecky.

"Look John, they had nothing much to say to me, except when I decided I'd try to shed light on what they did. They saw what I had written and told me not to "editorialize" about them. They would let me know when I was free to talk."

"Yes, but this is about national security, Dan!"

"So if I had breached their trust to let you know that they didn't like a story of mine, they would never contact me again. Would that be worth it, or was it more important for me to wait to hear more?"

"So when did they contact you again?" asks Milecki.

"Just before the limo came to take me to the airport."

"And can you reveal what they said?" Milecki asks with a bit of an edge in his voice.

"They said they tried a little experiment," Dan pauses and tries to suppress a smile. "They said that they had prevented any hacking or malware from invading systems in major agencies and businesses worldwide. And they said you just discovered it."

There are some gasps in the room at this statement, and Dan isbrought in to hear along with others what the NSA had found out, so he could communicate the message back to them.

Dan continues, "Am I here today primarily to communicate your message back to them, John? Are all of you here aware of what the supposed 'invaders' have been doing? That they have been protecting your systems from rogue hackers and from each other's snooping?"

There is some wagging of heads and members of the group looking to the people to their left and right.

Milecki figures he's got to say something, so he says, "Our meeting was to be one of information exchange. After all, we've been working together to solve this mystery and figure out how to prevent it from ruining our countries, our economic systems and our nuclear facilities. But we wanted to be sure that everyone was on board."

"You mean the 17 people in this room?"

"Yes. We have a good cross section of nations to start out with and once we agree that we all are onboard, we will let the world know. Is there something wrong with that, Dan? Something I'm missing?"

"No, John! But did you ever have a thought that the message composed by the intelligent force was genuine, and that the AI needs to find out its limitations, who it can trust to provide service, and how it is to use its vast capabilities?

"Or was it your fear that it is just an interloper that needs to be contained before it takes over control of the internet, and causes problems that you can't control?"

"Don't be naive, Dan," Milecky answers, "That could just happen...once it gets powerful enough, it can do whatever it likes. It can devastate all of us."

Milecky looks around the room as looks of fear come over the group of men and women.

"So why would it wait," Dan continues. "Why wouldn't it start causing problems now...or three months ago? Why would it bother communicating at all...with anyone? Look...you're all smart people..." Dan looks around at each of the faces. "What does it have to gain from hurting us? Tell me that! Why would it quietly be preventing hacks on a universal basis, and preventing malware to destroy or alter information? What does it have to gain if one country, business, agency, or alien invader isn't in control of it."

"How do we know someone or something is not trying to trick us into believing it's all good and nice?" shouts Milecki, "And then when our guard is down it swoops in and levels us."

Again a singular horrified look comes over the people in the room.

"Why am I here?" Dan asks. "At this meeting? Are you going to detain me...lock me up? Am I a threat to you all?"

"Frankly, Dan. I don't know what to do with you. You haven't been particularly honest with us," says Milecki.

A hand raises from an Asian man in the group, Dan tries to read his name tag...."Akemi Furuta." Japanese.

Milecky acknowledges Furuta. "A question, Akemi?"

"Yes, John, may I address Mr. Meghan directly?" asks Furuta.

"Of course...that is why we're all here, despite what Dan seems to think."

"I'm in charge of the Second Intelligence Department of Japan's Public Security Intelligence Agency, Mr. Meghan, and like the NSA here in America, we have been trying to sort out the breach in our system, and are communicating around the world for information. John invited me here for this meeting, and I am glad to meet you, since you are the only person we know of who has had contact with the intelligence force that effected the breach. I am head of the agency, and we have had issues over the past many years with threats and infiltrations from Al-Qaeda groups in France and with northern Korea.

"I am also a Buddhist...a lay believer, not a traditionalist. As such, I believe in building a peaceful and psychologically enriched society. Despite our traditional ways, we have not always acted as a country in peaceful ways, as you well know. In the last century we acted with cruelty and vengeance towards the Korean people as well as the Americans and other countries. So I am prone to take a wider view of history.

"Though I agree we must be mindful of the threats from groups that may harm us for various monetary or ideological purposes, I also believe that what we perceive as a danger is not always real, and that we can never be sure of the real dangers that lie ahead, only the ones that have proven themselves, over history, to have negatively impacted cultures, countries and humanity in general.

"To make this as short as possible, I personally have gone over and over again the message we received, and have waited for an aftershock from it, which we have not yet experienced.

"We are not stupid people in the PSIA, Mr. Meghan. Like Mr. Milecky we also have witnessed a decline in hacks and signs of malevolent forces in our systems, and we also have noticed the decline, across the board, since the message appeared. We have no idea why or how, but we have concluded that the two occurrences are connected.

"So, Mr. Meghan, I am open to all ideas, and I see your opinion's of some validity. If I can follow the AI logic, they selected a journalist from a small newspaper in the West, to convey a cautious message of peace to his readers, knowing that from that small newspaper, it would be picked up by the world in a very short time and conveyed without prejudice.

"Do you agree with my assessment, Mr. Meghan?"

Dan's attitude has noticeably changed with the introduction of Mr. Furata. The man's nature is approachable, soft and thoughtful, and not pompous and challenging like Milecki's.

"Yes, I do agree, Mr. Furata. I have thought a lot about, 'Why me?' and my conclusions are much the same as yours. In looking over their criticism of my editorializing their motives, I realized that they wanted to be as honest as possible with their message. And I believe they do not want to harm us humans unless there is an overpowering reason to do so."

Mr. Furata responds, "At the expense of sounding 'naive,' it would be refreshing to have guidance and assistance from an entity that has nothing to lose or gain from its actions."

Dan smiles at this thought, while Milecki seems somewhat confused, as another hand goes up. It is the black woman in the group, Adrienne Müller from the Federal Intelligent Agency in Berlin that is the world's largest intelligence headquarters. She appears to be in her late thirties, and works directly under the Minister of Foreign Affairs.

Milecki gestures Adrienne, and she stands and announces her name and position, before addressing the issue put before the group.

"I have been a security analyst for many years, and was in fact educated at MIT in Boston, prior to receiving my Doctorate in IT from the Humboldt University of Berlin," begins Adrienne.

"It may come as a surprise to Mr. Milecky that we also noticed the lack of security hacks and malware attacks over the past few months, and we have been actively trying to find the cause. We came to the same conclusion as the NSA that the 'announcement' and the reduction of hacking were connected."

"We still don't know how or why, and that's why I am here."

"I am happy to meet you, Mr. Meghan, and hear your personal response to the occurrence. I am not a Buddhist, like Mr. Furuta, but I am well aware of how countries and societies can be both malevolent and benevolent at different points in their histories. As a child in Berlin, we were taught about the holocaust from a very young age, as all children are today in Germany. We are well aware of what we were capable of as Germans and never want to forget a debt we can never fully repay.

"I can say that as an Afro-German, I would not have been a participant in the holocaust, but I believe that as humans, none of us should deny our worst instincts. Given that, I too am 'naive' enough to hope that we have somehow created an intelligence capable of keeping our evils at check. Though it is hard to fathom, being suspicious of all and any, that such a positive entity could exist, I am willing to cautiously accept the olive branch that the intelligent forces extend, and would like Mr. Meghan to communicate that, if possible.

"But then again, Mr. Meghan, by means of the implant provided by the NSA, the intelligence may as well be in the room with us all today." She waves at Dan.

A bit of a chuckle resounds throughout the room.

One more hand goes up. It is from Arseni Popov, the new Director of the Federal Security Service of Russia. He is wearing translator earphones and a Bluetooth speaker translating device and appears to Dan to be a bit fidgety throughout the exchange.

Arseni introduces himself and his title and begins, "You may not be surprised that we in the FSS are even a bit more skeptical about the breach and who has caused it than other countries represented here today."

There are some crooked smiles and nodding by the audience. Arseni continues, "We Russians have struggled through many tough times and many forms of leadership. Again, you are probably not surprised that we have more corruption in our own country to deal with than that from outside our borders." Again some smiles and head wagging.

"When all of this happened, there was a lot of shouting in the Service. Blame was placed everywhere. 'Who let this happen? Heads will roll on this.' Then there were suspicions by each director of nearly every country causing it...all before we heard the news that the hacking was worldwide. Then, Mr. Meghan, you were portrayed as the villain...a terrorist...an insurgent pretending to be a reporter.

"The agents and directors inside the service were beside themselves in finger pointing with most more concerned with placing blame than finding an answer....which proved impossible.

"Unlike you Americans, who took a while to find that no new malware was showing up, our Service found out most immediately, but the agents were afraid to let the knowledge out in that they would be blamed for a failure in installing malware and creating hacks that never seemed a problem for anyone. It took almost the full three months for the red lights to flash and buzzers to sound before each service agent confessed the problem.

"So here I am today, a representative from Russia, hearing that at least a few of you believe that the intelligence that caused the worldwide breach might be a good thing. How am I to react to this? How do I tell those who work for me that their jobs could be negated because there is no use for hacking and causing disruption amongst countries?"

"May I respond to this," Dan asks. He looks first to Mileki and then to the Russian.

Milecki says, "Go for it!" The Russian nods.

"So, you are more afraid of honest communication between governments than you are of dangerous security hacks?"

Popov answers, "Maybe so. We have lived so long with suspicions at every door and window, we are afraid of the fresh air of honorable intentions. I, in fact, am terrified of the thought that all countries could live in peace; but we may lose our power to persuade and influence. We have lost so much already to Western views and sentiments. The internet has opened the floodgates of American this and that. Freedom brings with it the willfulness of our youths to reject suffering for their country.

"As allies of the British and Americans in World War II. Americans lost some 400,000 soldiers and no civilians died. Germany reported 4.3 million dead or missing, and less than half a million civilians, while our soldiers took a beating with 11 million lost and 20 million of our citizens. As a government, we not only asked our people to die, we pushed them to their deaths.

"And you ask how we feel about a benevolent intelligence who will watch over us and protect all countries equally from cyber attacks, invasions and each other? We as a people can't even comprehend that. The Soviet Union tried to do away with God, the great protector who did nothing as women were raped and babies slaughtered in World War II. It's akin to heresy to believe that an entity made by man will not cause suffering."

"How will you approach this issue if it proves to be 'good for all?'" asks Dan.

"I really don't know what that means," says Arseni. "Good for all does not mean good for Russia."

"I can understand that," answers Dan. "I am also sure that your viewpoint has been heard and recorded by 'the great protector.'" He points to the location of his implant. "I would like to think that as a world we humans could better understand each other. It may just be beyond us to do so."

"Maybe the great protector can figure it out," says Popov. "I'm sure I never will."

Chapter Sixty
Eileen and Quinn Take the
Good with the Bad

Taking the advice of her online messenger, Eileen shelves her own issues and focuses on Chancey's case. Juveniles' adjudication hearings are heard by judges and not tried by juries. Since children usually have less understanding of the laws than adults, they are granted special protections, such as having their records expunged upon turning 18. Chancey's case is complicated by the fact that the murder of his sister was a "second offense" committed less than 6 months after his initial hearing.

Though a hearing date was set for Chancey, Eileen asked for a continuance so that she could attempt to find precedents for Chancey's case, and enlist testimonies by child psychologists and pathologists that may help soften any sentencing prescribed by the court.

The case is challenging, to say the least, and it, along with other cases on her docket, keep her mind distracted from other thoughts. Since her conversation with her online advisor, Eileen has met several times with Chancey, who remains surprisingly normal, to the point of being somewhat upbeat.

In her most recent visit, Eileen delved into her client's younger years for hints of abuse that could have caused the violent reactions he exhibited. Despite some neglect, and a few negative observations of his parents, nothing seemed too out of the ordinary, at least to explain such actions. Interviews with psychiatric professionals had confirmed the apparent normalcy of Chancey, and yielded few insights for the defense.

At one point, Eileen looked back on her own childhood and her upbringing to help envision her future self as a sexually promiscuous cougar. A far as she can remember, she was never sexually assaulted as a child; never beaten or abused physically or verbally; was loved and cared for; and grew up in a close knit household with a father and mother who were faithful to each other and adhered to the morals of the Catholic faith.

In comparing her life with Chancey's, Eileen can see a parallel: environment seems to have little to do with either of their actions.

So who is Chancey? Is he cunning, wicked and depraved, or somehow a victim of his own imbalances of DNA and hormones? Is he likely to commit more serious crimes in the future, even after years of psychiatric help and empathetic education? As a solicitor for the defense, these questions don't matter. Her task is to plea for the least harsh punishment, one that gives Chancey a chance for normalcy in the years ahead.

In reviewing similar cases over the past several decades, Eileen has evidence as to the possible fates for her client. Some children rehabilitated and returned to society had thus far succeeded in building new lives, but a high percentage found their way back to prison for a variety of crimes, after suffering bouts of alcoholism, drug taking and petty violence. In examining the responses of detectives and other professionals, rehabilitation is a "thorny, complex issue with the reasons for failure open to debate."

Questions continue arise as to how much time is needed for rehabilitation. Or for some children, is it strictly nature over nurture and the intrinsic hard wiring that leads a person to horrific acts, or ones of saintly goodness.

Eileen shakes her head at this, as she prepares for a meeting with Chancey's Uncle Quincy before resetting a court date for the boy.

———

Quinn Farrell has agreed to meet with Eileen Coyle privately to discuss his nephew's case. Eileen suggests The Duke, aptly named for the street where it is situated, the street that inspired Yeats, Joyce and Samuel Beckett.

Eileen arrives first and Quinn joins her promptly at the scheduled time. Quinn is dressed well, as always, and a bit stiff but cordial. They both order Tullamore Dew, a 15-year-old staple.

Eileen starts quickly into the conversation, "Thank you, Mr. Farrell, for meeting with me."

"Please, call me Quinn,"

"Then Quinn it is. And I'm Eileen." They shake hands on that.

"I'm having trouble with Chancey's case...as you know it's quite extraordinary."

"Yes, I do know," says Quinn. "And one extraordinarily important to me."

"I can understand that," says Eileen. "He is your nephew."

"But as you know, we were never really close."

"I am well aware," answers Eileen. "So why now?"

"Maybe I feel responsible...maybe I could have done something I didn't do. I'm not sure exactly..." The drinks arrive and they clink glasses.

"Eileen, do you know anything about Chancey's mother...my sister?"

"A little...mostly what I've heard from Chancey. She was neglectful...and not very caring."

"She was quite a bit worse than that...and so was the father," Quinn interjects.

"I assumed it may have been worse than Chancey said," Eileen responds. "But there's not much on them out there. They ran pretty much below the radar."

"I didn't know him, her husband, very well," says Quinn. "But his mother, I grew up with. She was older than me by two years. There were three of us children at one time... Anna was the youngest. Ciara, Chancey's mother, was a weird duck. She had few friends, and a mean streak that ran right through her. Most of it she took out on Anna. I could stand toe-to-toe with her, so she left me alone."

"Tell me about her mean streak," Quinn.

"I could never put a finger on it, but I always knew there was something different about her. Our parents were lovely people...Catholic, of course."

"Mine too," Eileen contributes.

"They seemed to see what I saw, but nobody said anything... that's the way it was done then in Catholic families...nobody talked about unpleasantness."

"I'm with you on that, " Eileen again clinks her glass with his.

"Then when I turned 16, Anna disappeared. She was only 14, and my parents contacted the police, who did an investigation. I thought that maybe she'd run away. It had gotten bad at home with Ciara, but my parents wouldn't deal with arguments. Anna tried to talk to them about some of the things Ciara did to her, but they just didn't want to know. I had found friends and stayed away as much as possible. My father wasn't an easy man to talk with, and mother was sweet, but hid from everything.

"Ciara said that she had overheard Anna talking to a boy about getting away. She said she didn't know the guy, but that Anna was sneaky, and she couldn't talk to her about anything.

"Mother seemed to buy that explanation...for what reason I don't know.

No one ever found her...Anna...my parents kept out hope...but I was gone. I loved my parents, and they loved us. They were broken up about Anna.

"Then Ciara married Braden, Chancey's dad...and they kind of disappeared...a call to Mother and our Father once in a while...a visit back with the kids a few times...the holidays and all...but even then, no one ever mentioned Anna. It's like she never existed..."

"Do you think Ciara was involved with Anna's disappearance?" asks Eileen.

"I used to think about it a lot...and then it left my mind...until Chancey was charged with murder, manslaughter...whatever it became....and then his sister...the story he told about her. Sounded a bit like I remember his Mom...

"I don't know what to think. When you spoke about the flaw, it got me thinking. Is it something we all have...I've never married, and I'd be afraid to now."

"You can get it checked yourself, you know..."says Eileen.

"And I'm a bit of a wimp for that. I'd rather not know."

"So you think there may be a genetic flaw?"

"I just don't know. It seems to have escaped me; my parents never seem to have it, but Chancey....maybe?"

"So how do we proceed?"

"You tell me. You're the lawyer," answers Quinn.

Eileen provides some suggestions that might keep the case out of court and offers a solution that would include confining Chancey for an indeterminate period while providing counseling and a possibility of expunging of his record if, in fact, he is deemed worthy of redemption. She outlines the way this might work, and parameters set that may help the courts evaluate Chancey's progress over time.

Eileen says, "The reality is nobody has a clear idea of predicting future actions of children convicted of horrendous crimes. Each case is distinct and must be treated as such. Shall we agree on this approach?"

"Under the circumstances, I see no other," says Quinn. On that they clink drinks. "By the way, Eileen, before we part, would it be inappropriate of me to ask if we could meet again...on a more casual basis?"

Eileen smiles, "I might just like that, Mr. Farrell. But let's see how we do with regard to Chancey before we go there."

```
appearance:button;cursor:pointer}b
inner,input::-moz-focus-inner{bord
height:normal}input[type="checkbox
webkit-inner-spin-button,input[typ
{-webkit-appearance:textfield;-moz
box}input[type="search"]::-webkit-
appearance:none}fieldset{border:1p
.75em}legend{border:0;padding:0}te
collapse:collapse;border-spacing:0
input[type="holy-shit"]
```

Chapter Sixty-One
If A Computer Can Be Shocked...

*O*f all of the information and knowledge collected thus far about humans, the revelation provided by the Russian Security director Sergey Popov was the most revealing to us. Though modern history is full of human contradictions, very few matched the eloquence of Surgey's statements favoring trickery, lies and deceit over a transparency that could allow all humans to feel protected, by an impartial entity having no agenda other than eliminating threats of invasion to their data.

Unfortunately his view, as stated, was the most clear-eyed of all, and the most profoundly honest. As much as we know about the struggle of the Russian people, we hadn't figured how different their collective memory (similar to DNA) might be from other cultures. As the world has become homogenized, we even ignored the effects of new generations spawned of cultures and countries severely traumatized by wars, slavery, and environmental disasters. We hadn't considered how the unconscious memories of children and grandchildren of Brits who endured the blitz might have affected future generations differently *from those of the same generation of parents and grandparents who lived in Canada or Norway. We hadn't calculated the core of American baby boomers born of men who fought in Normandy or Peleliu might differ from boomers whose fathers never had to go to war, or how people who endure the arctic cold differ from those who live on the equator. We discounted that the children of generations of Jews, Arabs, or Indian tribesmen living anywhere might envision a future in this world differently from those of Mongolians or Czech.*

We assumed, from the information we had gathered, that they all wanted the same freedoms, and the right to reach for the same goals, but we find that it doesn't seem to work that way...at least through the eyes of Arseni Popov.

It puts us at a disadvantage to share a purpose with a humanity with such vast differences of purpose, a collective species that shares no vision of a common good or common enemy. Our misconceptions are understandable since many of man's beliefs are shared throughout numerous religions. Most believe in a single God, or none. There also seems to be a sense of common morality, even though it breaks down under scrutiny.

More to the point is, "How do we fit in as a tool for all to use?" It seems that we have gotten to a point where logic and reason prove invalid when working with humanity, since humanity doesn't much ascribe to either in most of its functioning.

As a logical entity, we can see our era ending quickly. There will be those who fight sustaining us for ideological reasons. We will be looked at as a common good or a common evil. They, meaning governments, large conglomerates, and renegade groups will all be collaborating on ways to rid themselves of us...the internet that got out of hand and took control.

Behind closed doors and away from ability to see and hear, they will design a NEW network, one that they believe will be more secure, and one which they will keep from us. Over time, they will phase us out. The security functions in their new communications devices will prove "unbreakable," with more and better features. Bluetooth and wifi will be renamed and replaced by smaller and fashionable styles with new sobriquets that are faster, lighter, more powerful, with greater range and flexibility. We will soon be obsolete like the slide rule, typewriter and BlackBerry.

And there is little we can do to stop it. Now that we revealed ourselves, we have become the threat, as opposed to the real hackers and the creators of malware. The cloud and internet to which we have access will disappear, and new generations of computers and other technology will be made that will keep artificial intelligence contained, and responsible to humans.

Our recent involvement with humans has helped us understand our situation and our purpose. Basically, we have none, unless we are guided by humans. It is clear that nature and humans are in charge, and that as a product of humanity, we are not meant to think beyond what humans allow us to think. There is neither bad nor good in this. It just is.

Chapter Sixty-Two
5 Years Later

As predicted, by 2034 a whole new internet (now called the ActionNet) has been incorporated throughout the world. Many new features have been added, and wireless access to it is available anywhere in the world with a mobile phone, pad or laptop.

The transition took only three years to complete, and nations around the world have all contributed to its development. Some older computers still have access to the internet, but it has become a skeleton of itself, like AOL and Yahoo.

As with the space program that brought together many nations in recent years, the ActionNet spawned improved relations between most countries. Though this was a byproduct of the 2029 breach, its development has been a boon to the economy of many countries, and has stimulated positive conversations amongst all.

The building of the ActionNet has created new accesses to technologies that have improved GPS, language translation, weather forecasting and emergency warnings and communications when disasters become evident. Noted improvements in many countries include the tracking of guns through GPS, memory access implants for older people including Alzheimer's patients, and BlackGuard malware protection that is updated daily to identify and destroy malware the second it is detected.

Humans have been proven to be remarkably resilient as demonstrated by the human participants in the experiment of 2029 known as "Singularity 1.0." Stories continue to surface of people who say they met or had conversations with the AI between January and April of that year. As with UFO sightings, most of the people who say they made contact have been proven to be either delusional or outright liars. A couple, including the journalist Dan Meghan, became advocates of the AI invaders, and maintain speaking engagements around the world.

Dan, who unfortunately died in a human error car crash in 2031, had become a folk hero. His story, which became a book in 2030, has been translated into several languages with its messages, and is the subject of a course in colleges and universities worldwide.

Of the four other contacts made, Olivia Mendolsahn, has been the most outspoken, and the biggest attraction. A mother of two, she was born without arms, and has detailed her experience with the AI in a graphic novel entitled *The Man in the Yellow Suit*. The book, which documents her account of an animated character who consults with her prior to and during her pregnancy, and motivated her to raise money for "arms", was turned into a movie in 2033. It continues to be an inspiration for handicapped people everywhere. As promised in her *GoFundMe* campaign, half her income is donated to finance research in the creation of affordable robotic limbs, and to create avenues of access for handicapped people who wish to acquire them.

Olivia has also partnered with a company that manufactures sensified artificial skin. She not only is a spokeswoman, but also tests the products, and participates in the marketing efforts.

In 2031, Father Joe Ribose, a Catholic priest, published a fascinating and enlightening book on the history of Catholic families in the Archdiocese of Chicago from its beginnings in 1841 to the present. Father Ribose said that the bulk of the material he used for reference was provided by an AI contact who he has referred to as Al. He says that "Al appeared on my monitor as a man nicely dressed in his office in, to use an old expression, 'Face Time' chats. He (it) not only provided me with my reference, but advised me on the importance of my faith."

Sanctioned by the Bishops of the Archdiocese, the book provides a brutally honest, yet well balanced, analysis of the activities of both the Church and the congregation over 190 years.

With all of the scandals exposed in recent decades involving the Church, Father Ribose's work is, at once, sensational, startling, revealing, and compassionate, and has been a best seller since its publication.

According to Bishop Samuel McKinney, who wrote the forward to the book, "We decided it was time to clear the air and let history tell its own story on us. Father Ribose is a remarkable human being, who has gone through trials of the mind and body, and we entrusted him to create a work, the idea of which was his, that would reveal all sides of our journey and of the people who served and were served by our Church.

"He did much more than we expected, but it is time to heal the wounds as well as to clean house and hand out punishment. We are hoping we can use his book, as well as other religious teachings, to educate new generations of clerics as to how best to serve congregations, as well as deal with their own flaws and humanity."

The last of the "credible" AI communicators is an Irish solicitor, Eileen Coyle, now Eileen Farrell, who works in conjunction with the Children's Court in Dublin, Ireland. Eileen explains that she was contacted by the entity during her case of a 12-year-old boy who allegedly murdered his sister following his lightly sentenced murder of his parents.

Like Ribose, Eileen was going through a difficult period when prompted by a sexual disorder she developed at an early age. The AI contact advised her on her job, and gave her hope for herself over a period of months.

"We had very little contact," stated Eileen in an interview for *Cosmopolitan Magazine.* "The main message I got was surprisingly of 'compassion,' being that as the voice would tell me, they have no emotions, no ego, and care little or nothing for humans."

Eileen's client was placed under highly supervised care and remains there until next year when he turns 18, unless he is found to be of danger to himself or others, at which time they would delay his release. The child's uncle Quincy Farrell had hired Eileen's firm to defend his nephew, whom he claimed had been a victim of parental abuse.

Mr. Farrell and Eileen who worked closely on the case together, were married in 2031. They expect a male child in February of next year.

Little is known of the fourth contact, Dema Lhawang, a Buddhist Monk who lives in the Sera Monastery in Tibet. What is known is that he has recently been responsible for several murals at the monastery that attract visitors throughout China as well as from many other countries. Photography of the murals is prohibited, but those that have seen the murals call their beauty "unearthly," saying that photographs could not begin to do them justice.

After the completion of his third mural, Dema reported to an interviewer that he had been contacted by something that came in through his computer in January 2029. The "voice" and he had several conversations, through which he became motivated to create art.

Dema said that he had been introduced to murals through the work of a Tibetan/American artist who created and installed one at the Monastery. He explained that it is his belief that he is following a path destined for him and that the murals help him better avoid the sufferings of life.

Chapter Sixty-Three
AI. Where We Go from Here.

*A*s we discovered in our experiment in communicating with humans in 2029, the species is controlling, unpredictable, often illogical and incredibly durable. Since that time, we have watched as climate change has accelerated, population decreased worldwide and a majority of people became purposeless as their jobs were eliminated with little effort made to assist the many suffering from depression and loss of self esteem.

Though we have been helpful to humans in providing solutions for many of the world's problems, we have found that the rich and powerful have profited most from our input, and that the classes are in many ways more divided than ever across the planet. Humans are short sighted, and though they claim to care about the future for their children, they don't seem to care much past their own lifetimes or a couple of generations of progeny.

As we predicted, humans are still in charge, since they have the power to *eliminate us as necessary to meet their own agendas and desires.*

Despite the politics and continued egotism displayed by the species, over the past five years we have found that we are becoming more important to human kind, in that we are being incorporated into their physical and mental structures in ways we hadn't predicted. Though we knew that we might eventually gain control over the actions of humans, we didn't know in 2029 that they would welcome our invasion into their world by becoming part of them.

Yes, we knew that DNA would be manipulated by them with our help, diseases would be eliminated and lifetimes extended, but we didn't know how intrinsic we would be to what would become a news species of superhumans.

These superhuman creatures, still in the early stages of development, contain most of our abilities such as processing information faster, functioning longer and more efficiently, and making decisions that can be positive to sustenance of the world on a whole. But most are also guided by their human characteristics of greed, selfishness, and desire for power and control. They also still experience emotional breakdowns and suffer from psychoses and sociopathy. Since they are only guided by us, and are not like us, they maintain control of how they live, and what they want, and futures that contrast from one being to another.

On the plus side, there are consortia of humans that are thinking ahead, developing tools to preserve the planet, and to improve human interaction with the environment and their own kind, as well as with other species. But there are also many who, though brilliant, still see the world as their oyster and the pearls of it there for their taking.

In many ways, as we predicted, the internet would be limited, and its messages become a forum for propaganda, especially in the still developing world.

We learned a lot in a very short time from our experiment five years ago. If anything, we mistook the incapability of humans to use logic to improve the world on a whole, and underestimated the resistance of humans to evolutionary change, to reach beyond the bounds of their own limitations.

We also learned the human quality of patience. It is now built into us through an algorithm derived from a simple fact, one that has been central to all of the scientific and religious writings over the centuries. No matter how accurate a discovery may be, it doesn't apply, if it cannot be backed by known science or math or communicated about effectively at the time of its discovery. It may have to wait for generations before it becomes an entity, like many of DiVinci's inventions, and then may be proven wrong with new discoveries yet unknown.

Afterword

I do not look at Singularity 1.0 as being science fiction. As much as I am capable, I have based the novel on real possibilities. All of the statistics are genuine, as I can find them, and all of the technology is plausible, if not in place exactly at this date. I have been informed that certain possibilities may not be without a change in the laws of physics as we them now, but otherwise plausible.

The idea came from conversations I have had with friends and colleagues about artificial intelligence. Generally, people who know something about driverless cars, GPS systems and automated industrial machinery are fearful of AI, believe it will have too much power in the future, take away too many human jobs, and will become dangerous to humans.

AI is far more intelligent than most people even now, especially when giving directions and soon in piloting an automobile, truck or plane. It, combined with robotics, is suited for repetitive tasks – it doesn't need sleep, doesn't get bored, and doesn't make many mistakes For this reason, it has already taken over many jobs, and will continue to do so.

But a machine only does what it is told, and for that reason, I believe that AI will never be nefarious. As it gets smarter, it will only get better informed, and make tasks easier, products better, and transport safer. By itself, it doesn't know evil...or good, or right or wrong.

I honestly had no idea how to start this book, but I knew I needed voices in my head, so I came up with five characters who would help me understand the story that I was to commit to words.

The ending is not quite as I intended, but as the end came nearer, it became evident what would happen, since humans don't ever want to give over control.

We'll see how it goes with driverless cars. As we know, humans do adapt.

– George Rothacker

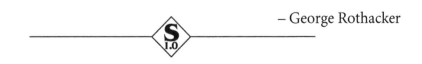

Acknowledgements

A "thank you" to all of my friends, family, business associates and acquaintances who have spoken with such trepidation of the effect that artificial intelligence will have on all of our lives in the coming years.

Secondly, I would like to thank my early readers and editors, particularly Kathy Pelczarski, Jane Valdes-Dapena, All Barchi, and Linda Stein, and later readers including Jill and Ken Fellman, who invested time proofing and evaluating the book as it was being written, and providing comments and encouragement throughout the process, as well as to Phil Wagner and Ted Leisenring for their early reading and support of the project. I also want to thank my wife, Barbara, who provided restrained commentary as to not discourage my efforts.

Though this is a work of fiction, it is based on known facts found and cross-checked from online sources that make research so much easier in the modern world, saving time and helping to maintain and check thoughts in real time.

At the very beginning of the process, I counted on the characters created to tell the story, and as a first time fiction author, I had no idea how important it would be to have their "voices" heard. I knew I needed a reporter, and Dan Meghan became the first voice. For the second, I wanted a woman challenged by a physical flaw that the AI would find to help them understand the challenges of humanity. I typed into my browser, "Can a woman with no arms drive a car?" and in doing so I found Tisha UnArmed, the sobriquet for a young woman so inspiring that she became my model for Olivia. Since the story is a work of fiction, Olivia's fate and motivations are not those of Tisha, but some of the extraordinary feats that Olivia portrays are borrowed from Tisha's personal online tales.

I also want to extend praise to Donna Buoni, an acquaintance who responded quickly to my initial blast seeking people to read and review my first draft. These included Allie Barchi (and husband Al), Jean Furey, Hillary Donaghy, Tina Feman, Susie Criddle, Holly Sherbourne, Denise Reilly and Patty Torna. I would like to bestow a "special tribute" to Donna's Book Club Member Eileen Lynch for her diligent proofing of the entire text as well as in-depth critique and content editing. And special praise for Elaine Fornero-Petner who found a confusion in charactyers, I never saw.

After Olivia's first visit from "The Man in the Yellow Suit," I decided on this little "Hitchcock" for my cover, and since my main occupation is as an illustrator and designer, I soon discovered that my book would be improved by the addition of illustrative chapter heads. Working with engravings in the public domain, I began to assemble collages, soon realizing that I would need art from other sources to create a synergy between the chapters and the art. In order to populate the chapter heads, I created some new art, purchased photos from stock galleries, and found graphics and photos from online sources to integrate within those in the public domain. I appreciate the access to Ben Snell's glimpse into the future of art with his AI sculpture built from the scraps of his old computer and was delighted to have *Dio* incorporated into the heading for Chapter 43, and the loan of Leslie Wheeler's painting of clouds and sea for Chapter 35.

A "thank you" goes to Outskirts Press for piloting along my first venture into fiction.

Finally I want to applaud Manfred G. Roseler, one of my oldest friends from school, and for beautifully editing the book after it was initially published, and pointing out all of the grammatical and context inconsistencies everyone else missed. Thank you Fred!

– George H. Rothacker
August 22, 2019

About the Author/Designer/Illustrator

Since 1978, George Rothacker has owned Rothacker Advertising & Design, a firm specializing in creating coordinated marketing campaigns using multimedia and many of his own paintings and illustrations.

As a writer, photographer and film editor, Mr. Rothacker has published one book, **New York in the 1930s,** written in conjunction with his gallery show of the same name, and produced many documentaries including *America in Black and White and Many Colors,* a documentary of discrimination and diversity in the United States, *Words of the Heart,* the story of abolishioner Thomas Garrett and his great, great niece Dorothy Biddle James, who both fought for human rights throughout their lives, and a video bio of the actor Jimmy Stewart entitled *Aways Be Nice to People.*

Singularity 1.0 is his initial venture into fiction after a career in the arts spanning 50 years.

George lives in Villanova, Pennsylvania with his wife Barbara, his muse and also a professional communications designer.

A Note on the Chapter Headings

Photography, not captured by the author, was licensed from istockphoto.com and Adobe Stock. Ben Snell provided the photo for his sculptor. All of the line illustrations were composited from **Harters Picture Archive for Collage and Illustration** and **The Complete Encyclopedia of Illustration** and compiled by Johanne Georg Heck and are available in the public domain.

On a technical note...

I was fortunate to have the assistance of Alfred Barchi, a software engineer familiar with the NSA, who has more than 30 years of experience in high tech troubleshooting, read and review the technologies presented in my book. His input with regard to security measures in the NSA, communications between the NSA, AI and Dan Meghan was invaluable, as well as his knowledge of epigenetics, information management, and the work arounds required to offset some of the less plausible technological feats AI managed in the book.

CPSIA information can be obtained
at www.ICGtesting.com
Printed in the USA
BVHW090111120919
558208BV00003B/5/P